Pleasing
the Dead

Books by Deborah Turrell Atkinson

Primitive Secrets
The Green Room
Fire Prayer
Pleasing the Dead

Pleasing
the Dead

Deborah Turrell Atkinson

Poisoned Pen Press

Poisoned
Pen
Press

Copyright © 2009 by Deborah Turrell Atkinson

First Edition 2009

10 9 8 7 6 5 4 3 2 1

Library of Congress Catalog Card Number: 2008931495

ISBN: 978-1-59058-597-9   Hardcover

Poisoned Pen Press
6962 E. First Ave., Ste. 103
Scottsdale, AZ 85251
www.poisonedpenpress.com
info@poisonedpenpress.com

Printed in the United States of America

This book is dedicated to George C. Crout,
principal of Wilson Elementary School,
Middletown, Ohio, 1960.

I was fortunate to be among the Fourth, Fifth,
and Sixth Grade students Mr. Crout inspired with
his innate kindness and his progressive views on education.
Thank you, Mr. Crout.

O Rose, thou are sick.
The invisible worm
That flies in the night,
In the howling storm,

Has found out thy bed
Of crimson joy,
And his dark secret love
Does thy life destroy.

—William Blake, *The Sick Rose*

Acknowledgments

Pounding out the twists and turns of a mystery at the keyboard may be a solitary aspect of writing, but the real stuff, the nitty-gritty, comes from the experts. Endless gratitude goes to my legal eagle friends: Claudia Turrell, Patty NaPier, Judy Pavey, Ron Johnson, and George Van Buren. Each of them has an impressive domain of expertise; I am awed. Any mistakes regarding legal and investigative procedure in this book are mine because I didn't know enough to ask. Thanks, guys!

Thank you to my advisors, readers, and fellow writers: Karen Huffman, Michelle Calabro-Hubbard, Michael Chapman, and Honey Pavel, who keep me on course. Many thanks to Barbara Peters, editor extraordinaire, without whom this book wouldn't reach its readership.

Hugs and salty kisses to all the Pink Hats, Maui's intrepid Masters Swimmers, especially Doug Rice and Christine Andrews. These patient people allowed me to slow them down, and then showed me the rare Hawksbill turtle and Bruce the shark, who did NOT charge anyone. We also learned not to put orange peels in our bathing suits. So much for trying not to litter. Ouch.

Mahalo to Celia at Hawaii Shark Encounters on Oahu's North Shore, for information on their dives and the types of sharks encountered. These folks wouldn't consider baiting the water.

Mahalo nui loa, everyone.

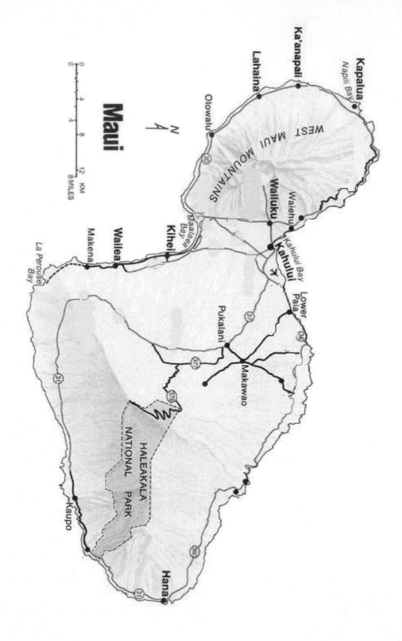

Maui

Chapter One

The silver Lexus turned left at the light, then glided a few blocks down Waine'e Street and slowed. It bumped into a pitted lot behind a small frame building. Though the bar looked closed and forlorn from the rear, a handful of dilapidated cars were parked on the worn gravel. A black Mercedes S600, isolated in the far corner, stood out like a tank at a peace demonstration.

The young man at the wheel of the Lexus gulped, and his eyes flicked to his father. Ichiru Tagama kept his gaze straight ahead, but a muscle twitched along his jaw.

Ryan Tagama parked the Lexus on the other side of the lot from the Mercedes. "I thought we were early."

The older Tagama grunted. Both men got out of the car, Ryan locked it with the remote, and adjusted the hang of his linen jacket. Tagama's broad face glistened and the tic in his jaw muscle pulsed.

Inside, father and son paused to let their eyes adapt to the dimly lit room, where a handful of male customers sat at small tables. Though Ryan watched to see if anyone noticed their entry, the customers' reddened eyes followed only the attractive, heavily made-up hostesses. Ryan watched to see if anyone noticed their entry, but the men only had eyes for the women.

There were more women than men, in assorted stages of dress. One wore a Chanel suit with a silk peony pinned to the lapel. Nearby, a very young woman wore a sheer pareau over a thong bikini in a vivid tropical print. She was less than five feet tall, with a couple of water balloons barely restrained by two tiny triangles, on her chest. Still another wore a short pleated plaid skirt, knee socks, and high heeled pumps. No one but the women smiled, and only when they faced a customer to set his drink on the table with a little curtsy or bow.

Chanel's perfect coiffure swiveled to the men coming through the door, and her mouth turned up in a smile that reached her smoky almond eyes a second or two after her red lips parted. "Tagama-san," she said in a husky voice. "Welcome."

"Yasuko, flower of Asia," Tagama said in his accented English.

"It's so good to see you again." Her sultry, warm gaze turned to Ryan. "And this is your handsome son."

"Yasuko, this is Ryan."

She gave a little bow, which Ryan returned. He bent deeper than she had.

"Come with me." She turned to lead them through a curtain of plastic beads and a blast of cold air from an overhead vent.

Ryan ducked his head and smoothed his hair. Tagama walked through the refrigerated air and the beads with the dignity of an old soldier. They entered a simple room that was unfurnished except for a table, two chairs, and a cluster of pachinko machines in the corner.

A tanned, beefy man dwarfed the table where he sat alone. Sunglasses hid his eyes. Two younger, brawny men, also wearing dark glasses, stood behind their boss.

The seated man wore an expensive Italian suit with a slight sheen, as if silk were mixed with the fine wool. He rolled his broad shoulders and nodded to his guests.

"Welcome, Tagama." The dark glasses flickered at the woman. "Thank you, Yasuko."

She backed from the room. Tagama bowed deeply. "Obake-san," Tagama said. "This is my son, Ryan."

Ryan took his cue and bowed. The man lowered his oversized head a fraction of an inch. His big hands spread flat on the table, three and a half fingers on each hand. The ends of both pinkies were missing.

"Thank you for coming." Obake pointed at the other chair. His dark lenses reflected a distortion of Tagama.

Tagama sat. "How is your health, Obake-san?"

"Good, thank you. The ocean keeps me fit. I swim a mile each morning, and again before the sun sets."

Ryan took a place behind his father in the manner of Obake's bodyguards. The elder Tagama spoke to his son. "Obake-san is a skilled swimmer and diver."

Ryan bowed again. "We would be honored to take you on a tour."

Obake didn't answer the young man, and with his eyes on the elder Tagama, waved his guards away. Tagama did not ask Ryan to leave and after a brief pause, Obake acted as if he and the older Tagama were the only people in the room.

Ryan watched the muscles around his father's eyes tighten, a reaction he doubted anyone else would notice. As a boy, it was a trait for which he'd learned to be on the lookout.

During the drive over, his father had shared information about this meeting. The few moments of candor were unusual, and Ryan was both flattered and unsettled by it. First, Tagama had told him that Obake would use an interpreter. Second, he'd revealed that Obake, who was a Japanese national, came to the U.S. several times a year, but supervised his financial empire from his home in Tokyo, and used an intermediary to carry out his negotiations. Tagama had been his agent on a few occasions, but he hadn't been a member of Obake's stable for several years.

Though Tagama never bragged, something in his voice told Ryan this hadn't been Obake's decision. Tagama did share that he was never certain about Obake's long term word, and he always made it his business to know what the Yakuza chief was up to in the islands. Secrets were more precious than diamonds when one dealt with Obake.

Ryan, chastened by Obake's snub, studied the face of the swarthy foreigner.

"We have a problem." Obake addressed Tagama in heavily accented English.

"I heard Tom Peters died in the explosion," said Tagama.

"I was the target." Obake took a long pull on his Marlboro.

Tagama squinted at the smoke. "No one knows you're here."

"Someone knew."

"Peters has enemies. I can think of several people who would like him to disappear."

"No." Obake slapped the surface of the table and the ashtray jumped. Tagama sat like a boulder, though Ryan twitched.

"They want me."

Ryan saw his father blink at this news, though he didn't speak.

"I only survive because I leave meeting early." Obake paused a moment, as if making a decision. "I get a warning."

"When?" Tagama asked.

"This morning, in Japan. Noboru sent a text message."

Tagama raised an eyebrow. Noboru was Obake's personal secretary, a man whose extensive tattoos proclaimed his loyalty to Obake and the businessman's clan.

Tagama took a deep breath and looked down at his folded hands. "May I ask what the message said?"

"It said, '*ikimasu.*'"

"'I'm coming?' One person?"

Obake nodded. "Not a native speaker, but it is someone who knows my business. He knew to contact Noboru, after all."

Tagama sat quietly for several seconds. "I will need a list of your business contacts."

"This is not a time to be devious. You know them." Obake removed his dark glasses and stared at Tagama, his murky brown eyes stones in the tanned mask of his face. "Find the leak, Tagama." *Fine da reek, Tagama.*

Neither the older Tagama nor Ryan found the butchered words amusing.

Chapter Two

Storm Kayama looked at the sticky linoleum floor of the car rental shack and remembered the legend of Māui, the Hawaiian god and mischief maker, and how he'd lassoed the sun to nourish the land. Right then, she thought he'd overdone it. It was way too hot for a Wednesday in April. It didn't help that the Kahului car rental office was packed and the air conditioning broken. In the stillness, no relief came through the propped-open doors.

Ahead of Storm in line, two parents and three of their children sagged against the rental counter and complained to the very young and very pregnant clerk. The fourth, a droopy-diapered tyke of about two sauntered up and down the line, scrutinizing the overheated customers with black eyes that dared anyone to meet them. Most people stared ahead, but Storm grinned at the kid, and wondered if it was a boy or a girl.

"Lexie," barked the mother, who turned from the counter. The woman's face glowed with heat and exasperation.

Lexie ignored her mom and stopped next to Storm. Was Lexie a girl's name or a boy's? In one hand, a paper cone of melting shave ice dripped virulent pink liquid onto the kid's toes. Ant battalions queued up across the grubby linoleum.

Storm broke eye contact with the toddler and shoved back damp, wavy strands of dark hair that had sprung free of her French braid. Everyone in line drooped with heat, and Lexie's feet made sucky sounds in the growing pink puddle. Ants, single-minded in their mission, outlined the nectar like someone had used a black pen.

The pregnant clerk, whose belly pulled the flowers on her company muʻumuʻu into amorphous blobs, had been explaining something to the family in a low voice, but now her whisper carried. "…are all blocked, anyway." Everyone in line leaned forward.

"Eh? The roads are blocked?" asked a man in front of Storm.

"That's what they're saying," said the clerk.

"All of them?" asked someone behind Storm.

"That's what I hear." The pregnant girl fanned herself with a rental contract.

"What happened?" Storm asked. From a couple miles away, the whine of sirens carried on the still air.

"I'm not sure—" the girl began, but the staccato snap of leather heels distracted her. Her eyes flitted to the door, and she ruffled through a stack of contracts resting on the countertop.

A woman in a navy suit and matching navy mid-heeled pumps marched up to the clerk. Four men, dressed in the masculine version of her outfit, followed. All of them wore Ray Bans. Their heels tapped their significance to the peons in line.

Lexie watched, mouth agape. Everyone in line bristled. The pregnant clerk fumbled a pile of keys and the waiting papers into the suited woman's outstretched hands. The suit veered away, with the four men following behind like imprinted ducklings.

The line of homogenous agents reminded Storm of the ants, except crisis was the agents' puddle of nirvana. And that meant there was a mountain of misery out there for someone. Without realizing it, Storm touched the emerald-eyed pig that hung on a gold chain on her neck. He was her *ʻaumakua*, or family totem, and Aunt Maile had given it to her for luck a few years ago.

One by one, the customers got their cars. The family obtained the van they needed. The mom scooped Lexie up and jammed a flowered pink elastic headband on her shining scalp. Lexie howled.

The man in front of Storm asked about the blocked roads. Now that the Feds had come and gone, the pregnant clerk was happy to chat. "An explosion in Kahului. Madelyn—you know—the sales manager over at Avis, said someone died. Might be a terrorist attack."

"Who were the suits?" Storm asked when she got to the counter.

"A federal task force."

"Makes sense if they're worried about terrorism."

"It's scary, isn't it?" The young woman didn't sound scared. "Row three, stall eleven. Good luck."

It only took two blocks for Storm to realize that she'd need that luck. No one was going anywhere fast. It was after five, rush hour, and cars were lined up as far as she could see.

Up to now, she'd been looking forward to the trip. She had a handful of paying clients on Maui, which was a gorgeous place to visit. The most intriguing was a job incorporating and overseeing liability issues regarding a new dive shop. The owner, a minor celebrity, had called out of the blue because a friend of a friend had recommended Storm's services. Word of mouth was a strong persuader in the islands.

Lara Farrell's name had sounded familiar to Storm, and the minute she'd hung up the phone with her new client, Storm Googled her. Sure enough, six or seven years ago, Lara made a name for herself in the windsurfing world. Maui's north shore beaches were among the world's most ideal sites, and Lara had been an internationally known competitor. She stopped suddenly five years ago, and though Storm spent almost two hours on the Internet (how did it gobble so much time?), she couldn't figure out why Lara had quit. She did find a reference to Lara's temper, however. Not enough to scare Storm off; temperamental people were more apt to annoy Storm than scare her.

She flipped through radio stations, searching for a news report that would explain the traffic jam. An explosion had occurred in a restaurant that morning, and streets were still jammed. Probably not an international terrorist, Storm thought, but crazy people are everywhere.

A tickling sensation bothered the back of her head, and Storm looked around at the other idling cars. Funny, she felt like she was being watched. But who could locate anyone in the parking lot that would normally be Dairy Road? There was a street cop, red-faced and sweating in his dark hat, uniform, and white gloves, a handful of pedestrians, and one brave or stupid bicyclist, who talked on his cell phone as he wove between cars.

Ahead of her, a child stared from the back window of a van. It was Lexie, who raised both hands to the window. Storm waved. Lexie frowned, then sat down. The feeling of being watched abated.

Storm sighed with exasperation, and crawled ahead. She hoped the car didn't overheat. There was no way she was going to make her dinner date with her new client. Not even close.

◇◇◇

Sergeant Carl Moana, Maui PD, didn't flinch at the blaring horns. His face a ruddy mask, he stood his ground in the middle of the intersection at Dairy Road and Hana Highway. Ignoring the sweat trickling across his burning scalp, he kept one gloved palm toward Hana Highway and waved the other like a metronome at the endless procession of heat-radiating, fuming vehicles that crept toward him.

His brain, however, raced like the engines that revved in frustration. Why were the police blocking *all* the streets leading into town? Every citizen in Wailuku and Kahului combined, all thirty thousand of them, seemed to be on the road. His nine-year-old could roller blade faster than these cars were moving. These people just wanted to get home for dinner. Plus, the top of his navy blue cap felt like a steam iron sat on it.

He was blocks from the explosion, which took out the side of the Blue Marine, a restaurant that was usually only open evenings for fine dining. Odd that they'd been serving breakfast, and certainly not to the general public. But he knew one thing: the worse the problem, the tighter the lid on the matter. There hadn't been a press release yet, and people were clamoring for news. As a result, the coconut wireless hummed. At least one person had died, maybe two. Word on the street had it that the dead guy was a contact for the Yakuza. He was also a member of the Maui Department of Liquor Control.

Moana knew better than to take gossip at face value. Someone else said that ATF, FBI, and representatives from the U.S. Attorney's office were on the way from Honolulu. His mouth twitched with that thought. Good luck if they were driving from the airport.

Sweat coursed down the side of Moana's face. But it wasn't just the navy blue uniform that cranked up the heat. Though Moana had trained for explosions, he'd never had to deal with one.

Just last week, his wife had sewn the third stripe on his sleeve, and they'd put their three kids to bed, drunk Korbel from jelly glasses, laughed, and made love. He'd studied hard for the sergeant's exam. And he wanted to work on this new crisis, but knew he had no connections. He had no relatives on the force or uncles in government. Kahului wasn't even his regular patrol district. Working overtime directing traffic was as close as he was going to get to this emergency. Especially since the federal heavies were on the way.

And what if the rumors of terrorism were accurate? It was a damn scary thought. Here on quiet, friendly Maui? What was going on?

Despite his apprehension, Carl wanted to make a difference in his community. And he wanted his kids to go to college someday. He needed to be noticed; he needed to be on the inside of a big case.

◇◇◇

The boss had been right, as usual. A bicycle was the way to go in this situation. The man sailed between the stalling, steaming cars. People were going to be steamed, too. He had what he'd come for; it was time to move out of this mess.

His mobile phone rang, and he dug it out of his shorts pocket. "She's here. Avis rental, white Chrysler Sebring, license MBW 9453. She's stuck along with the rest of these slobs."

"She's not a slob, she's a pit bull. Don't let the clothes or the free spirit act fool you."

"Right, boss." He hung up and avoided the rear bumper of a mini van. Some kid was leaving sticky hand prints all over the window. Slobs.

Chapter Three

"Lara? Mokulele Highway's jammed. I'm not going to make it to our dinner meeting."

There was a longer pause than Storm expected, which gave her a moment of concern. Storm had looked into the rumor about Lara's temper. It had taken some work, but finally an old friend who ran a windsurfing shop in Kailua told her that Lara's last windsurfing competition had been on Maui six years ago. The sponsors were big corporations, and Lara came in second to win a $2,500 purse. However, when she discovered that the man who came in second collected $15,000, she threw a fit that was broadcast on ESPN.

Storm felt sympathy for the woman. The prize difference was discriminatory, it sucked, and it still occurred in not only windsurfing, but many sports. As far as Storm was concerned, Lara's new business was a good indication that she'd recovered and moved on.

When Lara spoke, there was a hint of disappointment in her voice. "Shoots, I wanted you to meet my fiancé. He's a big part of the picture." She sighed. "But we'll do it later. Why don't we get together at the store tomorrow morning?"

"That would be perfect."

"We'll talk over coffee about the kind of legal help I had in mind." Lara gave Storm directions to the dive shop.

"Eight-thirty?" Storm asked.

"Better make it nine," Lara said, and Storm could hear a grin in her voice. That fiancé must be hot.

It took Storm nearly two hours to get out of Kahului and another forty-five minutes to cross to the south side of the island. By the time she got to her hotel in Kihei, it was dark. The hotel was on the beach, close to an area known as Makena, a still-pristine coastline of white sand beaches and the stark ruggedness of ancient lava flows. It was peaceful, and Storm found a quiet restaurant for dinner where she had to wait only five minutes for a table. Amazing. She used the time to call her partner, Ian Hamlin.

He was in Los Angeles, where it wasn't quite eleven, and his mobile phone was turned off. She doubted he was asleep. So where was he? With a grimace, she turned off her own phone and dropped it into the bottom of her purse. This was not the moment to think about Hamlin and his "break." She'd have plenty of time in the middle of the night, when a dream would wake her and she'd reach out to find she was alone. Then she'd remember the exact words he'd used when he told her he needed to get away and think about their relationship.

"Your table is ready," the hostess said, and Storm struggled to return her smile.

She placed her order, then slipped some legal briefs out of her oversized handbag. When her dinner arrived, she put them away and turned her attention to the succulent filet of monchong with sake-ginger beurre blanc.

The next morning, she woke early enough to have a cup of coffee at a little concession off the hotel lobby before heading out for a morning jog along Makena Alanui Drive, a narrow, winding road that ran parallel to the sea. On the other side of the road, interspersed with pastures, a handful of luxury houses stood in various stages of construction. Chickens still pecked and foraged in soon-to-be-landscaped gardens.

An hour later, Storm relaxed in the shower and began to prepare for her meeting with Lara. She'd found pictures of her new client on the internet, and she looked gorgeous. Consequently,

Storm spent at least fifteen minutes wrestling with the hotel's hair dryer, trying to get the frizz out of her dark shoulder-length hair. The underside was still wet when she gave up, dropped the dryer on the counter, and wove her hair into the usual French braid. If only she'd inherited her father's straight, Asian-type hair. But alas, the genes for Hawaiian hair had trumped the genes for silky Japanese tresses, and she had her mother's waves and curls.

Except for the occasional bout of insecurity—like this morning—she'd given up messing with her hair. In her teens, she'd fought it with soup-can rollers and salon chemicals. By sixteen, she was fed up, chopped it to an inch and a half, and died it purple. But in those days, she'd also worn a leather motorcycle jacket and used black laundry markers for eyeliner. One day, during her junior year in high school, she had a tattoo of her *'aumakua*, the *pua'a*, applied in a place where few people would see. Now, at thirty-one, she was still glad she had the little pig tattoo, but didn't bother with rebellious hair styles. She'd also moved on to subtle cosmetics, though a Sharpie would still do in a pinch if the lights were low.

Storm gathered some papers, a legal pad, and checked the charge on her mobile phone. Lara's directions were excellent and Storm arrived at the construction site a few minutes before nine.

The new dive shop was in Kihei at a strip mall one block back from the ocean. The space had previously been occupied by three small stores. Storm was surprised by how big it was. The lease rent would be substantial, maybe as much as $7,000 or $8,000 per month.

A workman was in the process of removing a somewhat faded sign for Aunty Piko's Puka Shells. His next task was probably to move his ladder ten feet to the right, remove the sign for Ice Scream, and proceed to demolish the one for Manny's Diner. The previous small business owners probably got priced out of the market. Too bad, Storm thought.

"Storm, come in." Lara offered a strong hand and a friendly grin. She was as beautiful as her pictures, though she was thinner than Storm had expected.

Lara gestured to a man holding a large roll of blueprints. "This is my contractor, Damon Lloyd. Damon, this is my lawyer, Storm Kayama."

"Storm?" Damon fumbled the blueprints, then grinned. "Last time I saw you, you were going out with Kimo Sutcliffe. When did you go to law school?"

"Not long after that. Last time I saw you, you were putting messages in fortune cookies."

Lara looked back and forth like she was watching a ping-pong match. Storm looked at her and shrugged. "You can't get away with anything in the islands."

Damon laughed. "I guess you didn't know I was working part time for B & W Construction back then. I've got my own license now."

"Me, too," Storm said.

"It's the old two degrees of separation," Lara said. She looked at her contractor. "You're from O'ahu?"

"No, I'm from Maui, but I was attending UH Mānoa back then."

Lara looked back at Storm. "I thought you went to college on the mainland."

"I did, but I had a couple years off between college and law school."

Lara glanced toward a crew of workers, and the amusement vanished from her expression. "Storm, excuse me for just a moment. Damon, I need a few minutes to finalize today's schedule."

She pointed to an area where workers were removing old sheet rock. "Check the plans. We need to move the wall over ten inches so we've got more storage space for hanging wet suits and storing equipment."

"Got it," Damon replied.

"And no change fee, right?"

"Just this time. I'm doing you a favor because the studs weren't installed yet."

A short, voluptuous woman approached Lara from the back of the store. Her eyes were shadowed by false eyelashes heavy as butterfly wings. Full red lips parted in a grin.

"Hey girl, you were going to take a break." She scolded Lara.

"Storm, this is Stella, my office manager."

"I'm the office *tita*. You know, the watchdog." She gave the deep husky laugh of a smoker.

"She's a poodle," Damon said, and dodged her punch.

Stella gave a very good imitation of a growl—a big dog's growl—and offered her hand to Storm with a grin that showed gold.

Storm's first impression was that the woman was in her sixties, but her second glance told her Stella was younger. She just hadn't led an easy life. The gold in her smile was due to a bridge. At some point, she'd had her front teeth knocked out. Her arms, however, were strong and tanned and Storm liked the sassy shine in her eyes.

Stella spoke to Lara. "As long as you're here, I've got a question. You want those cabinets along the back wall, right?"

"Definitely. Those have to go over the desks." She looked toward Damon. "They're being installed tomorrow, right?"

Damon nodded.

"Then we have a little glitch. The carpenter back there keeps measuring along the side," Stella said. "I don't think he understands me."

Damon frowned. "I'll take care of it." He disappeared behind the sheet rock.

Out of the women's view, his voice barked a few words of Japanese. Stella shrugged at Storm, while Lara folded her arms tightly across her chest. "Is Keiko here?"

"She's back there setting up your file system," Stella said, and a young woman appeared from back, carrying a file box piled with folders, topped with rolls of what looked like maps and building plans. "Speak of the devil," she said, and grinned at the young woman.

Stella went to Keiko and scooped the teetering rolls of paper from the top of the box. "Let's get this out of the way." She led the young woman to the table where Damon had his blueprints. "Set it here. We can't file any of it until the carpenters finish with the cabinets."

Keiko was a bit over five feet tall, with the body of a ten-year old. Her long sleeved man's shirt flapped like laundry on a line, and her low slung jeans revealed hipbones that jutted like a clothes hanger. She looked Japanese, though her shoulder-length, wavy hair was dyed reddish brown and she wore contact lenses so blue they were iridescent.

Damon's rising tone in the back room distracted the women, whose heads turned in unison toward his voice. He shouted in English. "No whisky, no beer, no sake tonight—nothing. Hiroki, I give you one more chance."

Damon walked through the door, followed by a pale, thin man who mumbled a few words in Japanese.

Damon looked over his shoulder. "I know you're sick—I can tell. And if you drink tonight, don't come back."

The worker kept his face pointed toward the floor. A heavy tool belt drooped from his hips, and he shifted it with a trembling hand. "I understand," he said in awkward, accented English. At the sight of Lara, he paled further and scurried away.

Damon waited a few moments for the sound of a drill and other electrical tools to cover his words. "Don't worry, Lara. He'll get it right. He's not a bad guy, and he's a skilled worker."

Lara's eyes narrowed. "You said that before, but he looks like a drunk to me."

"He's got problems."

"Yeah, I can see." She faced Damon. "Our grand opening is in a week. What am I paying him for if he can't do the job?"

"His work has been excellent." Damon looked over his shoulder and lowered his voice. "He arrived from Japan about four months ago, and he's a single dad with two young daughters. I want to give him another chance."

"On my project?" Her voice rose.

"You heard me, Lara. If he drinks a drop, he's done."

"He better be." Lara looked at her watch. "We have a deadline."

Damon picked up plans from a workbench. "We'll have that wall moved and the rest of the sheet rock up today. The mud will dry overnight and we can begin installing overhead cabinets tomorrow. We're on track."

Lara looked over at Stella, who had lit a cigarette and was leaning against a stud. Keiko hovered behind her. "Why don't you two go get a bite to eat? Check in with me in a couple of hours, okay?"

Stella winked and stubbed out the cigarette on the floor with a bunch of other butts. It looked like she wasn't the only smoker in the crowd. With an arm around Keiko's bony shoulders, she drew the young woman out the front door, where the women paused in the bright sunlight and shaded their eyes before heading down the street.

"You hungry?" Lara asked Storm. "We could get breakfast and talk about how we need your help."

"Sounds great. I'm starved."

"Good, I'll show you the plans."

"There's a lot I want to talk to you about. Your lease agreement, the terms of ownership, what happens if your fiancé—"

Damon approached the two. "Lara, phone's for you. It's Ken, calling about a dive group."

"Damn," Lara said. "I've got to get this."

Storm raised an eyebrow. She'd told Lara she'd handle her legal questions for a set fee, but as far as she was concerned, she was on the clock. "Since I was the one who cancelled last night's meeting, I'll agree. Remember, the fee we agreed on was for a four-day job. I'm going back to O'ahu on Sunday. Maybe we could meet for lunch instead?"

Fleeting annoyance crossed Lara's face, but she erased it. "Sounds good."

It was already ten. "I'll be back here at noon," Storm said.

Storm walked out and, like Stella and Keiko, shaded her eyes from the sun's blaze. She was too hungry to wait two more hours for a meal. There were a number of shops in the area, and Storm hoped there was a little family-owned restaurant like the now-defunct Manny's Diner.

There was, and it was right down the street. Storm could see two empty wrought iron tables in the tree-shaded outside seating area. The aromas wafting from the place made her stomach growl aloud and she lengthened her stride. A chalk board listed specials for the day: miniature poi pancakes with coconut syrup, salmon Benedict Florentine, huevos rancheros with crab and fresh guacamole, assorted homemade pastries. She nearly drooled.

Ten feet away, she saw why two tables were empty in an otherwise crowded establishment. The tables flanked another where two women sat, and one of them sobbed into the other's arms. Keiko's face was hidden in Stella's shoulder, and Stella looked sad despite the cluster of brilliant hibiscus pinned in her hair.

Storm kept walking.

Chapter Four

Ryan got behind the wheel of the Lexus and glanced over at his father, who hadn't said a word. He drove three miles in slow traffic before the old man spoke.

"What do you know of Beach Rescue Alliance?" Tagama asked.

"You mean BRA," Ryan said. "They protest laws like the ones that require women to wear bathing suit tops on public beaches."

Tagama made a noise like he was trying to dislodge a kernel of rice from his sinuses. "I heard they were feminists and other leftists who protest discrimination. Like unequal job opportunities in hotels and restaurants."

"No, BRA started as a joke. Lara got involved because one of her employees is active in it. I should never have said anything about them."

"Are they well organized? And what's Lara's employee like?"

"No, they're not well organized." Ryan's mouth twisted. "They were just trying to get people to think differently. Like, if men go topless on beaches, women should be able to."

Tagama thought for a long moment. "It's not an angry group? They wouldn't plant a bomb, would they?"

"No."

Despite the Lexus' luxury acoustics, the whine of the car's tires on hot pavement filled the air between them.

"We have different ways of looking at the same problem." Tagama's eyes were hidden behind his dark glasses. "This is good. The way a father and son should."

Ryan didn't respond. A mental picture of his mother's face when she put him on a plane to Tokyo the summer after his twelfth birthday flashed through his mind. Careful makeup couldn't conceal the puffy anxiety in her eyes.

"You don't have to worry about anyone in BRA setting off a bomb," Ryan said after a few long moments. "Really, Dad, they're a little self-righteous, but harmless."

Ryan stopped at a red light, waited, and proceeded when the light changed. He kept his eyes on the road ahead.

Tagama broke the silence. "How is your fiancée? Are plans going well?"

A worm of apprehension burrowed in Ryan's chest, but he hid it. "She's busy with the shop."

"Protecting our interests?"

"Father—"

"What?"

"Lara is sensitive about this." Ryan's knuckles whitened on the steering wheel.

"Maybe she needs a reminder that she wouldn't have a shop without us."

Ryan swallowed. He'd already approached the topic, and the result had been a temper tantrum. Emotion in women made him feel as if his skin were shrinking until it got so tight he could barely breathe. Like when his mother got the phone call from his dad, asking for—well, demanding—that summer visit.

His father had nothing to worry about. Lara knew the terms of her lease were excellent, and Ryan was there to oversee the operation and keep an eye on his father's investment. He knew Lara wouldn't like the term "our interests," but she didn't understand that his father's lack of tact reflected the fact that English was his second language.

It was, however, time to shift the topic and ask a few of his own questions. Ryan knew his father would hold back; keeping secrets was deeply ingrained in him.

"Wasn't the guy who died in the explosion under investigation for a conflict of interest on the Liquor Council?"

Tagama's mouth twitched in the beginnings of a smile. "People in government accuse each other all the time. Everyone points a finger. It distracts people's attention, especially the journalists."

They rode for a while before Tagama spoke gently, as if letting Ryan in on a secret. "Don't lose sight of the big picture."

"You think the guy who died had a connection to the Yakuza?"

"Could be. Local law enforcement thinks so." Tagama turned his black lenses toward his son. "Even so, let's not talk about this to anyone else."

"Of course." Ryan shifted his hands on the steering wheel. "What about you? You still on the list of suspected local Yakuza?"

"Probably." Tagama sounded nonchalant. For years, federal officers had surveilled him, and at one time, he'd sweated under their scrutiny. Ryan was aware the pressure was no longer an issue; he assumed it was because his father was aging. It also could be due to the fact that his father started a small commercial real estate company with local, well-known investors six or seven years ago. They'd been open and charitable in their business arrangements.

"You think the bombers were trying to kill Obake?"

Tagama frowned. "There were four people in that room, plus restaurant staff."

"Obake and his guards were three of them, and they left early."

"Yes, and for some reason, the one man lingered. He may have been waiting for someone."

"Maybe it was a timed device."

Tagama nodded. "I wondered about that, too. We'll have that information soon. We still won't know if Obake was a target or the instigator."

"When he told us about Noboru's message, I believed him."

"Then you think Obake was the target."

Tagama paused. "I believe he's nervous about something. I'm not sure what that is."

Ryan thought a moment. "How do you feel about working for him again?"

"He has a big ego, especially if women are involved." Tagama gave his son an oblique glance.

"Don't worry, I won't let Lara get anyplace near him," Ryan said.

"Good. We must be very careful, though I think the old shark's teeth are getting dull."

Ryan wondered about that. Obake looked like a powerful man, both physically and professionally. So did the bodyguards. Despite what his father said, Obake looked like a shark whose teeth were still formidable.

Ryan was embarrassed that he'd revealed his nervousness at the meeting. He hoped he hadn't shamed his father, for whom showing anxiety would be a weakness. These men cultivated their inscrutability; they spun webs of deceit, layered with pawns and operators—and sometimes sacrifices.

Ryan's eyes flitted to his father. Tagama would know about using fear to get his way.

Ryan grew up in Beverly Hills with his Caucasian mother, whom he'd considered doting and high-strung. One afternoon after picking him up from school, she'd whispered about a man she claimed had been following her for weeks. Ryan wasn't inclined to listen to his mother's complaints, but that time he'd gone along with her. They ducked into a dress store and pretended to shop so they could observe the sidewalk.

To Ryan's surprise, a man with tattoos peeking from the sleeves of his dark, shiny suit passed by the window and smiled right at them. Two weeks later, she'd put him on the plane to Japan. Her eyes had been dilated with terror.

"You okay?" Tagama asked.

"Yeah, just thinking about what you said." He kept his voice level, but his mind raced. A few years ago, his mother had remarried and was finally happy. Ryan was delighted for her, but he felt suspended between his parents, and his father was still a mystery.

Chapter Five

Storm picked up a newspaper at a sidewalk stand and found a cozy restaurant several blocks down from where Stella and Keiko had been. She ordered scrambled eggs, toast, and a big pot of coffee.

Two tables away, a man yakked into his mobile phone. "The hernia's gone, but my balls are black and blue," he said, oblivious that his sense of privacy was a fantasy.

Storm ordered, then slipped into the women's room to phone a couple of clients and set up appointments. She got back to the table as her food arrived. She'd finished off her eggs and was salivating over the toasted homemade bread. Just as she took a giant bite, her mobile rang.

"Storm?" a familiar voice asked.

"Mmmph."

"It's Damon."

Storm washed the toast down with the remains of her coffee mug. "Hey, it was nice seeing you again."

"Yeah. Hey, you want to get together later and catch up on things?"

"Sure." Storm was pleasantly surprised.

"I won't get away until around six. Let's meet at seven at The Fiddler Crab."

"In Kihei?"

"Lahaina. You mind the drive?"

"No, see you then." Storm dropped her phone into her purse.

She tucked the newspaper under her arm and went outside. Her rented car was still parked at Lara's shop, but there was a cute bathing suit shop around the corner, and though buying a bikini after eating was a humbling prospect, the store was enticing.

It was about half the square footage of Lara's shop and the walls were artfully hung with women's beachwear. Storm picked out a handful of bathing suits and went into a dressing room. The first three were microscopic, and she took one look over her shoulder into the mirror and peeled them off with haste. The little *pua'a* tattoo was supposed to be hidden. Storm suddenly felt old. She almost put on her clothes at that point, but decided to give the last one a try. This one looked good, and Storm headed for the cash register with a smile.

"You're quick," the clerk said. "Most women spend an hour or so in there."

"That would be torture." Storm handed over a charge card. "Have you been open long?"

"A month."

"You've got great taste. All the teenage girls are going to come. But I bet the lease rent is high in this area."

"It is, though it's a great location. I'm getting a lot of tourist business."

"My friend is opening a dive shop a few blocks from here. You mind my asking what you pay?"

"Four thousand a month. My step dad knows the realtor and got me a good deal." The young woman nearly whispered, as if she couldn't believe it herself.

No wonder the bikini was five dollars a square inch. "It's what, about a thousand square feet?"

"Almost. But my accountant says I can make it work."

"Sell sunscreen with those Brazilian thongs."

The owner laughed. "Designer sunscreen."

"In luscious scents. I'll send some friends your way. Good luck."

Storm walked back out into the hot sunlight. That woman was getting a discount, and her store was less than half the size of Lara's. Plus, Lara's shop was more centrally located, which would make the rent higher.

Storm headed down the street back toward Lara's shop. On the way, her phone rang. "Where are you?" Lara asked.

"A couple blocks from your shop. I got a new bathing suit. You should check out this cute store."

"I will. We could send customers to each other. Want to meet me at Dina's for lunch?"

"I'll be there soon." That was the place Stella and Keiko had been. This might be interesting.

Lara's employees were no longer there. The table Storm had eyed earlier was now in the sun, so Storm chose one inside. Lara got there two minutes after Storm sat down. She looked around the room, still wearing her big dark glasses, as if looking for someone.

"Is your fiancé coming?" Storm asked.

"Yes, but he's running a few minutes late. That's good, we can talk." She pushed her glasses to the top of her head.

"You're opening in a week?" Storm asked.

"Yes, but we're already doing PR. We've planned a catered party for the afternoon and some important customers are invited for a special dive tomorrow."

"Hotel managers, tour guides, and people like that?"

"You've got it." Lara grinned, and leaned into the table. "People are calling to book dives already."

"You still windsurf?"

"No, I just dive now, both snorkeling and scuba diving. I love it."

A handsome young man in a navy linen sports jacket appeared at the table.

Lara took his hand and steered him toward the seat next to her. "Ryan, this is Storm."

"Ryan Tagama." He shook Storm's hand, then shrugged out of the jacket and sat down. "It's good to meet you."

"He and his father have a commercial real estate company."
Lara grinned widely and patted his hand. "Storm's going to help
us with the liability issues."

"Good. We need that." He put an arm around Lara and she
leaned into him. "Her windsurfing fame has people lining up.
We've got one dive boat booked solid for the next two months
and we're not yet officially open. We're trying to find a captain
for the second boat."

"That's wonderful. Though if you're already taking people out
on the boats, we need to get your liability insurance established.
I'd like to take a look at the paperwork you've got so far."

"We can show you that," Lara said.

"Setting up a Limited Liability Company would be the best
way to protect you if you're sued by a client. We'll need to discuss who the major shareholders are, and what their portions
of the stock will be."

Lara's smile grew a little stiff. "We've already—"

Ryan patted her hand. "She's right, Lara. I asked a friend
about it when we first started renovating." He glanced apologeti-
cally at Storm, who shrugged. She would have done the same in
his position. "He told us the LLC would protect our personal
assets if we're sued."

"Who holds the lease agreement on the property?" Storm
asked. "The owner of the shopping center?"

"You don't need to get into that," Lara said.

"I do, though. The lease agreement can affect how I set up
the business. It's part of your overhead. For example, who's
responsible for water and electricity? Is that divided among the
tenants of the property? I noticed two other tenants, but your
store is the biggest in the shopping center."

"Water—well, we're putting in new copper pipes. New
wiring, too. It'll help the other stores," Lara said.

Storm smiled at her. "Do you know if the utilities come from
the street? Are they on public property?"

Lara looked at Ryan, who played with his water glass.

"I'll check on that," Lara said.

Storm wondered if they doubted her experience. "You can check with other attorneys if you like."

"No, we trust you," Ryan said. "You set up Steve O'Donnell's restaurant and Riley Murakami's tattoo parlor. You come highly recommended."

"I'm glad you're checking around," Storm said. "But now I'm curious, are Steve and Riley friends of yours?"

"Riley and I knew each other in California. Steve's a friend of Riley's, and I called him."

"Good. I wish more of my clients asked for references and did background checks." She winced at a memory. "And checked employee records before hiring."

Storm had recalled a specific—and unfortunate—incident, so it took her a moment to notice that Lara looked a shade paler than she had a moment before.

"Anything wrong?" Storm asked.

"No," Lara said. "That's good advice."

A waitress appeared to take their order, and Storm figured since Damon's phone call had kept her from finishing her breakfast toast, she'd have the warm chocolate brownie with vanilla-flecked ice cream. Lara ordered an avocado filled with crab salad and Ryan ordered katsu curry rice with chicken and four gyoza.

"You can share my gyoza," he said, and looked first at Lara, then Storm.

"I just ate an hour ago," Storm said, though the offer was tempting. Storm loved the little fried dumplings.

"I have to fit into my wedding dress," Lara said.

While they ate, they discussed the upcoming wedding, which was in mid-July, three months away. Not long after his cup of coffee arrived, Ryan peeked at his gold watch.

"I've got to go."

"You do?" Lara looked up at him and her voice took on a wry note. "Meeting your dad again?"

"And some business associates. We're looking at a condominium in Kapalua."

"Good hunting," Lara said.

"It was great to meet you," Storm said. "I'll see you again soon."

"Yes, let's sit down tomorrow or the next day to set up details on the corporation."

The women watched him leave, then Storm sprawled back in her chair with a sigh. "That brownie was wonderful."

"I'm full too." Lara thought for a brief moment. "Damon's got the shop covered this afternoon. Are you busy? If you're off the clock, would you like to go snorkeling? I'll show you my favorite spots down by Makena, where we're going to take some tours. Two of my favorite sightings are at Turtle Town and Bruce the shark."

"Bruce the shark?" Storm straightened. "Do I want to see him?"

"Sure. Bruce is a four-foot, white-tipped reef shark. They're harmless." Lara cocked her head. "He's accustomed to divers, plus the shark is my *'aumakua*."

"It is?" Storm grimaced. "I'll have to rely on you for protection, because my *'aumakua* is the *pua'a*. I don't think a pig will be much help in the water."

"Pigs are known for their cleverness," Lara said, though Storm picked up a note of condescension in her voice. People whose *'aumakua* were the *manō* tended to think other *'aumakua* didn't measure up.

She'd have to check with Aunt Maile, who was well versed in Hawaiian lore, as to how the animal totems interacted. Maybe they practiced some kind of amnesty. If you believed in that stuff to begin with.

"You sure Bruce is safe?"

"You could hand-feed him, though we don't, because he needs to hunt on his own. White-tips aren't aggressive to people. And they don't have very big teeth." She grimaced. "Probably not as bad as getting bit by my mom's toy poodle. In fact, I'd say Bruce has a better personality."

"Ouch. You have to deal with the poodle often?"

"No, he died last year, at sixteen."

"How'd your mom handle that?"

"Not too well." Lara pushed back from the table. "But everyone else felt like celebrating."

"Get her a replacement. A nice one."

"Yeah, maybe." Lara sounded like she'd rather change the subject. "Let's gather some dive gear and go for a swim. You can see first hand what my clients are experiencing."

Chapter Six

Back at the dive shop, Lara went to a cabinet along the wall in the front room and began to sort through skin diving gear.

"Damon," she called out over the buzz of an electric sander in the back room. "We're going for a swim."

A man's voice answered over the noise, and Lara frowned. "Damon?"

"Not Damon," said a tall, tanned man who came through the door from the back. His denim jeans were nearly white with age, though his T-shirt and baseball cap were new and had Lara's Aquatic Adventures emblazoned on them. The brilliant turquoise shirt matched his eyes.

"He's wearing ear plugs," the man said. "Can't hear you."

"Ken, what are you doing here?" Lara handed a set of fins to Storm. "I thought we had a group going to Molokini this afternoon."

"They wanted to switch to tomorrow. We weren't busy, so I went for it." He grinned at her. "For a ten percent change fee."

Lara frowned. "Don't chase my customers away."

"It's in the contract. You know that." Ken's penetrating gaze drifted to Storm's curious one. White teeth gleamed under a full, rakish moustache. "Who's your friend?"

"Storm, meet the captain of my two-boat fleet. This is Ken McClure."

Storm put out her hand. "Nice to meet you."

Ken's hand was warm and dry. "Pleasure's mine."

"What's the schedule tomorrow?" Lara got back to business.

"The rescheduled group goes out at seven, and we'll be back before noon. The sunset cruise leaves at two." His eyes crinkled at her. "Don't worry, we've got it handled."

"Is Stella going out with you?"

"She's doing the morning group. I'll check with her about the afternoon run. If she can't go, Susan can."

"Susan's paid by the hour, so she's expensive," Lara said with a grimace. "How's Keiko coming along?"

"She still won't go without Stella. But I think she'll come along tomorrow morning. She's good at setting up the tanks and equipment."

Lara nodded, and for a moment Storm thought she saw concern flash across Lara's face, but it disappeared quickly. Running a small business is a huge job, Storm reminded herself. In some ways like her small law firm, but with more people to supervise. And Storm didn't have to deal with construction work going on at the same time. It was as if Lara had to supervise two separate work teams, complete with the personal issues that come with them. The carpenter's drinking, Keiko's distress (whatever that was about), dry wall dust over everything, and who knew what else? She'd been here all of a day.

"I'll talk to them," Lara said.

Ken nodded cheerfully. "I'll see you around lunchtime tomorrow?"

"Yes, at least call and give me a report."

"Have a nice swim." He cheerfully pointed to the fins Storm held. "I'll tell Damon you're going."

"Thanks, let him know I'll see him in the morning."

Lara handed Storm a dive mask. "See if this fits."

For the first time, Storm noticed crow's feet around Lara's perfectly made up eyes. Her client looked tired, and Storm could imagine why.

She put the mask to her face and checked the seal. "It's fine, but we don't have to do this today. Want to go tomorrow instead?"

Lara shook her head. "It's only getting busier." She jerked her head toward the back room. "If Damon and his crew get the cabinets up today, we'll start putting things away tomorrow." Her shoulders slumped a bit. "Of course, we'll be working around the painters."

"Can you delay the opening? Or open without having the back room finished?"

Lara's mouth twisted. "No, we'll get it done. It's just disorganized right now."

"Damon seems capable."

"Yeah, he is." She put fins, masks, and snorkels in two net bags with drawstrings and handed one to Storm. "Let's go. I can use the break."

"Ken McClure looks familiar somehow."

Lara's good humor returned. "Women often say that."

"No, I mean it."

"He's involved in a group called Beach Rescue Alliance. They got some print not long ago when about twenty protesters turned up on a beach and half the women marched topless."

"That could be it," Storm said.

"Probably," Lara laughed. "We'd better drive separately. I have to meet Ryan later."

Storm got into her rented oven and seared her leg on the chrome seatbelt buckle. She yelped, rolled down all the windows, and turned the air conditioner to maximum. A moment later, a white Corvette convertible rolled around the corner. Lara wore sunglasses and a wide brimmed hat. She looked as cool as a polar bear on an ice floe.

Storm wiped a rivulet of sweat from her eyes and pulled out onto South Kihei Road. She followed Lara to Pi'ilani Highway, then south through the golf courses in Wailea. A quarter mile past the turn to Storm's hotel, Lara turned onto a public access road to the beach and then into a gravel parking lot.

Storm parked next to her. Lara got out of her car, tossed her hat onto the front seat, and put the top up. "You're going to love this."

Both women went into the bathhouse to put on bathing suits, then pulled their snorkeling gear from the net bags and headed the last fifty yards to the gently lapping ocean. It was a calm day and people were scattered along the white sand, but the beach was far from crowded. A few snorkels bobbed around visible coral heads. Every now and then a lazy swim fin broke the surface.

"Tourists usually stay in close." Lara pointed to the nearby divers. "Some of the local swimmers are quite adventurous, though."

"Are we meeting any of them?"

"Not now. The pink hats usually go out in the morning." Lara fitted her mask on her face.

"Pink hats?"

"It's a group of local swimmers. They're all ages, but most of them are members of U.S. Masters Swimming, and they wear pink racing caps. I've been encouraging Stella and Keiko to join them."

"Are Stella and Keiko good swimmers?" Storm pulled on her fins and splashed into the water. She wanted to ask what their story was, but thought she'd get further if she eased into the topic. It would be best if Lara volunteered it.

"Stella's quite a good swimmer, though Keiko needs more experience. Stella is already leading some of my snorkeling groups. Easy stuff, not the scuba dives. Come on, I'll show you." Lara dove in, ending the conversation for the time being.

Storm stroked after her into deeper water, finding it easy to follow. Storm was a surfer, and paddling her board kept her in shape for this kind of outing. The water was so calm and warm she felt at ease, and looked around with delight at the increasing life below.

Coral colonies squatted like condominiums on the rippled sandy bottom. There were handfuls of fish hovering over each one, cleaning and foraging. The water, which was clear and bright, allowed her to see at least fifty feet in any direction, and the shadows of bigger coral heads loomed in the deeper water ahead.

As she found her swimming rhythm and began to breathe more comfortably, Storm imagined herself flying above a new and exciting landscape with inhabitants that paralleled the world of legs. Clusters of bright butterfly fish, and *humuhumu-nukunukuāpuaʻa,* the reef trigger fish, a small fellow with a long name, went about their business indifferent to the creatures passing above.

Not indifferent, Storm reminded herself. They knew she and Lara were there; they just weren't threatened. The *humuhumu's* bright, flat eyes checked their progress, but the fish continued to peck along the rippled sandy bottom. Storm enjoyed spotting these animals, not only because they were the unofficial Hawaiʻi state fish, but the name translated to "trigger fish with a snout like a pig." Lara's *ʻaumakua* may have been the big, bad shark, but Storm trusted pigs.

The women swam nearly side by side, though Storm let Lara set both the pace and the direction. Lara wore a red flowered bikini, and her mask, snorkel, and fins were a yellow that matched the brilliant Yellow Tangs darting among the coral formations ten to fifteen feet below them.

They stayed in twenty to thirty feet of water as they rounded a point of lava rock that pitched from the shoreline into the ocean at a sharp angle. Above water, it was craggy, black, and forbidding. Beneath the surface, it teamed with life: algae, coral, *opihi,* little shrimp, eels, limpet, and other organisms in their own tidal ecosystem. It was the underwater version of the steep, high inland cliffs, known as the *pali,* formed by ancient volcanic eruptions and eroded by thousands of years of wind and rain into precipices of pleated green velvet.

Lara popped her head up and pulled the snorkel out of her mouth. "How're you doing?"

"I love it."

"It gets better. Just up ahead is an arch we can dive through. It's only about ten feet deep. Follow me."

Lara set out with Storm close behind. Right away, Storm spotted the arch of stone on the bottom, and three turtles, two larger ones and a juvenile, swam on the other side of it. Storm squealed with delight into her snorkel. Lara heard her and turned, her teeth showing in a smile around the snorkel. She looked a little like her shark totem.

Lara pointed to the turtles and dived. Storm pinched her nose to equalize her ears and went after her, keeping enough distance to avoid Lara's fins. Though Storm had a moment of trepidation, the arch wasn't far and she reached it before her breath ran out. Plenty of time to sail through and surface on the other side.

The turtles glided out of the way. It was as if they were watching the fun. Silly humans, look how hard they have to work out here.

Through the clear porthole of her mask, Storm observed two more turtles in the shadow of a rock formation, then three more lingering near the bottom. Lara grunted into her mask and pointed with excitement at a single turtle that was feeding along a slope of jagged lava rock. Like the fish, the animal watched the humans, but continued with his activity.

Lara popped her head out of the water and removed the snorkel from her mouth. "It's a Hawksbill. They're an extremely rare, endangered species. You can tell by its beaked mouth and the scalloping of his shell along the back edge."

Storm situated her mask and plunged her head back into the water. The Hawksbill scraped at a chunk of rock, though she knew the animal watched her carefully.

She surfaced and pushed the mask to the top of her head. "It's beautiful."

Lara's eyes gleamed. "I have to tell Stella and Keiko. Keiko will be thrilled." She scanned the coastline to get her bearings, then pulled her mask down and set out again.

Storm watched for other Hawksbills, and saw more of the larger Green turtles, but the Hawksbill was an exceptional sighting. Swimming with long, easy strokes, a sense of contentment filled Storm. She was aware that she and Lara were guests in this universe, and she was pleased that her passage above the turtle's world hadn't seemed to disturb it.

Lara swam for ten or fifteen minutes without comment, and Storm trailed behind and listened to the calls of Humpback whales in the distance. It was a mournful sound when heard from under water. A few of the great mammals lingered at the end of the season, probably mothers waiting until their calves were strong enough to make the long trek to their Alaskan feeding grounds.

Lara was at least fifteen feet ahead of Storm and had slowed at an outcropping of rocks. She dived, came up for air, and then dived again, deeper this time, and waved for Storm to follow. Storm took a deep breath and descended.

Lara hovered with her hands waving, like a skydiver floating on an air current, and grinned toward Storm. She pointed downward at an indentation still another ten feet below her. Because Storm was still on the other side of the rocks, she couldn't see what Lara was looking at, but she assumed Lara wanted to share another wildlife sighting. She hoped it was another Hawksbill, perhaps a mate to the one they'd seen, and she swam forward slowly, careful not to bang against rocks in the backwash from the surf.

Lara rounded the rock's jutting corner. The tips of her yellow fins fluttered about ten feet deeper than Storm, and Storm stroked to catch up.

Suddenly, Lara exploded from behind the jagged notch as if she'd been shot from a howitzer. Something else blasted past, too, with a force so strong it caused Storm to somersault, arms and legs flailing. Lara, folded into a multicolor ball of rolling limbs, caromed against her and knocked Storm's mask awry, but Storm caught a glimpse of Lara's face before she lost her mask. Her client's mouth was wide with terror, the mouthpiece to her yellow snorkel flopping uselessly in her streaming hair.

A split second later, something fast and muscular bumped Lara again, driving her into Storm's side. Lara made a noise like a drowning kitten, a plaintive cry that penetrated their underwater realm.

The women raced to the surface. Rarely had Storm felt so puny and helpless. Later, she would reflect that all their thrashing had been pretty dumb. Sharks are attracted to disturbances and signs of distress, and she and Lara were splashing like a couple of speared octopuses.

Once they were within ten feet of the rocky and difficult shore, the women faced each other. Each of them heaved for air, and Storm wondered if her eyes bulged as much as Lara's, whose pupils were dilated and black as gun barrels. Neither wanted to swim back the way they'd come.

"Bruce has never done that."

"We must have startled him. Maybe Bruce is a mom." Storm struggled to keep up. Lara had already stood up. Her knees were pumping as she high-stepped across the rocky bottom.

All they needed now was for one of them to step in a hole. They were probably all filled with Moray eels and sharp-spined *wana,* or sea urchins.

"Careful," Storm called.

Lara plunged ahead. "You don't understand." She held her mask and snorkel in one hand and her arms flapped with effort. "He's my *'aumakua.* My family totem. He should never have done that."

Storm tried to keep her feet from scraping across the sharp lava in the surging tide. "Lara, let's swim down shore a bit, where there's a sandy bottom."

Lara didn't seem to hear, so Storm set her jaw and followed with tentative, careful steps. Each one hurt. Not only were the black rocks sharp, but on shore they were hot as skillets.

"Lara, don't take it personally. We scared it. Maybe it's a she—with babies to protect."

"It's *supposed* to protect me." Lara's voice held a sense of betrayal.

"Ouch." Storm stepped on a sharp rock. "It's a wild animal. A wild pig would chase me, too, if it had to defend its nest." She didn't mention that she'd be disappointed, though she didn't expect a sow to protect her over her own young. That was asking too much.

It was true that many Hawaiians had great faith in their *'aumakua.* If a pig chased Storm, she'd find the experience distressing. But there were a lot of very good reasons it could happen.

"Shit," Lara said, and picked up her foot. Storm could see a drop of blood on the pad of her big toe. Meanwhile, Storm's heel had a tender stone bruise. A spot of soft sand loomed ahead, an oasis in a lava field.

Storm headed for it. "Where are we going?"

Lara hobbled on. "The road."

"How far are we from our cars?"

Lara's shoulders rose and fell. "About a mile."

The hot sun beat down on the top of Storm's head, and a contusion over her eye stung. Must have been from when Lara banged into her, when the mask came off, which was why salt water still ran from her nose.

She picked her way carefully across another pitted lava spill. The irregular surface had holes filled with fine white sand, which gave it a polka-dotted appearance. At high tide, those *puka* would be filled with salt water and tiny forms of life, but now they were cushions for her sore feet.

The women limped inland to the narrow, paved road. Storm recognized the area from this morning's jog.

Lara perked up. "We're close."

"Good." Storm hopped from foot to foot. She could fry an egg on the tarry asphalt. "My feet are killing me."

"Me, too." Lara cocked her head. A truck was lumbering down the road, and Lara waved at it. "I know these guys. They work at one of the houses down near La Perouse Bay."

"There's a lot of construction going on, isn't there?" Storm asked.

"Only a handful now, but there will be." Lara hopped on the hot pavement. "Hey, Charlie! Got room for two more?"

Two men sat in the cab and two more in the bed of the pickup. They were shirtless and wore bandanas over their dark hair. One guy's arms and chest were covered with writhing dragons, mermaids, and geishas. It was hard to make the scenes out without staring. Not staring wasn't easy, either. The other guy merely had tribal bands around both biceps. He looked tame by comparison.

Storm felt self-conscious in her bikini. Lara let Tribal pull her into the cab, but Storm hopped in before either man could grab her. The truck bed was grubby with clumps of earth, and she'd bet the metal was hot as a frying pan. Not wanting to add her butt to her growing list of sore spots, she sat on her swim fins.

The ride wasn't long and the men dropped Storm and Lara at their cars. Storm pointed to the outside shower. "I'm going to rinse the salt off."

Lara eyed the green moss around its base for a tenth of a second. "I'm taking off. I've got to meet Ryan for dinner."

Storm checked the angle of the sun, and then looked at her diver's watch. It was five-fifteen. "Hey, the swim was great. Thanks for taking me."

Lara looked out of the corner of her eye. "Right."

"I mean it. Stop worrying about the shark. Your *'aumakua* must be the *manō hae*, the fighter. Not a dinky reef shark."

That got a small smile. "See you tomorrow."

Storm stood in the cool shower while Lara walked to her car. Lara didn't have the same confident spring to her step that she'd had when they'd started their swim.

Chapter Seven

Storm didn't have much time if she wanted to meet Damon at seven. Depending on traffic, Lahaina could be a half-hour drive or more. The public shower's cool water had revived her, especially her burning feet, and she took another shower back in her hotel room, where she washed and conditioned her hair and slathered on the hotel's skin lotion.

A little lip gloss and mascara, and a black jersey tank dress with a short, flared skirt that was both comfortable and jazzy. Flat, strappy sandals. No way was she putting her beat-up feet into closed shoes.

She glanced at her watch again, and decided she had a few minutes. She dialed Hamlin's mobile phone.

He answered, and the sound of his voice was a comfort. "I'm glad you called," he said. "I've been leaving messages for you."

She peeked at the screen of her phone. Sure enough, there were three. "I've been trying to call you, too."

"I've been worried—. No, no. I miss you."

Storm was surprised when her heart leaped. "That's nice to hear."

"I have a lot to talk to you about."

"Are you coming home?"

"Soon. Do you have a minute now?"

"I'm meeting an old friend for dinner."

"How long are you going to stay on Maui? Grace told me you left yesterday."

"I thought I'd stay through the weekend."

Storm's secretary Grace, who wore a voluminous mu'u mu'u and an array of fresh flowers in her hair every day, was a romantic. She also was efficient and watched Storm like a brood mare watches her colt.

"I don't blame you." Hamlin sounded wistful.

"When will you be back?" Storm asked.

"Next week, if all goes well."

"Good, I should be back by then, too."

"I can't wait to see you." His words were soft.

"I'll call you." Storm slowly put the phone back in her purse. None of the old anger had been in his voice.

He'd gone to the Mainland for a few weeks and stayed two months. Part of the delay was due to the death of his mother, whose estate he'd needed to settle. After that, he'd had an excellent offer on a special project with a law firm in California.

Storm was no longer certain how he felt about her. Though they talked a couple times a week, reserve hovered between them like a screen.

Hamlin had been injured trying to protect Storm. When she was looking into the death of her uncle, the killer injected him with succinylcholine, a curare-like agent, and he nearly died. Another time, he'd fallen off a horse on Moloka'i and injured his shoulder. That time they'd been working cases that coincided eerily, but the horseback ride had been all her idea.

Hamlin told her he couldn't bear to watch her wander into life-threatening situations. But she sensed anger, and believed his reservations about their relationship went beyond concern for her welfare.

She wondered if he felt their backgrounds were too different. She'd known since she was twelve and her mother took an overdose of sleeping pills that her welfare was her own responsibility. She couldn't rely on other people to protect her if her own mother would not.

Eme Kayama, who suffered from depression, had planned her suicide for weeks. It was a form of desertion, and Storm had grown up with the belief that people couldn't rescue one another. She had never asked Hamlin to be her white knight. Lover, partner, friend, yes. Protector, no.

His voice had brought a surge of warmth and hope, but by the time she'd walked to her car, her throat had tightened with anger and sorrow, feelings she still had trouble separating. She tried to shake off the negative emotions. Upsetting her was the last thing Hamlin wanted to do. He'd told her he missed her, and that was what she needed to think about.

◇◇◇

It was a few minutes before seven when Storm reached The Fiddler Crab, and found she'd arrived before Damon. The hostess told her their table would take a few minutes to prepare and directed her to the bar, which overlooked the beach.

She sat on a stool with an unimpeded view of the fading day. The bartender brought a glass of wine, and she watched the eastern sky glow indigo, while gentle Venus climbed the darkening vastness. How appropriate, Storm thought, that the Greeks believed this mistress of sensuality sprang from the foam of the sea.

"Storm?"

She jerked around. "Damon, hi."

"You were far away."

She had been. "The view is wonderful."

"That it is." He sat down next to her, ordered a draught, and looked out at the water.

The bartender served his beer just as the hostess appeared to tell them their table was ready. They followed her to an outside table.

Damon studied Storm's face. "Life agrees with you." He looked tired and older than she'd remembered.

"Thanks. I had time for a long, hot shower after the swim."

"Lara didn't look as relaxed as you do."

"She came by the shop?" Storm asked. "Then she was probably late for her dinner with Ryan."

Damon sat back in his chair. "She's got a lot on her mind."

"How's the construction project going?"

"It's fine. We're on schedule." But his expression belied his words.

"So what's wrong?" Storm asked.

Damon gave a shrug and drained his beer.

"Planning the wedding is probably getting to her," Storm said. "People tell me they're stressful."

Damon tried to smile, but it didn't work. "That and her mom."

"Because the dog died?"

Damon looked confused. "I didn't know about that. I was talking about the new home. She hasn't adjusted."

"Lara's parents moved?"

"Her dad died a few years ago, and her mom's health went down hill." He waved down the waitress and ordered another beer. "Maybe I shouldn't talk about this."

Storm had the feeling he wanted to share his concerns, though. Whatever pressures were mounting in the dive shop seemed to be taking their toll on him, too. She sat back in her chair and took a slow sip from her wine glass.

After a moment, Damon filled the silence. "Her mom's in one of those assisted living places. Way I hear it, Barb doesn't always recognize Lara. She thinks Lara is her sister."

"Lara resembles her aunt?"

"No, Lara's younger sister. I don't know if they looked alike, but from what I've heard, their personalities were quite different."

Storm leaned toward him. "You're speaking of her in the past."

Damon set his beer down gently. "Angela died about five years ago."

"That's awful," Storm said. "Poor Lara." She remembered how quickly Lara changed the subject when Storm had suggested getting the mother a new dog. She felt a wave of embarrassment for the glibness of the comment.

"No kidding." He wiped condensation from his beer glass. "Her mom is lost in the past. This is when your mother is supposed to help you buy a dress and bug you about the guest list, isn't it?"

"From what I've heard." Storm pushed back a lock of wayward hair. "Does Lara's mom realize she's getting married?"

"I don't know." He raised his eyes to Storm's. "So what's your secret to happiness? You look great."

Storm gave a snort of laughter. "Nice stab at changing the subject."

"C'mon. Who's the love of your life?"

"Damon, please. You haven't seen me for years. Why are you asking?" She squinted at him. "I heard you got married."

"Yeah." He took a long swallow from his beer glass, and then centered it on its coaster without looking up at her. "I did. Then she left. Took our two daughters with her."

"That has to be tough. Do you get to see them?"

"She moved to Kauai. I get to see them once a month and they spend summers with me." He showed his teeth in a grin that didn't reach his eyes.

"This wasn't an amicable split, I gather. What happened?"

"The usual." He heaved a sigh. "I was working too hard and staying out late. She fell in love with her doctor." He winced. "Her gynecologist."

"Oof." In the candlelight, Storm could see the reddened capillaries in his nose and remembered the way he'd given the hung-over carpenter at Lara's shop another chance. Damon may have faced some demons in the bottle, too. Which could be another reason for the marriage breaking up.

"How old are your daughters?"

He smiled. "Maile's nine and Emily is twelve." He extracted his wallet and dug out two pictures, which he handed to Storm.

"They're adorable. What grades are they in?"

After the waiter took their orders, Damon launched into stories about their school exploits, sports events, and how much he looked forward to the summer soccer league. As he related his experiences, his eyes brightened and he straightened in his chair. He loved talking about his kids, just like most of the good dads she knew.

Over dinner, she found herself talking about Hamlin and how he'd dislocated his shoulder falling from a horse during her last case, when a high school friend living on Moloka'i asked for her help. The friend had neglected to tell her about a smoldering feud that involved betrayal and death.

"He thinks the accident was your fault?"

"He thinks I take unnecessary risks."

"Do you?"

She shrugged. "Maybe. I do what I have to do. It's a matter of perception." She searched his face. "Isn't it?"

"It sounds like something only the two of you would know."

A disturbance from the bar distracted them. A dozen or so people had clustered around one of the televisions on the wall. Instead of sports, a local news program was broadcasting live. The bartender turned up the volume just as one of the patrons approached Damon.

"Hey, Damon. Isn't that one of your guys?" He pointed to the TV screen.

"Huh?" Damon squinted at the distant television and the agitated reporter who dominated the screen. "That guy?"

"No, your new employee."

Damon and Storm stared at the television. A wailing police car added to the confusion on the screen. Over the commotion, the reporter blurted the names Hiroki Yoshinaka and Lloyd Construction Enterprises. The camera panned out to show a small, dilapidated frame house. The front door gaped like an open mouth.

"Jesus." Damon shot to his feet and threw money on the table. He grabbed Storm's arm. "Come with me. Please?"

No one noticed their exit. Everyone was looking at the TV.

They jumped in Damon's pickup truck. "He lives nearby," Damon said, and accelerated out of the restaurant parking lot.

An ambulance wailed behind them. Damon cursed and pulled over to let it pass. A few minutes later, he drove onto the dry front lawn of a small home. Both he and Storm jumped from the truck. The ambulance had arrived a minute ahead of them, and the policeman on the scene waved the attendants into the house. He held up his hand to stop Storm and Damon from going any farther, and then turned on the reporter. "Out by the street. Now."

"C'mon, Sarge. I called it in."

"Now!" the cop roared, and the news crew backed up.

Storm leaned against the truck, self-conscious. The name Hiroki Yoshinaka had come to her; it was the carpenter with the hangover. Why in the world had she come with Damon? It was an impulse she wished she'd ignored.

She looked down at her feet, at the patchy, dry grass. A doll, whose long blond hair tangled in the weeds, lay near her foot. Its staring blue eyes caught the glare of headlights. Storm picked it up and smoothed the toy's hair. Yoshinaka had two young daughters, didn't he? A wave of dread washed through her.

The cop spoke into a radio and turned to Damon, who stood about six feet away. "Hey man, this isn't a good time."

"Yoshinaka works for me. You know his girls play with mine. Can I help?"

"It looks bad, buddy." The cop spoke into his radio, turned back to Damon. "Hang on, okay?"

Two ambulance attendants burst from the front door carrying a gurney. As it passed, Storm saw a web of black hair against a face so white it was almost lost against the sheets. A third attendant kept the small form in place, and held his hand firmly over a spreading red stain on the white cover.

The cop walked over to Damon, his eyes on Storm. "Who's your friend?"

"Storm Kayama. Storm, this is my friend Carl Moana. Our girls play soccer together." Damon shot a nervous glance at Storm and turned to Moana. "I hope she'll be Hiroki's lawyer."

The cop looked between the two of them. "Hiroki won't need a lawyer." He rubbed his face as if he wanted to erase the words. Storm noticed the tremble in his hand.

"Carl, what happened in there?" Damon asked.

"Hiroki's dead. So is the younger daughter." He covered a break in his voice by clearing his throat. "Don't know how bad the older one is yet."

"Jesus," Damon's broken whisper carried above the sound of the disappearing siren.

"Damon, we might need to talk to you about Hiroki. He was holding the gun."

Damon didn't react right away. His eyes tracked the arrival of another ambulance and three more police vehicles. When he met Sergeant Moana's gaze, the confusion on his face was being replaced by anger.

"No, he wouldn't do that. He couldn't. He loved his girls, and he was getting better at work. It's just not possible."

Chapter Eight

The police insisted on talking to Damon about his employee, and Storm sat in the truck, miserable and unable to forget the image of the little girl being loaded, bleeding and alone, into the ambulance. Did she know her father and sister were dead? Where was the mother? What demons possessed a man to make him kill his children?

Damon came back looking as if he'd been gutted. The cop friend was with him and opened the truck door. Storm was about ready to offer to drive, but Damon glared ahead through the windshield. He turned the key and peered, red-eyed, at Sergeant Moana. "I can't believe it."

"I know." Moana kicked at a clump of dry grass. "But it's the way it looks. And we've seen it before, guys who get depressed, drink too much, get hopeless."

"She's Maile's age." Damon's voice broke.

"You don't have to tell your daughters yet," Moana said.

"What about Carmen?" Damon rubbed his face. "She gonna be okay?"

"Don't know yet." Moana looked almost as sad as Damon.

Storm watched the devastation on the faces of both men. They knew these girls. Damon had mentioned a summer soccer league; the girls probably all played together.

Moana looked around for his colleagues, and then said softly, "I'll call you tomorrow. Get a good night's sleep. We're all going to need it."

Damon backed out of the yard, drove down the street to the stop sign.

"You want me to drive?" Storm asked. "I'll buy you a drink and take you home."

Damon sat for a moment. They were alone at the stop sign, though people had gathered in the street in front of the small, neglected house. Blue police lights pulsed through the dark.

"I'm okay to drive—it's not far, but I'd like to sit down for a while. We've got to pick up your car anyway."

There was little conversation the rest of the drive. When they got to the restaurant, Damon pulled in next to Storm's car. "People in there are going to ask me stuff, and I don't want to talk about it."

"You want to go somewhere else?"

"Yeah, there's a quiet place a couple blocks from here."

"I'll follow you." Storm got into her own car. Damon waited until she turned around, and then headed down Front Street to a narrow side road and a municipal parking lot. They parked and Damon led the way to a small bar called The Surf Line.

The place was busy. Damon and Storm drew only brief glances from the patrons and sat at the last empty table under a big screen showing non-stop surfing movies. Damon's face flickered in the blue light, and when the waitress came to take their order, her short white apron fluoresced above long brown legs.

"Gordon Biersch pale ale," Damon said.

"I'll have one, too," Storm said.

Damon slumped back in his chair and heaved a sigh. The waitress came back right away with their order.

"I'm sorry—"they both said, as soon as she was out of earshot.

"I shouldn't have gone with you," Storm said. She had felt like a voyeur, an unwelcome crasher witnessing a stranger's dire misfortune.

"I asked you to go, and now I'm sorry you had to see it." Damon rubbed at the condensation on his glass. "But I'm glad you were there. I might have yelled at Carl or something. Just the idea that Hiroki could actually—" Damon drank half his beer.

Murder his daughters? Storm understood Damon's disbelief, but she knew that Hiroki, if he'd done it, hadn't been the first. For Damon, the idea was unthinkable, but Sergeant Moana, who looked as miserable as Damon, had to consider it.

"Did he talk to you this afternoon?" Storm asked.

"He didn't talk much. Language barrier." His lips twisted as if his drink was bitter. "Crystal did a lot of interpreting for him."

He drained the rest of his beer, caught the eye of their waitress, and gestured for a refill. Storm had only taken a few swallows of her ale. The waitress anticipated it, and only brought one.

"Where's the mother?"

"Dead. I think she had cancer." He took a long swallow. "But, like I said, it was hard to get Hiroki to talk."

Damon ran a finger along initials carved in the wood table top. For several minutes, he was lost in thought. His face was pale and blue semicircles underscored his eyes.

Storm wasn't sure how to alleviate his distress. "You knew the girls pretty well."

"Yeah, they're good friends with my daughters. I don't know how I can tell Maile that Crystal...that she's dead." His voice broke on the little girl's name, Crystal.

"You think it will be in the paper?"

"Oh, shit." Damon set his glass down with a crack. "I have to tell her tomorrow, don't I?"

"Probably. Will their mother tell them?" Storm finished her beer and the waitress brought another before she looked up.

"She will or someone else. People know my girls are from Maui." He rubbed his eyes. "This really sucks."

"Yeah."

Long minutes passed before Storm broke into his thoughts again. He'd almost finished his third—fourth?—beer. She'd lost track of her own, let alone his, but she knew her eyes were starting to droop.

"Damon, remember what Moana told you. You need to get a good rest tonight if you can. Can I drive you home?"

"I'm not ready to go yet."

"It's after midnight. I need to go and I don't want to leave you here." She reached out to touch his arm. "Let me drive you."

"Not yet. I'm okay."

"I'm tired. You must be, too."

"Don't worry about me."

The waitress had appeared at their table. "We start closing up in about an hour. Someone will drive him home. We've done it before." The smile she gave Damon was kind.

◇◇◇

Raging thirst, a thumping headache, and a stomach that rocked and rolled awoke Storm at seven-thirty. She decided not to go for a morning jog. Three cups of strong coffee, a dry bagel, and a dip in the ocean improved her outlook, but she still regretted that second beer. Or was it the third?

She got to the dive shop around nine-thirty, and found she'd arrived before Lara. Stella and Keiko were busy moving files and boxes into the back room. The fresh plumeria in Stella's bright blonde hair smelled wonderful. One of her gold teeth glinted in a smile. "I'm glad you're helping Lara. She needs it, and we heard good things about you."

"Thanks." Storm blinked. "What kind of help do you think she needs most?"

"Picking men," Keiko said, then flushed.

"Ryan's good for her." Stella flashed a look at Keiko, who shrugged. "Keiko and I knew her last boyfriend, and he wasn't so nice."

"His name is Greg Wilson," Keiko said as if Storm might have met him.

"Never heard of him," Storm said.

"You can mention his name," Stella said. "She'll only be mad at me for about a tenth of a second and she needs the reminder."

"You sure? I don't like to reveal a source."

"I'm sure. It'll do her some good." Stella looked like she meant it.

"Stella introduced Ryan to Lara," Keiko said.

Stella gave her a playful slap on the arm. "Oh, hush."

"Do you know where she is?" Storm asked.

"Talking to the florist," Stella said, and headed for the back room. The aromas of sweet flowers and old cigarettes wafted along with her.

"For the wedding?" Storm asked.

"Either that or the opening," said Keiko. "It's hard to keep track right now."

This conversation was the first time Storm had heard the young woman speak. She had a low, soft voice with a hint of an accent. One of Storm's friends had moved from Asia to Hawai'i at the age of twelve, and Keiko sounded like her. Storm guessed Keiko to be around twenty.

Storm picked up a box from the stack waiting to be taken to the back office. "How do you know about Lara's old boyfriend?" She trailed behind Keiko. The box was heavy, probably filled with papers and files.

She set it on a table next to Stella's last load. The older woman gave her a half-smile. "I've known Lara since she was a kid." She left to carry more boxes from the front room.

Damon was at the other end of the office space, carefully measuring for the installation of a cabinet that sat on the floor.

"You okay this morning?"

"Getting by." He sounded bad and looked worse. "My daughters called this morning. They heard it on the car radio going to school."

"That sucks."

"You're telling me. So then my ex gets the idea it might be too dangerous for the girls to come stay with me this summer."

"Not going to happen. She can't do that."

Damon's face brightened. That is, it went from burgundy to a capillary-webbed cherry. "She can't?"

"Hiroki's and his daughters' situation isn't relevant to your child custody agreement. You didn't cause it; your girls aren't in danger."

"Will you represent me if she makes trouble?"

"You'd be better off using your divorce lawyer. He or she knows the original agreement. If that person can't help, I'll take a look."

Storm felt a wave of relief when Damon nodded in agreement.

"Yeah, that makes sense. I'll call him this afternoon."

Storm watched a painter, a face she hadn't seen yesterday, trim around a window casing. "New guy?"

Damon shook his head. "No, he was scheduled today. I'm doing Hiroki's work."

"You heard anything about his daughter?"

"I called Carl this morning and left a message. He hasn't called back."

"He's busy."

"Yeah, I don't envy him."

"Storm?" Lara's voice rang out and Storm went out front to see her. Lara looked nearly as tired as Damon.

Storm greeted her. "I came by to talk business. We've got to get insurance papers filed if you're already running dive tours."

"Yeah, I know." Lara slumped into a desk chair. "So much going on at once."

"This is important. If something happens on one of your boats, you don't want to be liable."

"Ken's a great captain. He's real careful."

"What if someone falls down the steps? Claims you should have had a sign up that warned they could be slippery?"

Lara looked aghast. "Could that happen?"

"Sure, and that's not as serious as someone panicking underwater and claiming your dive equipment was faulty. Lara, we have to talk about how your corporation is set up, what the terms of your land-lease agreement are, and a whole list of other things."

"Ryan should be here for that."

"When can we do it?"

Lara picked at her thumb nail, which was painted shell pink. "He's tied up all day with appointments."

"Your insurance company is going to want this information, too."

"We've got some insurance."

"What kind?"

Lara chipped away more nail polish. "Ryan and his dad own the property. They've got insurance."

"It probably doesn't cover diving or boating accidents."

"Ryan told me it would until we got started."

"You've started." Storm folded her arms across her chest. "Lara, Stella wanted me to remind you about Greg Wilson."

Lara jumped out of the chair, hands on her hips. "That bitch."

"She cares a great deal about you."

She dropped back into the chair, legs stuck out straight. "She cares about her point of view, not mine. She thinks I'm still a kid."

"So who's Greg Wilson?"

"Some pig I dated a couple of years ago. When I broke up with him, he claimed he trained me and wanted half of my winnings. When the asshole moved out, he took all my autographed sports stuff. I had a soccer ball signed by David Beckham."

"Did he train you?"

"Of course not." Her eyes flashed. "I met him a few months before I quit."

"But I gather you were with him for a while."

"Longer than I should have been." She shuddered.

"I've had a relationship or two I've regretted, too."

"As in total brain lapse?"

"Utter stupidity. Can't imagine what I saw in him."

Lara's face lit up. "Thank God I'm not the only one."

"We're not alone."

Lara looked at her through wings of sleek hair. "You don't know the half of it."

"I'm sure I don't. But the stakes are higher for you now. I want to make sure you don't have any regrets. Lawyers, contrary to popular belief, want to prevent train wrecks."

"But we're getting married. Ryan wouldn't endanger my business because it will affect his own."

"I hope he won't for other reasons, too." As in he adores you and wants the best for you. "Lara, it's a business. You need to protect yourself."

Lara looked away, as if there might be an answer painted on the wall behind Storm. All of the workers had evaporated into the back room.

"He'd never do anything to hurt me."

Storm had heard that before. In fact, she'd said it about her own ex, who ran the bar where Storm worked after college. He was so handsome all of her girlfriends had been envious—until he'd shown himself to be creepier than a Moray eel. Gorgeous to look at, but manipulative, slimy, and scheming.

Chapter Nine

Ryan and Tagama stood inside an empty warehouse in Kahului, not far from the airport. It was only eight o'clock, and they'd left Wailea at seven. Ryan held an extra large Starbucks cup. Whatever that size was called. Vente? He wished It came with an intravenous drip.

He and Lara had shared a bottle of wine last night, which was more than he usually drank. After that they began to argue, softly in the restaurant and much louder on the way home. That lasted until two, when he went to sleep on the couch.

Friends had told him about the stresses of a wedding, but he hadn't thought they would apply to them. The friends' stories revolved around overbearing future mothers-in-law, but Lara's mother couldn't even get her name right half the time, let alone force a china pattern down their throats.

Nor did Lara nag about crystal like his friends' wives had. No, she wanted real estate. She wanted the deed to the whole goddamned strip mall. Ryan kept telling her it would be in the family once they got married. It was part of Mālua LLC, Tagama and son's business. Lara wasn't the only one with a new corporation.

Lara's Aquatic Adventures took up two-thirds of the prime real estate space in the mall, which was worth over a million. The amount of her lease rent was for property half the value— and she knew it. There was even room for future expansion; the only stores left were an art gallery, an upscale wine shop, and an organic coffee/sandwich shop whose bread tasted like sawdust and the coffee like road tar.

"...this afternoon." Tagama narrowed his eyes. "You listening?"

"Sorry. Didn't get enough sleep last night. What did you say?"

"Can you show the wrought iron people the other half of the warehouse this afternoon?"

"The sculptor's willing to share it?"

"They use some of the same equipment."

"It's a great location." Ryan looked around the high, wide space. "And clean. Must have been expensive. How'd you find it?"

"Heard about a Chapter 11. Bank was going to repossess it, so I made an offer."

"Where we going now?" Ryan wondered if he might get another cup of coffee on the way.

"A shopping center about a mile from here. We bought it about the same time as the warehouse."

That "we" sounded very good.

"Has a good family restaurant in it. Home-cooked food, popular with the locals."

"Nice. Have we closed on the properties?"

"A few days ago."

"Great," Ryan said.

He was amazed. They were worth millions, as in multiple millions. He wondered where his father got that much money.

Until five months ago, Tagama would invite Ryan to dinner and take him to his golf club once a month, but they didn't interact much. They didn't talk about business, and often his father's colleagues, foreigners with vague but important titles, were around.

When Tagama invited his son to join Mālua LLC as a principal partner, the timing couldn't have been better. Ryan and a friend had just decided their gelato business wouldn't support the two of them. He thought he might have to persuade Lara to move to Honolulu, where jobs were more plentiful, and he'd been in turmoil at the prospect. But Tagama said he wanted to work with his son, get to know him as a man, and leave him a legacy for the future.

"Did you turn over some other properties to buy these?" Ryan asked.

Tagama gave Ryan a sideways glance, but answered. "I had two houses in Kahala and two on Waialae Iki Ridge. Nice, desirable neighborhoods on Oʻahu. Made some good money."

Ryan didn't ask how his father had bought those. He knew the areas. One of his friends, a lawyer, had bought a ridge home a year ago for two million.

Ryan knew his father had made astute investments over the years, and was delighted to be his partner in commercial real estate. His income had skyrocketed to the point that he hardly knew what to do with it. Brokerage houses loved him; someone from Merrill Lynch called at least once a week.

He played it down around his old friends. Marini, in particular, was still barely scraping by with gelato. Riley Murakami's tattoo parlor was marginal, too. These were good guys, and Ryan hoped they got out of the hole. Maybe he could help them out some day.

Chapter Ten

Stella interrupted the conversation about toxic ex-boyfriends with a call for Lara to get the phone. Lara shot from her chair as if springs had fired her into the air. Storm could hear her book a string of dive outings, the relief in her voice resonating at a level that would leave her customers delighted.

The morning session had obviously come to an end. That was okay; Storm had plenty on her mind. The Hawaii State Family Court had appointed her *guardian ad litem* for an O'ahu child, but the grandparents, with whom she needed to speak, lived in Kahului. She'd called earlier and set up an appointment.

On the way out of the shop, she paused to look at the progress in the large front room, where a worker was laying ceramic tile the color of the ocean. In a side room, wet suits and BCDs hung to dry and scuba tanks lined a wall. Ken McClure was busy in there with an assistant, some buff, bare-chested guy in surf trunks with a big eagle tattoo on his arm. It was heavy work, and they were sweating as they arranged equipment and loaded supplies into the back of a van with Lara's Aquatic Adventures emblazoned on the side. The shop even had its own air compressor for filling the tanks to exact safety standards. Hundreds of thousands of dollars were going into Lara's new business.

Damon emerged from the back room and headed outside to his truck. Storm followed him. "I'm going to Kahului on other business. Do you know if Carmen was taken to Maui Memorial Hospital?"

He gathered a load of tarpaulins and paint rollers. "Probably. That's where I'd go. You think she's covered by Hiroki's insurance?"

"You pay his premiums, right?"

Damon nodded.

"I'll check and let you know."

"The hospital's in Wailuku, not Kahului."

"No problem, they're close."

Storm drove out to Pi'ilani Highway, then pulled into the parking lot at Elleair Golf Club where she could make a couple of calls on her cell phone without running red lights or rear-ending someone. One of the calls was to a Honolulu number.

"Bureau of Conveyances," the operator answered.

"Mike Chilworth, please." Storm hoped he was in the office and not out on a site.

Mike picked up, and Storm went through the usual pleasantries regarding his wife and kids before she got to business. "Mike, how do I check who holds a land lease on a strip mall in Maui? It's in Kihei."

"You on Maui? You're one lucky wahine."

"Like I've got time to enjoy it."

"Not surfing?"

"I wish." Storm could hear Mike flipping through papers.

"Okay, here we go. You want the Maui County Real Property Assessment Division in Kahului. Here's the number. Ask for Sally—tell her I sent you." He chuckled. "Maybe you can finish early and go to Ho'okipa."

"I'm not holding my breath about getting to the beach, even if it is Ho'okipa."

Storm smiled at Mike's teasing, but it faded when she remembered one of the errands she wanted to accomplish. Visiting a twelve-year-old orphan with a gunshot wound wasn't going to be easy.

She had to drive around a bit before she found the Property Assessment offices, and in doing so, she made a detour around a badly damaged, once-elegant restaurant surrounded by warning signs, crime tape, and a handful of official-looking people.

The site of the explosion that had tied up traffic on Wednesday. Still under investigation, and it probably would be for days. She parked a few blocks away and walked by the place. The whole left corner of the building had been ripped off, revealing a scattering of dining tables and tattered linens, along with part of the sign, which now said "—lue Marine."

When she got to the Property Assessment offices, she was sweating from the bright, hot sun. Inside, though, the air conditioning was set to January in Nova Scotia. The clerk who told Storm that Sally was at lunch wore a sweater buttoned to the neck.

"She should be back in a half hour."

In her sleeveless linen blouse, Storm was covered with goose bumps, so she headed back outside. On the other side of the shattered restaurant was a small mall, which was sure to have a sandwich or coffee shop. She skirted the yellow crime tape, but along with all the other pedestrians, ignored the signs to use the sidewalk on the other side of the street.

It was hard not to stare at the destruction. The missing wall reminded her of the open side of a doll house where the petulant owner had reached in and tossed furniture, draperies, and wiring into a violent tangle. The dangling table linens were blackened and torn and dining chairs leaned, askew. Storm looked away from the dark stains on the carpeting.

Three police officers, alert but not vigilant to the point of obsession, patrolled the area and watched pedestrians and traffic. They weren't fiddling with the holsters on their hips, or speaking into radios.

Storm squinted in their direction. One of the cops looked like the guy she'd seen last night. And how had Damon introduced him? Moana. She remembered because it meant *ocean* in Hawaiian. A soft word for a man with a hard job.

She waved at him. All three officers' heads swung her direction, but only Moana walked over.

"No stopping, please." He pointed at the signs directing people across the street, through the busy traffic. The closest crosswalk was a block away.

"I met you last night. I was with Damon."

"Oh, yeah." Sadness softened the authority in his eyes. "Sorry, I forgot your name."

"Storm Kayama. You're Sergeant Moana, right?" He nodded, and Storm asked what had been on her mind all day. "How's the little girl?"

"I called the hospital this morning. She should be okay, barring infection or other complications. She got shot through the shoulder. Lucky, considering."

"Does she know about her dad and sister?"

"Yeah. We talked to her." He looked down at his shoes, somewhat dusty from the bomb detritus. "I thought I'd take my daughters to see her this afternoon."

"I can't help thinking about her. You think I could drop off a little gift?"

"Sure, any support would be good. Though she's getting a lot of attention from the hospital personnel."

"Does she know what happened?"

"She's been told, but I'm not sure she understands. Hell, I'm not sure I do." He wiped sweat from his forehead, but Storm thought he might be trying to hide anguish that had crossed his face. He braced himself and continued. "She told us her dad was crying, and that he had a gun. She started to run away, and heard the shots. She keeps asking," Moana cleared his throat, "about her sister."

Storm looked at the ground. If she looked in his eyes, she'd tear up. "That's terrible."

"It is. Seems Yoshinaka had gambling debts and had missed a couple rent payments. It looks like he just got real depressed. He had high blood alcohol levels."

"Any chance he was into a loan shark?"

"Could be." Moana's gaze slid away from hers.

For sure, Storm thought. He just can't talk about it. "Poor kid's going to need all the help she can get."

"We're trying to find family in Japan," Moana said, then looked over his shoulder. A big sedan had pulled into the building's parking lot, right up to a strip of crime tape. Four doors popped open and four suits emerged from the car.

"I've gotta go."

Storm watched Moana hurry off. If the coconut wireless was operating at full efficiency and the pregnant clerk's information was accurate, those were the JTTF agents.

Storm found a sandwich shop, picked up a copy of the newspaper, and sat on a bench to eat. The front page was covered with a photograph of Hiroki Yoshinaka's house, with police cars, two ambulances, and Damon's pickup on the front lawn. Storm could see her own shadowy form in the front seat of the truck. Unidentifiable, thank goodness. The story of the murder/suicide continued onto page two, and Storm didn't read it.

On her way back to the Property Assessment office, only one police officer hung around outside the restaurant, but the sedan still sat in the parking lot. She could imagine Moana and his colleague picking their way through the rubble with the Federal agents.

Sally was back from lunch and was happy to look up the land lease records for Lara's shop. "It's held by Mālua LLC."

"Do you have the names of the corporate officers?"

"Ichiru and Ryan Tagama are the president and chief operating officer, respectively." Sally read over the fine print. "They do have another investor in the property," she said. "Paradise Consortium holds ten percent."

"I'm helping Lara Farrell set up the corporation. Are there any liens on the land?"

"Not that I can see here. It looks as if it's owned clean and free."

"Thanks," Storm said, and began to leave, but turned back. "Say, what was the name of the restaurant that was bombed?"

Sally didn't have to look that up. "Blue Marine. Fine dining, known for their seafood. They weren't normally open for breakfast."

"You wouldn't know who owns it, would you?"

Sally typed in information on her computer. After a minute or so, she hit the print button, scooped up some papers and said, "Paradise Consortium."

"Who are the officers and owners?"

"That's coming out in the news. Some conglomerate, a combination of local guys—I have their names—and a couple big investors from Japan."

Storm was a decent upside-down reader, so she could see the address of the corporate headquarters, here in Kahului. If she had time after her morning appointments, she might drop by. "Who are the local investors?"

Sally mentioned three names that were unfamiliar to Storm, but the fourth was Ichiru Tagama. Ryan's dad.

"Does the company own other businesses?" Storm asked.

"Let me see here." She tapped away on her keyboard, and her eyes flicked across the screen.

"It's public knowledge?"

"Sure. But sometimes the companies are owned by other companies and so on. I might have to dig around."

"Shell corporations?" Storm asked.

"Depends if they have any assets or operations. It happens, especially when foreign investors are sheltering taxable money in local investments." She paused. "Looks like Paradise Consortium owns two hotels, a handful of restaurants and bars, and two or three residential properties."

Sally seemed to enjoy gossiping about elusive property owners, so when the thought came to her, Storm decided to ask one more question. She unfolded the newspaper she'd picked up earlier and pointed to the murder/suicide story. "Any chance we could find out who owned this house?"

"Wow, I heard about that. Sad, yeah? You know the address?"

Both women leaned over the paper. The mailbox was visible, and the number 4028 was easy to read, even in the grainy photo.

"I need the street name, too," Sally said.

"I saw the name—it's a fish. Kumu? Kamanu?"

Sally typed, then scanned the computer screen. "Those poor little girls." She sighed, but stopped mid-inhale. "Oh, that's interesting."

"What?" Storm asked.

"I went back to the screen with Paradise Consortium's local holdings." She hit the print button, then handed a sheet of paper to Storm. "Look, Paradise Consortium holds the title on 4028 Kumu Street."

Storm stared at it.

Sally pointed to the list. "Same group that owns Blue Marine."

Chapter Eleven

The address for Paradise Consortium was located a few blocks from the Property Assessment offices, and Storm drove right by it the first time. It was one of those multi-story storage units that were springing up throughout the state. Big, expensive buildings on prime real estate. She pulled into the nearly empty parking lot and checked the street number again. This was an office for a conglomerate that owned millions of dollars of real estate? Her curiosity was piqued.

A front office with a wide, open window was just inside the front door. A bell to get attention sat on the countertop, along with a lineup of Plexiglas business card holders. It looked like there were a number of businesses located here.

In the office, a man with a cell phone pressed to his ear paced back and forth on the industrial carpeting. He spoke loudly in Japanese-accented English and gesticulated with his free hand. Storm didn't want to interrupt, so she took a step back and looked around.

Doors appeared at regular intervals down a long corridor, which was lit by caged light bulbs dangling on long wires. The concrete floor was clean, but lacked any pretense of comfort or luxury, and the hall ended in a steel door that was stenciled with a sign, "Exit Stair." Perhaps there was an elevator down there, too, but Storm couldn't tell because the ceiling light at the end of the passageway had burned out. If light hadn't spilled from one of the unit doors, it would be quite dark.

The clerk hadn't acknowledged her presence, so Storm ambled toward the open unit. She was about halfway down the corridor when the man in the office noticed.

"Hey, stop!" He slammed the office door and dashed down the hallway. "No entry without authorization."

Storm turned around. "Sorry, you were busy. I'm interested in renting a unit."

"We protect the privacy of our clients," he panted. "Come to the office. I'll show you rates." Sweat trickled from his hairline. "What are you storing?"

"Antiques," Storm said. "My mother left me some very nice pieces. I'm going to open a shop."

"Our security is excellent."

"Obviously."

"Let me show you some available units." They were back at the office and the man let himself in while Storm waited at the counter.

"What size unit do you need?" he asked from the other side of the counter.

"Some of the furniture is quite large. I'll need at least seventy or eighty square feet."

"We have units that size."

"I may need a phone line, too. Is that possible?"

"Yes, we can set up phone and fax facilities. For a fee, you can have wireless internet access."

"How about a mailing address?" Storm asked.

"Yes, of course. You would pick up mail here." He gestured to a series of cubbyholes at the back of the office. "Let me get our rate list and floor plan for you."

He slapped a document on the counter and turned it for her to see. It was a diagram of units, but what drew her attention were his hands. Both pinkies were chopped off at the first knuckle.

"Could I see an ID, please?" he asked.

Storm dragged her attention from the missing fingers. "Um, I don't want to move furniture to the second floor. Do you have something on the first floor?"

"Maybe. The ID?"

Storm dug around in her bag. "I must have left it in the car." She dumped a hairbrush, a compact, and two lipsticks on the counter.

He looked doubtful. "Security. I must see ID."

Storm had heard stories about missing fingers as a sign of allegiance to the Yakuza. Ten or fifteen years ago, the organization had been quite active in the islands, particularly in real estate adventures, as it was an effective way to launder large amounts of cash.

She eyed the guy. No tattoos crawling up his neck, but his collar was buttoned and the shirt had long sleeves. She was leery of handing her ID over to this guy.

"I don't have it right now. I can give it to you when we sign the contract." Storm scooped her things back into her purse. "I need references from some of your customers."

The phone rang again, and the man answered it. Storm hesitated a moment, then folded the contract and put it into her bag with the hairbrush and lipsticks. She gave the man a little wave, but he was speaking to someone in Japanese and had resumed pacing and gesturing.

Outside the building, she hopped into her rental, turned the ignition, rolled down all the windows, and set the air conditioner to high. A turkey could roast in there, and she was beginning to. Drops of sweat crept down the sides of her face.

She readjusted the vent and took a moment to remove the contract from her purse. Nothing too interesting about it. Across the top of the torn paper was Maʻalahi Storage, with phone and fax numbers, in both English and Japanese. There was also a hand-written doodle in Japanese that Storm couldn't read, followed by $18,765. Apparently the office manager had been using the contract for scratch paper.

Storm shrugged to herself, rolled up the windows and exited onto the main thoroughfare. She didn't look back, so she didn't see the office clerk at the building's entrance. He watched her drive away and chattered into his cell phone.

◇◇◇

At a red light, Storm called the office and made a report of her day to her ever-protective and efficient secretary.

"Two things," Grace told her. "Call your Aunt Maile and Hamlin's on his way home."

"He is? That's great news."

"I thought so, too. Finish up with the dive shop and get back here. Don't forget your aunt, either, or she'll be on the next plane to Maui."

That part was true, Storm thought. "I'll call her. But the dive shop business is a little more complicated than I originally thought."

"I've heard that before." Grace hung up.

On her way to Maui Memorial Hospital, Storm had a chance to ponder the ball of tangled ends she was trying to unravel. Lara hadn't been forthcoming with the information Storm needed to set up liability protection. Instead of volunteering that Ryan and his father owned the land under the shop, Lara had mentioned it as if it were afterthought, even as Storm was begging for the information. Ryan was a little better, but he'd ducked out before Storm got the specifics about water, electricity, and the other stores in the little mall.

It was not the kind of thing she could let go. What if, God forbid, there was a lawsuit against the shop? Not only would Lara and Ryan blame her, she could be sued for legal malpractice.

Several other things niggled at her, more misgivings than specifics. Damon had quickly changed the subject when they'd talked about Lara's family. Storm supposed he felt it wasn't his place to discuss it, but there'd been something in the way he'd clammed up after bringing up the death of Lara's sister.

Another concern was the fact that the older Tagama did business with Paradise Consortium. It could be nothing, as he seemed to be a wealthy, well-connected businessman. Local bars and restaurants would be logical investments. But when the pushy, chop-fingered clerk in the storage facility where Paradise Consortium had its office insisted on her ID, alarm bells sounded.

She needed to find answers to a long list of questions, but by the time Storm drove into the hospital parking lot, her mind was on the child with the gunshot wound. This visit had little to do with her legal clients. Storm had been twelve, the same age as Carmen, when her mother killed herself. It had affected everything in her life, just as this event would color Carmen's life. This visit was for herself and, she hoped, another little girl.

A volunteer at the information desk in the lobby gave her directions to Carmen Yoshinaka's room. Despite her nervousness and the desire to turn around and leave, Storm knew why she was there.

Storm's father died four years after her mother. For most of those four years, her father had been moody and preoccupied. Even if he was staring across the dinner table at her, he'd been elsewhere. Aunt Maile and Uncle Keone, recognizing his despair, had stepped in. Storm had had her rebellious period—the purple hair and tattoo—but they'd been there. And they still were. This twelve-year-old had no one.

Worse yet, Carmen's father had tried to kill her. The kid probably recognized this on some level, even if she couldn't tell the police about it. Storm's parents may have left her, but they didn't try and take her with them.

There were two nurses in Carmen's room. One sat on her bed and read a story from a children's book.

Storm had picked up a big white teddy bear in the hospital gift shop. It was half the size of the child on the bed. The nurses smiled, but Carmen looked surprised. "Aunt Kiki?"

"You look a little like her aunt," one of the nurses explained.

Storm was buoyed by the idea of the child having an aunt. "No, I'm a friend. My name is Storm. Your dad worked with some people I know, and I heard you got hurt."

She handed the furry bear to the little girl. "I hope you feel better soon."

Carmen's eyes were very large in her pale face. "Where's Daddy? And Crystal?"

Storm was glad Carmen didn't see the anguish on the face of the nurse with the book. The other one froze in the act of adjusting the window blinds.

The nurse put down the book and hugged Carmen. "They can't come visit," she said. She motioned for Storm to take her chair by the bed, and she tiptoed from the room.

Storm remembered her mother's death. She'd been the one to find her mother in bed, and had phoned for help when she couldn't rouse her. She still remembered how one of her mother's friends had patted her head and told her that her mother would wake up. Storm's hopes had soared, then plummeted into loathing.

"Do you like animals?" Storm stroked the bear's fur.

Carmen's eyes stayed wide, and after a moment she nodded. "I have a kitten."

Storm sat up a little straighter. "A real kitty? Um, the kind who has to go outside?"

"Her name is Neko."

"What color is she?"

"Orange."

Storm drew a careful breath. "Do you leave water and food out for her?"

Carmen frowned. "No, silly. She lives on my bed. Daddy won't let me take water in my room."

"I see," Storm said, and hoped she really did. "Do you think she'll like your bear?"

Carmen thought for a moment, then nodded. "Can you bring Neko to me?"

"Yes, I'll do that," Storm said.

The nurses came back with a doctor. All three wore concerned expressions.

"I'll see you later, Carmen."

"Will you help me go home?"

"Yes." Storm nearly choked on the word. Where would home be for this child? She stood up to give the doctor her place at Carmen's bedside, but she would be back. After all, she had to find Neko.

On the drive back to Wailea, her mobile phone rang, but she didn't reach for it. Whoever it was could leave a message. She was wrapped in empathy for Carmen Yoshinaka. The child's sad eyes had left a piercing ache in Storm's chest.

Chapter Twelve

Stella unloaded the take-out from Ono Saimin onto the kitchen table in the apartment she and Keiko shared. The smell made her mouth water, and had drawn Keiko from her slump on the battered living room sofa, where she'd been since Stella dropped her off.

"Got plenty char siu?" Keiko asked, and Stella beamed. Success.

"Yours does. I have high cholesterol, remember? No pork for me. I got Pono's veggie special."

Keiko peered into Stella's bowl. "I see fish cake and egg."

Stella put her hands on her hips. "I can cheat a little."

Keiko actually smiled, which made Stella happier. The phone rang and Stella rolled her eyes with mock exasperation.

"Hello? Hey, Pauline. What's up?" Stella handed Keiko a flat-bottomed Japanese spoon and motioned for her to begin. "It's Auntie Piko," she whispered to Keiko.

"You hear about that explosion yesterday?" Pauline warbled with excitement. She could hardly wait to pass the news.

"Who didn't?"

"My son was supposed to be there. His associate went instead at the last minute, and he was killed."

"God, Pauline. I'm sorry to hear that." Stella was sorry for Pauline, though she didn't care for Wayne Harding. He had a smarmy smile and eyes that never settled on a face.

"You talked to Ichiru Tagama lately?" Pauline asked.

"No. Why are you asking?"

Keiko put down her spoon. Stella made a placating motion and walked around the corner, out of the kitchen.

"He met with Obake."

"He doesn't work for Obake anymore." If voices had temperatures, Stella's dropped thirty degrees. "Pauline, you know you can't always believe Yasuko. She has to say whatever Obake tells her to say."

"Hey, she didn't have to call."

Stella made a snorting noise.

"You forget, she helped Keiko."

Stella peeked around the corner at the young woman, who sat in a chair, twisted the cuffs of her sleeves around her wrists, and stared into her lap. She hadn't touched her soup since the phone rang.

"She had to. It was damage control."

Pauline didn't respond. They'd been down this road before.

Stella spoke first. "Hey, Pauline. Sorry I take it out on you."

"S'okay." Pauline's voice was soft. "But keep in mind, Yasuko didn't have to call you." She paused. "And there wasn't nothing you could do before."

When Stella answered, her voice was a hoarse whisper. "You're wrong. I should have helped Angela. I should have been there for her."

"You going to live your whole life with regret? It wasn't fair of Barb to lay that responsibility on you."

"Barb couldn't do anything. I let Angela down, and I have to live with that."

Pauline sighed. "Yeah, well. That's why I called. I wanted to let you know Obake was in town. Keiko's going to hear about it."

"How do you know he wasn't behind that explosion?"

"How can you say that? It was an attempt on his life. His body-guards barely got him out in time."

"Yasuko told you that?"

"No, Wayne did. You know what a softie my son is. He was pretty upset."

Sure, Wayne was soft and cozy as lava rock.

"Thanks for calling, Pauline." Stella hung up the phone and dragged herself back to the kitchen. She sat down in the chair opposite Keiko and propped her head, which felt as heavy as an iron skillet, in her hands. She should have known. Keiko met her gaze with brimming eyes.

"You knew, didn't you? Why didn't you tell me Obake was in town?"

"It would just worry you." Keiko grasped her own wrists and twisted as if she were trying to unscrew her hands from her arms.

Stella reached out and pulled Keiko's sleeve up. Vertical scars ran the length of her arms. Some of them were thickened and distorted by keloids.

"You're making the scars angrier." Stella stroked Keiko's arms. "Just tell me. You get one of your funny feelings, you *got* to tell me."

Stella waited until Keiko's breathing had calmed. "How did you know Obake was here?" she asked.

"I guessed because of those little girls and their father."

Stella's gaze sharpened. "What do you mean?"

"My father should have done the same thing."

Stella drew a sharp breath, but waited a beat so her voice wouldn't reflect her alarm. Keiko had avoided talking about how she'd gone to work for Obake, though Stella knew enough about the business to draw conclusions.

She took Keiko's cold hand in hers. "Did your father owe him money?"

Keiko whispered a word that Stella couldn't hear, but Stella saw the dark head nod. It was a common story. Most of the women who worked for him had been forced by one means or another.

"It's not your fault," Stella whispered to her. "Not your fault. And it's over. You run your life now. Only you." She smiled. "Your friends are here to help you."

Keiko nodded and twisted again at her arms.

"Stop doing that and eat," Stella commanded. "You're getting healthy. You're gaining weight and you got your period back. It's your life—don't give him control."

Keiko picked up her spoon and chopsticks and took a delicate bite.

Stella piled noodles onto her spoon and slurped in a mouthful. "I'm glad you told me what you were thinking."

"What about the little girl? Carmen?"

"She's safe in the hospital."

Keiko wasn't reassured, and her face showed it.

"Eat, you need to get stronger."

Keiko put a spoonful of noodles in her mouth and chewed thoughtfully. The women ate in silence for a moment.

"Good for you," Stella said, and made a show of slurping a large mouthful. "No need to be sad."

Then Keiko did something unusual. She met Stella's eyes with a stare that didn't slide away, though when she spoke, her voice was soft and gentle. "Look who's talking about being sad."

Stella's hand stopped midair on the way to her mouth and stayed there. After a long moment, she gave Keiko a small smile. "You're right."

Chapter Thirteen

"I have some information," Tagama said.

"Sit." Obake gestured at the chair across the bar table. At nine in the morning, they were alone in the hostess bar. Yasuko had unlocked the entrance for Tagama, then disappeared.

"Yasuko will bring us some tea. Or would you like a whiskey?"

"Tea will be excellent, thank you."

"How is your son? He's a handsome boy," Obake said.

"He is slow to learn the business." Tagama practiced the Asian custom of disparaging that which he was most proud. To do otherwise would bring misfortune.

Obake lowered his head in approval. "My son will never run a business." He shook his head, as if in despair. "He will stay a body guard."

Tagama knew Obake was doing more than playing down his son's worth. He was sending a layered message, which emphasized his strength and the depth of his knowledge.

Tagama had discovered that Obake, a word that referred to a faceless ghost in local Japanese folklore, was a pseudonym for Akira Kudo. Akira Kudo had a wife and three daughters in Japan, aged thirteen to nineteen.

Steven Kudo, the bodyguard son to whom Obake referred, was the son of one of Obake's mistresses. Tagama had hit a wall when he'd tried to track the woman down; she'd disappeared.

Steven had been born and raised on Maui, and had a rap sheet long as a roll of toilet paper. Among his transgressions were aggravated assault, gambling, and cockfighting.

"Sons are difficult to rear. They take longer to mature than daughters. You have a daughter?" Tagama's voice oozed innocence.

Tagama knew that he wasn't the only one gathering information. For that reason, Tagama was glad Ryan's attempt at the gelato business had been a flop, as failure was apt to relax Obake's attention. Even Ryan's mother, though she'd remarried five or six years ago, could be vulnerable. Her new husband was a dot-com success story who'd sold his software company at the right time and retired to sail up and down the coast of California, doting on his new wife. She was probably out of reach, which relieved Tagama.

Age and experience had mellowed Tagama's feelings for his ex. For years after she left him, when Ryan was small, he'd had her followed. Now her happiness pleased Ryan, which enhanced his relationship with his father. The down side of this, however, meant that if Obake wanted leverage, she could be a weak link in Tagama's armor.

Obake replied, with a proper amount of ruefulness, that he had no daughter. It was time for Tagama to share his information.

"I have asked about the leak you suspected."

Obake merely raised a tiny teacup to his lips.

"The word on the street is that Tom Peters, the Deputy Director of Liquor Control, was the only target. The people who set the bomb eliminated the person they wanted."

Obake raised one thin eyebrow to show his skepticism. In his suntanned face, the white creases that radiated from Obake's eyes looked like a child's drawing of black suns. They annoyed Tagama, perhaps of their false sense of jollity, but it could be because the man was nut brown from his twice-daily swims. Obake wasn't good looking, but he cultivated a façade of virility, and he preened before women.

Tagama had to remind himself that some of his disgruntle-
ment came from the fact that his own skin was white and his
arms puny.

"Why would anyone care about Tom Peters?" Obake asked.
"And what else do your spies tell you?"

Tagama took a sip of his tea. He would ask the same questions in Obake's position. "They tell me the bomber is an
independent."

"Who?"

"People suspect the husband of the woman he was having an
affair with," Tagama said.

"Go on." Obake's voice was like gravel.

Tagama watched him carefully. Had Obake relaxed an iota?
"Information was leaked to your secretary, Noboru. You were
meant to escape."

Obake's thick fingers played with his tiny teacup. The severed
pinkies stuck out like Vienna sausages. "Peters was a liquor commissioner and also served on the Maui Restaurant Association
board."

Tagama nodded. "The special breakfast meeting was to assure
that bars and restaurants operated by Paradise Consortium had
unimpeded access to liquor licenses. Commissioners would
overlook past legal problems, yes?"

Obake's eyes narrowed. "So? Peters was helping my interests.
Yours, too. He was a small part of a big plan."

Tagama knew Obake saw himself as the center of his universe.
No one else was as important; why would anyone else be the
target of an assassination attempt?

"An intricate watch stops operating when a tiny wheel breaks,"
Tagama maintained the deference in his tone.

Obake's voice was like gravel. "Who told my enemies that
I'd be there?"

"So far, no one seems to know. Not even rumors are floating
around. Perhaps you have some insight?"

Tagama stared into Obake's eyes and waited. This was a small
but significant test. It was Obake's chance to tell Tagama that

Steven had worked at Blue Marine. He'd quit when his father flew in from Japan, about a week before the explosion. Tagama found the connection suspicious.

Obake's face darkened. "You and I have history, Tagama."

Tagama had wanted to push the man, but he might have gone too far. "I have never forgotten, Obake-san."

"Your past can be used against you."

"Of course," Tagama said, and rose to leave.

"I want more information."

"Yes, Obake-san."

"One more thing."

Tagama turned.

"Your daughter-in-law wants ownership of the land under her shop." Obake's brown face widened in a sneer.

Someone close to Tagama had talked. Funny thing was, he was thinking about giving it to her and Ryan as a wedding present. But now Tagama knew he had a rat in his own camp, and Obake had access to him—or her.

Chapter Fourteen

Keiko didn't want to come in. She preferred sitting in the car, though they couldn't find parking in the shade. Stella told her the faded blue Toyota was going to get damned steamy.

Despite the air-conditioning vents that were aimed right at her face, sweat was already beading on Keiko's forehead. Stella rolled down the windows and turned off the car.

"You sure about this?" Stella asked. "There's a lobby where you can wait. No one will bother you."

Keiko only grabbed her wrists and twisted her hands, winding her long sleeves into a mummy's wrap.

"Okay, okay. I won't be long."

She didn't add that how long she would visit depended on Barb's state of mind. Some days there was a light in Barb's eyes and she knew where she was and to whom she was talking. Other days, Barb's entire demeanor sagged. In her mid-fifties, she looked at least twenty years older. Her once-lustrous black hair hung lank and stringy, and the eyes that gazed at Stella could be as blank as a doll's.

A doll with thinning hair and sagging jowls, Stella thought. Nobody made dolls like that. Just syrupy babies or the ones with huge tits and tiny feet. She wondered what would happen if someone made a sweet-faced grandma doll. Would anyone tuck her into bed at night?

Stella blinked hard and passed through the wide double doors that opened at her approach. It was a decent place; there were a lot worse, she knew. Lara was taking the best care of her mom that she could. Stella signed the visitor registry and followed the nurse down the halls. She tried to ignore the odors that clung to the back of her throat. Disinfectant, overlaid with smells of illness and incontinence.

Barb sat in a wing chair and gazed at the blaring television set. Her roommate was on her side in bed, snoring softly. The nurse adjusted the shawl around Barb's thin shoulders and turned down the volume.

"Barb, your friend is here." She took Barb's hand in hers and smoothed her hair.

"She's having a good day," she said to Stella.

Stella swallowed hard. "Hey, Boomer. I brought you something."

Stella handed Barb a pot of cattleya orchids. Purple, a color she knew Barb loved.

Barb made a little gasp and reached for them. Her lips parted in a smile and her teeth, as always, were white and unblemished. Stella ran her tongue over her bridge, which rubbed sores on her gums from time to time. Better her mind than her teeth, but what a choice.

"Like our prom corsages," Barb said.

Stella felt a pang. Memories of high school had not been what she'd wanted to evoke. Though Barb had been a popular cheerleader before they both got kicked out for—what was it back then?—moral laxity?

The scandal had spread through the small town of Wailuku like a brush fire, but Barb had always longed to return to their Catholic girls' school. Not Stella, who wasn't the type to turn her anger inward. St. Mark's, whose motto was Forgiveness, Charity, and Hope. Yeah, sure.

"We screwed up, didn't we?" Barb's voice was sad.

"We made a bad choice," Stella said slowly. Barb hadn't spoken of this for decades. It was a big step to recognize Stella, let alone to bring up the past. Maybe Barb was on some kind of new medicine. Stella looked for the nurse, but the woman had slipped out of the room.

"We danced." Barb giggled.

"That's right."

A cloud passed through Barb's eyes. "The old man didn't speak any English."

Stella's pulse rate increased. She didn't want to disagree, but she also didn't want to go in this direction. "You're right, he didn't." She forced a smile. "We drank too many screwdrivers. Remember?"

"Remember the young guy?"

This conversation was definitely going in the wrong direction. "Do you remember your date for the prom?"

"Missing fingers." Barb's eyes looked far into the past. "He paid us a lot of money."

Stella remembered. He'd given them each a hundred dollar bill. Neither of the girls had seen one before. That was the first time, when they'd been invited to come in their St. Mark's uniforms, pleated navy skirts and sailor blouses with a long tie. That day, they'd worn panty hose, partly to see if the nuns would notice and make them take the stockings off. They hadn't, and the girls were still wearing them when they got to hostess bar. They'd thought it was pretty funny when the head hostess asked them to replace the stockings with knee socks and high-heeled pumps. Barb's shoes had been too big, which had prompted lots of giggles. Too bad the giggles didn't last. So much for the girls' wild streak. They were trapped, and their next visit was no fun at all.

A cloud passed through Barb's eyes. "The ghost. He hurt me." She dropped the orchid pot on the floor. The pot was plastic, but cinders scattered and a blossom broke off.

"I know." Stella did her best to scoop up the dirt. "Tell me a cheer. You remember, don't you?"

Barb stared for several long moments.

Stella put her hand on top of her friend's, which was cold and damp. "Barb, you're safe. You're with me."

"Angela?" Barb's voice was a whisper.

"I'm Stella." Her voice quavered.

"Angela, why did you stay away so long?"

Stella didn't hear the footsteps until Lara came through the door.

"Stella, what are you doing here? Who's at the shop?" Lara asked. "Hi Mom," she added in the same breath, and gave her mother a kiss on the cheek. She set down a pot of gardenias and pinned two blossoms in her mother's hair.

Barb smiled at her, reached up and touched the fragrant flowers.

"Ken and Damon are there," Stella said. "Keiko and I were getting lunch, and I wanted to visit."

"You can't leave those guys alone. Damon's wearing ear plugs and Ken probably won't bother to answer the phone."

"It'll be okay for a half hour or so."

"Mom, I brought you something else." Lara handed her mother a can of cold guava juice. Barb reached for it and took a swallow.

Lara patted Barb's hand and gave her mother a bland smile, but the words that came out of her mouth were aimed at Stella and had an edge. "You didn't have to blab to Storm about Greg Wilson. She may be my lawyer, but she doesn't have to know my life history."

"She doesn't. Believe me."

Lara glared at her, her lips pressed into a tight line. "Just because you're my godmother, it doesn't give you rights."

"It gives me the right to do what I can to protect you. Barb asked me to."

Both women looked at Barb, who had finished the can of juice. She was pale and looked up at Lara as if their mother-daughter roles were reversed. "Angela, do you still have that land Daddy and I gave you?" she asked.

"Yes," Lara said, and she sounded both tired and sad. "Mom, I'm Lara."

Chapter Fifteen

By the time Storm got back to her hotel, it was late afternoon. Carmen's dark, frightened eyes still haunted her. She flopped back on the bed and punched in Aunt Maile's phone number on the Big Island.

"You sound a bit blue," said her aunt.

"Right now, I wish I were in Pa'auilo with you and Uncle Keone." Storm told her about Carmen.

"Storm, there's a reason you keep finding needy children."

"Orphans, you mean."

"Not always. You're a good friend to Robbie." Robbie was Storm's best friend's son. Leila owned a popular bakery in Honolulu, and Storm often helped her pick up or drop off Robbie from school.

"Except for the time we tried skateboarding down his driveway." Leila was working one Saturday morning, and Storm ended up calling her from Queen's Hospital. Robbie had a broken wrist, and Storm a badly sprained ankle.

"You were the first to sign each others' casts." Aunt Maile chuckled.

"I'd rather forget that incident." So Storm told her about Lara's 'aumakua and how the shark had chased them.

"Do you have your little pua'a with you?"

"I wear it all the time." Storm touched the emerald-eyed pig.

"Good."

Storm detected the relief in Maile's voice. "Lara was very upset."

"She'd better pay attention. It's a warning."

"What kind of warning?"

"I don't know yet." Maile paused. "You'll figure that out before I do." She didn't sound happy. "Is she a friend?"

"She's a client, but I like her. We're about the same age and we have things in common." Storm asked about Uncle Keone, who got on the phone for a few minutes to send his love. When she hung up, Storm felt much better. She called Hamlin, left a message on his voice mail, splashed some water on her face and grabbed her handbag. She was getting her appetite back, and there was a casual restaurant not far from the hotel.

The restaurant's bar was an open lanai that fronted the dining room and looked out onto the ocean. Twenty feet away, the sea glittered a deep sapphire in the fiery obliqueness of the waning sun. Elongated shadows in the dining room kept Storm from seeing Lara until the hostess came back and pointed her out.

"You're meeting a friend? She's waving at you."

Storm had been expecting a quiet dinner with a paperback she'd stuffed in her purse, but this option looked like more fun. "Sure."

The hostess led her to Lara's table. "I'll check back with you in a while."

"Are you waiting for someone?" Storm asked.

"Ryan had to cancel." Lara gestured at the chair. "Join me? I hate eating alone."

"Sure, thanks." Storm admired Lara's sleek, upswept hair as she turned her head to catch the eye of the waitress. The tendrils that strayed were strategic. Storm patted at the fluff that was springing free of her French braid. She hadn't touched her hair since that morning. Beauty takes time and effort.

The waitress came over. "You like Cosmopolitans?" Lara asked, and pointed to her drink.

"Never had one."

"Two, please," Lara said. The waitress took away Lara's empty glass and returned in about two minutes with a couple of pink concoctions in martini glasses. Lara sank her chin into the palm of one hand and lifted the fresh drink to Storm.

"I'm glad you showed up." Her tone was wry.

"Does this happen often?" Storm asked.

Lara gave the pink liquid in her martini glass a swirl. "He and his dad have a handful of new clients."

Storm hoped the smile she offered was some consolation, but she wondered how long a person could drink alone, even at candlelit tables in nice restaurants. Storm faced the bar, and it seemed as if at least four guys were eyeing Lara. One of them caught Storm's eye and smiled. She took a quick gulp of her drink, which was delicious.

Lara looked lazily over her shoulder, then back at Storm. "His dad is kind of demanding, but I guess he's teaching Ryan about the family business." She sighed. "Your boyfriend ever do this to you?"

"Not really." That was true, and the admission made her miss Hamlin. "Our arguments are about whether I take too many chances." This popped out before Storm's brain had a chance to put on the brakes. "And how differently we run the business," she added.

Lara raised an elegant eyebrow. "Sounds manageable." She sipped her drink. "And as if he cares about you. What's his name?"

"Ian Hamlin."

"He's on Oʻahu?"

"Right now, he's in L.A." Storm made a face. "Taking a break."

"Really? What happened?"

Storm told her about Uncle Miles' death. Everyone but Storm thought he'd died of old age. Even Hamlin, but despite his doubts, he'd stuck by Storm through the investigation. Because he'd tried to help her, he'd almost died.

"Did he save you?" Lara looked much happier than when Storm had first entered. Her cheeks were pink and she signaled for another drink.

"Yes," Storm said. "And then I helped him."

"How romantic." Lara acknowledged the arrival of her fresh cocktail. "You'll work it out."

She leaned forward and Storm reflected that Lara might have had more than one Cosmo before Storm had arrived. "So, what do you think of Ryan?" Lara asked.

"Handsome guy, and he seems to adore you."

"If he adores me, why'd he go out to dinner with his dad?"

"Because it's his dad. Plus, guys approach work differently than women. We multitask better."

"What does your dad do?"

"He worked for Hamakua Sugar Plantation, but he died a while ago."

"What happened?"

Storm opted for the short answer. "He had a kidney disease."

"Do you miss him?"

"Yes, I do."

"We never stop, do we?"

"I guess not. Your dad died, too?"

"Yes." Lara's eyes grew distant, as if she could see into the past. "Four years ago."

"How'd it happen?"

"A broken heart." Lara finished her Cosmo. The pink in her cheeks had faded.

"Marriage troubles?" Storm's voice was soft. She could have said her dad died of a broken heart, too.

"No, my parents worshipped each other. He saved my mom." She looked at Storm over the rim of her glass. "Kind of like your boyfriend did for you."

"What happened?"

Storm wanted to hear how Lara's father had saved her mother, but Lara waved her empty martini glass around the bar. "You like this place?"

"Sure, it's nice. The view's great."

"It should have been my dad's."

"Really?" Storm used an old technique of Aunt Maile's—make a few encouraging noises and people will tell you a lot.

"He was on the verge of buying it."

"He decided not to?"

A frown cast a deep shadow on Lara's face. "No, he got squeezed out of the deal." She drained half of her Cosmo. "He was in business with friends, but it turns out they weren't friends."

"I guess not." Storm watched the clouds build in Lara's eyes. "That hurts."

"Yeah." Lara's voice was thick. "A week later, he had a heart attack."

"I'm so sorry."

"Me, too." Lara's consonants were getting a bit mushy. "But I'm going to fix it."

"How?"

"I'm thinking of buying the place." Lara grinned at Storm. "Will you do the legal work for me?"

"Sure, but let's get your dive shop settled. We still have some things to finish up—"

"Sunday. Can't do it tomorrow, I'm taking out a dive group."

"I need to get back to O'ahu on Sunday."

"Sunday morning, I promise."

"Right." Storm's brain was feeling soft and she'd only had two Cosmos. These things were sneaky.

Lara directed a manicured finger at Storm's chest. "I noticed your pig necklace on our swim yesterday. He's beautiful. Did your boyfriend give it to you?"

"No, my aunt did. He's my 'aumakua." Storm looked down at her necklace, which was set off by the black cotton V-neck sweater she wore. His emerald eyes winked in the candlelight.

"Oh yeah, I remember." One side of Lara's mouth turned up, more of a smirk than a smile. "My 'aumakua was giving me a hard time."

"Probably wasn't the right animal. Lara, let's order some food."

"I'm not hungry. Ryan is going to pick me up." She lifted her drink. "I'll wait for him."

Storm looked around for the waitress, who was busy at a table across the room. Instead, a young man appeared.

"Lara, who's your friend?" he asked.

"Casey, this is Storm." Lara gave him a melting smile, then slid her eyes to Storm. "Casey likes the new girls."

Storm slowly sat back in her chair and gathered her fuzzy thoughts. Lara's words reminded her of another incident. She'd been sixteen, a self-conscious high school transplant from the "country." A basketball player had asked to join her in the school cafeteria. A cheerleader type had walked by the lunch table and said in a loud voice, "Brian, she won't be new for long." As if she'd be used goods in a week. No one stays new.

As it had back then, an uncomfortable silence settled over both Storm and the young man. Storm pasted a placid smile on her face. "Nice to meet you, Casey. I was just telling Lara it was time for me to go."

She stood, put money on the table and walked away. She was pretty sure she moved in a straight line.

Back in her hotel room, she called room service and ordered a hamburger, a tossed salad, and a pitcher of ice water. After gulping dinner, she booted up her lap top to catch up on email. Fifteen minutes later, she'd nodded off. Her computer put itself to sleep, too.

When her cell phone woke her, bright light streamed through the crack between the heavy draperies. It took several rings before she found the phone next to the bathroom sink, where she'd left it after checking for messages the night before.

It was Hamlin. "How's the dive shop business?"

"Interesting, in more ways than one."

"Want to tell me about it?"

"Very much," Storm said. His organized, rational outlook would be a welcome sounding board. "When will you be home?"

"I'll be in Honolulu tomorrow afternoon. I could come join you, if you want company."

"That would be great," she said, and hung up with a big smile.

That smile turned into a grimace when she glanced into the bathroom mirror. Her hair stuck out at all angles, and creases in the pillow had embedded a tic-tac-toe grid on the side of her face. Dehydrated from last night's drinks, she swilled a gallon of water directly from the tap, showered, and put on a fresh outfit. She got her mobile phone from the bathroom counter and went to the dresser to put it in her handbag.

Except her purse wasn't on the dresser. Nor was it in her open suitcase, which was beginning to look like a magpie nest. Not on the back of the toilet, and though the white countertops were scattered with mascara, toothpaste, and other small items, there was nothing the size of her handbag. She looked under the beds, and straightened the rumpled sheets where she'd slept. No purse.

Despite the Cosmo-fog, she remembered lifting her handbag from the back of her chair at the restaurant. She'd taken money from her wallet to pay for the drinks, and then put the bag over her shoulder. Not only that, she'd used her room key to let herself into the room. She'd also tipped the room service guy a couple of bucks. No, her purse had been with her in the room.

That's when she saw the rental car keys sitting on the dresser top. They sat on top of her driver's license, which should have been in her wallet. Startled, she grabbed the keys. A piece of hotel stationery fluttered to the floor. It said "GO HOME" in block letters.

Storm's mouth went dry. The room key was an electronic card, and the door locked automatically, though she didn't remember fastening the dead bolt. Someone had been able to open the door without making a sound, no scratching or fumbling. Slick as an eel on the reef.

Another revelation hit her, and it was even worse than her missing purse. She ran to the bed and ripped back the sheets. Her lap top was gone. When she'd fallen asleep last night, it had been right next to her. Not only had someone broken into her room, he'd been a foot from her head.

Chapter Sixteen

Ryan insisted on stopping for a large cup of very strong coffee before they arrived at The Red Light. The cooks wouldn't be working yet at the hostess bar, and he hadn't had much sleep again. When he'd picked up Lara last night, she'd been drunk and madder than a cornered barracuda. Mostly she was pissed at him for standing her up for dinner, but he had the feeling there was more to the story. He'd spent the night on the sofa, neck cricked at one end, feet hanging over the other.

He left before she was up this morning, and that wasn't going to please her, either. His father seemed to take the stop at Starbucks in stride.

"You want anything?" Ryan asked before he got out of the car.

"Sure, I'll take one of those green tea lattes," Tagama answered, and rolled down his window to wait in the car.

That's a first, reflected Ryan, right before the barista took his order. He ordered two blueberry scones to go.

Tagama was eating the scone with gusto when his mobile phone rang. Ryan couldn't make out what the person on the other end of the call was saying, but he could tell it was a woman's voice, and he could hear it rise and fall with dismay. Tagama grunted a few times into the phone then snapped it closed. He tossed his green tea latte and the half-eaten scone, paper bag and all, out the car window.

Ryan kept his eyes on the road. His father's face was a dangerous red. Neither man spoke, and when Ryan bumped into the rutted gravel lot behind the hostess bar, Tagama was out of the car before Ryan had shifted into park. While Ryan fumbled the key out of the ignition, Tagama squared his shoulders as if he were a gladiator entering the arena.

Yasuko greeted them at the back entrance, where her obsequious bows were stiff. Her face was paler than usual, a white mask. Tagama's gaze lingered on her as if reading a message. His glower then moved toward the meeting room. No "Flower of Japan" endearments this time.

Because his father had seemed to watch Yasuko for a signal, Ryan observed her, too. He saw the dark shadow under her left eye, which her makeup couldn't quite conceal. Nor could the crimson lipstick hide the swollen upper lip. Yasuko turned away from him.

In the meeting room, Obake sat at the same table. His body guard son stood behind him. "Sit," he commanded.

Tagama sat across from him, and Ryan stood behind his father. Ryan avoided the hooded, smoldering gaze of Steven Kudo. What was going on? Hostility hung in the air like ozone at a thunderstorm.

Not that Obake had been welcoming the first time, but his demeanor had been neutral and he'd sent his body guards away. Ryan was learning that every motion, gesture, and word this man presented had significance. Keeping a body guard in the room sent a blatant message.

Who'd made the phone call to his dad? Yasuko? He could tell from what little he'd heard that the speaker was troubled, but he hadn't been able to identify her.

"Keiko." Obake snarled the word.

"Keiko?" Tagama said. "I just met her."

"Stella called you." Obake slapped the table for emphasis.

"Keiko just recently came to my attention. My future daughter-in-law's new employee." Tagama, whose face was more flushed than Ryan liked to see, responded as if he and Obake were discussing which friend to include in their weekly golf four-some. Not that he'd ever seen his father play golf with Obake. "Why would Stella call me?"

Ryan felt a breath of cold air along the back of his neck. Keiko? The first he'd seen of the girl was when Lara hired her a couple of months ago. She was a thin wisp who barely made a sound. He hadn't given much thought to her, except to wonder about the fact that she didn't swim very well. He'd asked Lara about it. She'd assured him Stella would teach her, and Keiko was cheap—a few cents over hourly minimum wage.

"You cannot play me, Tagama." Obake's voice cut through Ryan's thoughts.

"Nor would I want to." Tagama sounded calm and sincere.

"I have kept the doctor's report."

Ryan felt his father stiffen. "That was a long time ago. The statute of limitation in Hawai'i—"

"Is worthless. Rape is a Class A felony, and the doctor will say it was five years ago." Obake's fat brown face was hard as a plate. No jolly tan lines now.

Ryan was frozen in place. At one level, he knew Obake was playing to him as the stunned audience. On another level, he was so shocked he couldn't process the information he was receiving. Rape? His father?

He'd never seen his father on the defensive. He'd never seen him react in front of anyone like this, particularly an adversary like Obake.

"I have reformed. She knows this." Tagama's spine was as straight as a fence post. "She will not testify."

Ryan had to brace himself by putting a hand on the back of his father's chair. Through the roaring in his ears, he realized that Obake had picked up on his shock, and the thug was pleased by it.

A flush of shame spread from his chest and up his neck. Burning, he gathered himself and met Steven Kudo's leer with eyes like obsidian. His pallor might betray his angst, but he wouldn't give them anything else.

"She doesn't have to. Someone else will."

Tagama opened his mouth, then closed it without making a sound. Ryan's chest ached, and he knew he had been holding his breath. He exhaled slowly. His mind began to work through what he was hearing.

"The young woman has defied me," said Obake.

"Stella?" Tagama asked.

"No! Keiko." Obake slammed the table with his fist, then lowered his rumbling voice so Tagama unconsciously leaned toward him. "Stella knows better."

Ryan observed the man's performance. It was masterful, every gesture and tonal inflection. Even the accent, a reminder of his fearsome status in his own country.

"Keiko, then. What has she done?" Tagama's voice was agreeable, though Ryan knew a razor-sharp wire vibrated through it.

"She has stolen from me. You will find her."

"I need more information."

"You'll get it yourself, and have Keiko and the—property—," he paused for emphasis, "back here tonight." Obake rose, a dismissal.

But he had one more knife to twist. He turned to his son. "We're a few minutes late, but Wayne Harding and Larry Johns will wait." His capped teeth gleamed against his tanned skin in a sneer. "I don't want these people to make me late for my sunset swim." He stood and rolled his oversized head in the direction of the Tagamas.

"Let's go." Steven Kudo sounded as if they were leaving excrement on the floor.

Though Ryan's feet seemed to be cemented in place, he didn't expect his father to sit still for this. Yet the older Tagama stayed in his chair until Obake and his son left the room. Ichiru Tagama's expression betrayed no strain; he looked, if anything, thoughtful.

Ryan knew the names Obake had thrown at them. Larry Johns was Maui County Commissioner and Wayne Harding had just assumed the late Tom Peters' position as Deputy Director of Liquor Control. He'd filled his boss' shoes in no time.

Obake was letting Tagama know that his contacts had more power than any Tagama could scrounge together. His message was that few would believe Tagama if it came to Obake's word against his. And even if they did believe Tagama, they'd be too afraid to say so.

Chapter Seventeen

Two police officers arrived in Storm's hotel room, along with the head of the hotel's security. The security man was concerned to the point of defensiveness.

"The electronic key card is changed after each guest. Did you lose your key?"

"No," Storm said. "I had one copy and it was in my purse. Someone got the security code."

"Impossible."

"Not if this person had access to the front desk," said Storm. She was in no mood to be the simpering pushover the security man hoped for.

One of the police, a short lean man, had the door propped open and examined the lock mechanism. "No sign of forced entry."

The security man had nothing to say.

The other officer, tall and tan, asked if he could dust her car keys and driver's license. "Though I doubt we'll find anything."

"Let's check the door, too," said the smaller cop.

The security man watched the cops work and stayed out of the way. There wasn't much for him to do. "I'll need a copy of the report," he said.

"Of course," the tall cop said.

Meanwhile, Storm filled out her part of the report, which included her lap top computer and everything that was in her handbag.

"Call us if you think of anything else that's missing," said the short cop. "Most people don't remember everything the first go-round."

"Any idea what he was after?" the tall cop asked.

"I had about a hundred dollars in cash, but my laptop is worth more than that." Storm thought a minute. "It's encrypted, but someone might want information I've got stored on it."

"Hope your encryption holds up," the tall cop said.

"Me, too."

"He left you just enough to get home." The short cop had just finished dusting her driver's license and keys. "You need your ID at the airport and your car keys to get there."

About a half-hour later, the police were finished, and Storm called Grace's cell phone. The ever-dependable secretary was in the office on a Saturday morning.

"What's wrong?" Grace asked. She and Aunt Maile must keep each other up to date with the latest in telepathic techniques.

"Why are you in the office?"

"I thought I'd catch up on some filing."

Storm told her the problem.

Five minutes later, Storm had a list of her credit card companies, and Grace had called the front desk of the hotel for a cash advance on the credit card Storm had used to check in. Grace's efficiency cut through most of Storm's confusion and fear. The burglary was a pain in the ass, but Storm could function for a day or two before she had to fly home and work on replacing everything.

"Call the companies, but I doubt this person wants your credit cards," Grace said. "He wants you to leave."

"I hate being manipulated."

"I know, but this is not the time to be obstinate."

"I can't do it today. I've got some details to nail down with the dive shop."

"What about the guardian ad litem case?"

"I've talked to the grandparents. Everything looks good."

"Any chance you can finish with the dive shop this afternoon?"

"No." Storm told her about Lara's dive that afternoon. "We'll wrap it up tomorrow."

"At the latest."

"Grace?"

"What?" Grace sounded like she knew.

"Do me a favor. Don't tell Hamlin about my purse." Grace sighed loudly, but Storm was reassured.

As they'd talked, other ideas had come to Storm. Her next call was to Sergeant Carl Moana, who was working a Lahaina art gallery after a break-in. She told him about her conversation with Carmen.

"Any chance I could go to her house and get her toy cat?"

"The house is still secured." He paused. "Can I call you back?"

Storm was in the car on the way to breakfast, when he phoned. "I can meet you in an hour and a half. You remember where the house is?"

"Sure, I'll be there."

By now Storm's stomach growled audibly, and a Cosmo-induced headache was digging in behind her eyeballs. Food was what she needed, and lots of water.

She went to Dina's, the restaurant near Lara's shop, where she'd seen Stella console a crying Keiko. Storm didn't recognize anyone this visit, but the menu was as enticing as it had been before. She ordered the omelet with pesto, goat cheese, and sun-dried tomatoes. Maybe she'd skip lunch.

The waitress was friendly, knowledgeable, and stayed close to keep Storm's coffee mug full of fresh brew, which prompted Storm to strike up a conversation.

"Do you remember Manny's Diner, Ice Scream, and Auntie Piko's Puka Shells?"

"Sure, the dive shop people bought them out." Storm picked up a note of disdain.

"Who owned the stores? Did they retire?"

"Bucky Silva died." The waitress didn't hide her distress with that pronouncement.

"Which store was his?"

"Ice Scream." The waitress, whose name tag said Louise, ignored Storm's raised hand and poured more coffee.

"That's sad." Storm added milk to her brimming coffee mug. "What about Manny? And Auntie Piko?"

"They're around. Auntie Piko is Pauline Harding. She lives up Makawao way. Manny Barrolo is in Lahaina." Louise looked thoughtful. "I heard he opened an Italian deli. I need to go visit."

"Sounds good. I will, too," Storm said.

"We have to support local shop owners, right?"

"Aren't the dive shop people local folks?"

"Lara Farrell is." Her tone implied that Lara was the only one.

Storm had an hour before she was to meet Sergeant Moana. Since Carmen's house was in Lahaina, she had time to drop by Manny Barrolo's new deli. She wasn't sure yet how she'd frame her questions, but she wanted inside, local rumor-mill type info on how the previous shop owners had been treated. She wanted to know if the new buyer was a faceless consortium, or whether Ryan Tagama or his father had negotiated the sale. But even more, she wanted intangible particulars. The sort Louise was giving her now, about how the owners were perceived in the community. Whether their business practices were on the level, opportunistic, or downright dirty. It was a small community, and the coconut wireless should have the scoop.

Manny Barrolo had thinning black hair, liver spots, and the lumpy, veined nose of a man who'd enjoyed his wine for a long, long time. He had a tall glass of iced tea next to the cash register and he raised it often. At first, Storm thought it was more than iced tea, but she couldn't pick up the scent of anything but tea and lemon.

"Joey, cut this lovely *wahine* a slice of that imported salami." Manny shouted over his shoulder at the young man behind the counter without taking his eyes from Storm's face.

"No thanks, I just—"

"You must. I get it straight from my cousin in Genoa. He sends a box every two weeks."

Joey put three paper-thin slices on a piece of wax paper and slid it across the top of the glass display case. His enthusiastic grin and flopping ginger hair reminded Storm of a happy golden retriever. He didn't look at all like Manny.

Storm put one in her mouth. It melted like spiced butter on her tongue. "That is delicious." She ate the other two.

"Told you." Manny slapped the counter with one hand, raised his iced tea with the other. "Joey, give her one of those fresh mozzarella balls."

Storm had to laugh. "I can't. But I promise I'll come back for lunch."

"What are you here for?"

"I wanted to ask you about Manny's Diner."

His shoulders slumped.

"Bad topic?" Storm asked.

"Kinda. Whaddya need to know?"

"I've got a client who's going into that space, and I need to find out if this person's business might be at risk."

"Probably." Manny's voice was bitter. He glanced over his shoulder at Joey.

"It's okay, Uncle Manny. I'll handle these customers." The bell over the door rang as a group of three entered.

"Let's sit down," Manny said. "Joey, can you get me another iced tea? And one for *la bellezza*." He took her arm and guided her to a chair.

"I try not to think of that place," he said when they sat down. "Not good for my health. But I'm gonna tell you about it. Part of my recovery is full disclosure, especially if it will help someone else."

"What happened?"

"A lot." Manny sighed. "Including my wife left me."

Joey glanced over, a frown erasing his previous enthusiasm.

"It's okay, Joey. I have to admit my wrongs." Manny took a sip of iced tea. "It's part of the twelve steps. I've been going to AA since this happened."

"Good for you." She, too, had friends who had turned their lives around with the help of AA or NA.

"Yeah, but."

Storm waited while Manny made circles on the table with the condensation on the outside of his glass. He seemed to muster his courage.

"I had some other problems. The guy that bought the shopping center pressured me."

"Pressured you?"

"Yeah." Manny wasn't meeting her eyes. "To sell."

"He had something on you?"

"Part of it was real and part of it wasn't," Manny rushed to say.

"Did you make a mistake because of alcohol?" Storm asked.

Manny nodded. He waited a long moment. "Do I have to tell you?"

"It would help if I knew what he had on you. And what he made up."

"I had an affair with one of the waitresses."

"You wouldn't be the first."

Manny sounded miserable. "Yeah, well." He didn't look up. "It was my wife's second cousin. She was twenty."

"Ouch," Storm said.

"But she instigated it," He added quickly. "She'd always been trouble. The whole family said so—my brother told me not to hire her in the first place."

Storm was beginning to see where this was going. She sat quietly and let him continue.

"Then the guy threatened me. Said he'd get her to say she was raped." He popped the knuckles on his left hand as if he'd like to tear off his fingers. "I didn't do that."

"I believe you," Storm said, and did. "What did this guy look like?"

"Big heavy guy, dark tan."

Storm didn't know what Ryan Tagama's dad looked like, but it certainly wasn't Ryan.

"My wife had already moved out. This guy was going to send me to jail," Manny's voice was a whisper, "just to get my store. But I was done with that." He finally met Storm's eyes. "You know?"

"Yeah, I know."

"You believe me?"

"Yes, I do. And Manny, this stays with me." Storm stood up and offered her hand. "Thanks for your honesty."

He looked surprised, then shook it.

Walking back to the car, she was so lost in thinking about Manny's sad story that she almost collided with a skate boarder. The boarder kept going, lost in the cacophony of his iPod, but Storm looked back to see if she needed to shout a warning to the elderly woman she'd passed a few yards back. Fortunately, the woman was safely backed up against a store front.

But that's how Storm spotted the two suits hustling out of an unremarkable building across the street. Not only was the dark attire unusual for laid-back Lahaina, but their black Mercedes sedan, flanked by two rusting Toyotas, stuck out like a shark in an aquarium. Both men had stocky, bowed legs. The taller of the two, whose jacket pulled across his back, looked like his heavy thighs would soon chafe through his slacks. His thick arms stuck out from his sides like Gumby's. Probably on steroids. The shorter, older man had a very dark tan.

The windows of the Mercedes were tinted so darkly she couldn't see the men when they drove out of the parking lot. But she did recognize the next pair that exited the back of the building. They wore jackets over aloha shirts, still dressy, but common island business attire. The taller of these two was Ryan, Lara's fiancé. Storm figured the older man, who was thin and pale with brush-cut silver hair, was Ryan's father.

She sauntered to the corner to get a look at which real estate office they were leaving. But it wasn't a real estate office, it was a bar. The Red Light's neon sign wasn't turned on, but it was easy to read. So were the Budweiser and Kirin beer signs.

Perhaps the four men had been brokering a deal in a bar before opening hours, but it seemed odd. Even more significant was Ryan's and his father's demeanor. If they'd been brokering a deal, they'd wound up on the losing end.

Chapter Eighteen

Storm didn't have time to dwell on the Tagamas and the closed bar. Commercial real estate was their business, after all, and she didn't want to be late to her meeting with Sergeant Moana.

Ten minutes later, when she pulled into the driveway of the Yoshinaka's modest house, the sight of the pink bicycle on the lawn stung her eyes. Was it Carmen's? Would she ever want to play with it again?

Moana had already arrived. He leaned against the door of his patrol car and talked on his cell phone. A fuzzy, stuffed orange cat sat on the car's roof.

"Sorry I'm late," Storm said when he disconnected.

"No worries, I just got here, too." He put the phone in his pocket and handed the fluffy toy cat to her.

"You knew the family, didn't you?"

"My daughters played in a soccer league with Carmen and Crystal."

"Did you know the father?"

"Not well. He didn't speak much English. Seemed like a caring dad, though I couldn't exactly talk story with him."

"I heard he had some debts. You think he shot himself because of those?"

Moana scuffed his feet in the dry grass. "This is going to come out in the paper, but you can't say a word until it does." He looked around, though no one was there. "Yoshinaka had a gambling problem."

"Cards? Cock fights?"

"He's small time, so probably cards and Pachinko."

"Pachinko?"

"Kind of a cross between a slot machine and pin ball."

Storm frowned. "Small time?"

"He was down about eighteen grand—as opposed to white collar shakedowns, which run into the hundreds of thousands. Millions, for that matter."

Eighteen grand. Storm wondered if she would look foolish telling him about last night's experience, but decided not telling him was worse. "I've got to tell you a story. Don't know if it means anything, but you can decide for yourself." She told him about her visit to Ma'alahi Storage and the owners, the $18,765 handwritten note on the contract, and how her room had been broken into while she slept.

"My purse was stolen, except for my driver's license and the car keys. There was a note telling me to go home."

"This happened soon after you visited that storage place? Because that's the amount of Yoshinaka's debt."

Storm nodded.

"Your only connection to these storage owners is through Lara's Aquatic Adventures?"

"Lara's future father-in-law owns the property under the dive shop. He's also on the board of the consortium that owns Blue Marine and the Yoshinaka's house."

Moana screwed up his face. "He's a pretty big commercial real estate investor, but I'll look into it." He thought for a minute. "You're sure about the dollar amount?"

"I remember the descending numbers."

"Me, too." He squinted into the distance. "Let me speak to the cops who went to your room this morning. I'll also check on that storage facility."

"Will you let me know?" Storm asked.

"If I can." He got in his car.

Storm watched him pull away. He'd follow up on her question, but he probably wasn't going to give her much information.

She was curious about those Pachinko machines. Who ran gambling machines on this island? They probably weren't in private homes. The back rooms of bars? Hotels? Storage facilities?

Wait, she didn't want to get into this. She'd retrieved Neko the kitty, and done her duty by telling Moana what she knew. Now all she had to do was finish setting up Lara's corporation in a manner that protected her from liability and fraud. She could finish that project tomorrow morning and still have the rest of the day with Hamlin. It was perfect timing.

Storm was getting in her car when her mobile phone rang. It was a Maui number, not one she recognized.

"Storm? Is that you? It's Stella. You have a few minutes? I'd like to talk to you."

"You caught me at a pretty good time. What's up?"

"Uh, is there any chance you could pick me up? Keiko took the car this morning and hasn't come back and Lara wants me at the shop by noon."

Storm remembered how Stella had confided in her about Lara's struggles with her ex-boyfriend. She'd also told Storm a friend had recommended her services to Lara, so Stella must feel a level of trust. On one hand, this could be a big fat hassle. On the other, Stella would be a good source of information regarding the dive shop.

Storm stifled a sigh. At least she'd have a captive interviewee. Could be worse. "Where do you live?"

She got the address, which was off Mokulele Avenue, not far from Kahului.

It took Storm about twenty minutes to get there. On the way, she wondered why Stella didn't just take a bus or a cab, but the edge to the woman's normally easy-going voice made her think there was a reason for the call. Sure enough, when Storm got to the condominium, Stella was pacing in the parking lot. She pulled on a cigarette as if it were a pacifier.

She ground out the cigarette and got in the car, flushed and sweating. The smell of smoke clung to her. "Thanks for coming." Her fingernails were chewed to nubs. "I need to talk to you."

"Where's Keiko?"

"I don't know." Stella's hair, usually pinned up with fresh flowers, hung limp. Dark circles underscored her eyes.

"What time did she leave?"

"Around nine, I think. I was having coffee and reading the paper. It took me a while to notice she was gone."

"She didn't ask you for the keys?"

"No, but they're usually on the table by the front door. I thought she was in the bathroom. She liked to take long, hot baths."

"Anything unusual happen? Did she make any phone calls or receive any?"

"I don't think so. Not that I knew of."

"Does she take off very often?"

"No, and I think it's— " Stella drew a deep breath. "If I hire you, you're bound to confidentiality, right?"

"Yes."

"Can I hire you on someone's behalf?"

"Yes, but if you're not my client, what you tell me isn't confidential."

"Shit."

Storm thought a moment. "But personal is personal. It'll take a subpoena to squeeze it out of me."

"Okay." Stella slumped in the seat. "I have to talk to someone."

Storm put the car in park, but left the air conditioner running. "Is this about Keiko?"

Stella nodded. "She's had a hard life."

"What's she done?"

"I'm not sure. Well, I think— " She wrung her hands. "I have to give you some background."

"I'm okay with that." Storm kept her voice calm and reassuring.

Stella drew a deep breath. "She was in the *mizu shobai*. The water trade."

Storm didn't know the term.

"You know. Night-time entertainment."

"Prostitution?"

Stella flushed. "Look, she didn't have a choice." Her hands were curled into tight fists.

"Tell me about this." Storm kept her voice very soft.

"She's Chinese," Stella stared out the windshield at a distance Storm couldn't see. "Her real name is Yuan Ling, and her parents sold her to cover debts."

Stella had to clear her voice twice, but she went on. "The Yakuza pays about $5000 for young girls in China and the Philippines. They're told they'll be given good jobs."

Her upper lip curled and her tormented eyes slid to gauge Storm's reaction. Storm worked to keep the shock off her face, and the effort must have been effective because Stella kept talking.

"The men like them very young, you know. Before they get their periods. They call it selling spring."

"Jesus." Storm could no longer keep her dismay hidden.

"They make the girls wear school outfits, like short pleated skirts and knee socks. Sometimes with high heels."

Storm winced and followed Stella's gaze to the horizon. The older woman's face was waxy and pale, and she seemed to be revisiting a memory beyond the cane fields.

"How did you get Keiko away from them?" Storm whispered. She wasn't just asking about Keiko, and Stella knew it.

"I knew something about one of the men."

"Good for you."

Stella picked at a hangnail. "But Keiko tried to escape another way. She cut her arms and nearly bled to death."

"You were with her?"

"No, I got out years ago. This was about eight months ago." She chewed her thumb. "Someone called me about her."

"Someone from the, uh…"

"Club. They're called clubs."

Storm grimaced at the euphemism. "Who called you?"

Stella looked nervous. "You wouldn't know her."

Storm assumed it was one of the prostitutes. "Okay, but why you?"

"Keiko is my goddaughter's age. Twenty-three. The woman who called knew Angela."

"Angela was in the same business?"

"Yes, and she died of a drug overdose. It was a means of escape." Stella swallowed so hard Storm could hear it. "I'm afraid Keiko will try the same thing."

Storm found her own hands curling into fists. "Did something happen over the last few days to upset her? That would make her take your car and leave?"

Stella returned from the world of the past, and turned reddened eyes to Storm. "Yesterday, I went to see an old friend of mine. It upsets Keiko—she won't go inside."

"Inside her home?"

"She's in a nursing facility."

Hadn't Damon mentioned that Lara's mother was in a nursing home? Storm considered that connection.

"You think that's what made her take the car and leave?"

"That and Hiroki Yoshinaka's suicide."

"Because he killed his daughter?"

Stella's eyes slid to Storm. "She's concerned about the sister."

Debts, Storm thought. "You think she might have, um, done something with Carmen?"

"I'd like to check and make sure."

"Stella, is gambling part of the water trade?"

Stella's eyes grew round. "You know about Hiroki's gambling debts?"

"I suspected."

"It used to be part of the club scene, but I'm not sure anymore. Keiko ended up in the water trade because of her own father's debts."

And Keiko preferred death over life in Obake's establishment. Apparently, Hiroki Yoshinaka had made a similar choice. Would Keiko have the nerve to do what Hiroki had attempted? Storm put the car in gear, her grip tight on the steering wheel.

"You want to go visit Carmen?"

"I called the hospital earlier, and Keiko hadn't been there."

"When did you call?"

"Ten or ten-thirty."

Storm checked her watch. "Didn't you say Lara wanted you in the shop by noon? You're going to be very late."

Stella's shoulders drooped.

Storm felt for her. "Look, I need to call Lara to make an appointment to finish setting up her business. I can also find out if she's expecting you right away."

The phone rang a long time. Storm was about ready to disconnect when Damon's voice came on.

"Did you get my message?" he asked.

"Shoots, I'm sorry," Storm said. "My purse got stolen sometime last night and I completely forgot to call you back."

"I thought you were mad at me."

"No, I got distracted. Why'd you call?"

"I can't remember now." He laughed.

"Okay." If you say so. "Say, I'd like to talk to you. You free tonight after work?"

"Are you asking me on a date?" Damon sounded a bit too eager.

"Nice try. It's a professional date. I don't play golf."

He chuckled again. "Neither do I. The Fiddler Crab again? I can meet you at six."

"Sounds good. Is Lara around?"

"She and Ken took a group of travel agents out diving. Good promotional opportunity, you know."

"When will she be back? I need to talk to her."

"Late afternoon, I'd guess."

Storm could tell that Stella understood the gist of the conversation. "Is there any reason Stella needs to come to the shop right now? She needs some personal time."

"She could come in and answer this damned phone," Damon said.

"She'll be there in an hour. Meanwhile, practice your social skills."

Damon made a noise somewhere between a snort and a honk and hung up.

Ten minutes later, Storm and Stella pulled into the hospital parking lot. They went past the nursing station, straight to Carmen's room. The bed was rumpled and no one was in it.

"She could be in the bathroom." Stella's words rang with concern.

Storm had already turned back toward the nursing station. "We came to see Carmen Yoshinaka."

The desk clerk looked up with a practiced smile. "We released her to her auntie. Poor thing. Her only relative here in the U.S."

"What's the aunt's name?" Storm asked.

The clerk fluttered through a pile of papers. "Here." She handed a form to Storm.

Storm grabbed the paper, and Stella looked over her shoulder. The signature was illegible to Storm, but Stella recognized it.

"That's Keiko's," she said.

Stella waited until they were in Storm's car to speak. "I'm afraid of what Keiko might do."

"How far will she go to protect Carmen?"

Stella, her skin papery and grey, merely clenched her hands together.

Chapter Nineteen

"I'll take the helm," Lara said.

Ken adjusted his sunglasses against the glare. "My turn in the cage?"

She nodded.

"You still spooked from the encounter with the reef shark?"

"No." She grabbed the wheel of the thirty-six foot Newton. "I went last time, remember?"

Ken gave her a nudge. "That was a five-minute test run."

She cut the throttle on the twin inboard diesels to cruise. He waited for an answer, but she didn't speak.

"Suit yourself," he said, and turned from the helm.

"Did you drop some bait yesterday?"

Ken glanced over his shoulder at the five people waiting in the stern seating area. No one was listening to them; the engine noise would make it difficult even if someone was trying to. One reporter and four travel agents peered over the side of the boat with a mixture of excitement and nerves. One of the travel agents cradled his face, which had taken on a greenish-gray cast, in his arms.

"They know the sound of the engines," Ken said. "Four showed up before I even dropped the fish over the side. But keep your voice low—we're inside the intercoastal limit."

"One mile, three miles, you see anybody measuring?" Lara shrugged. "We're out far enough."

Ken glanced toward the coast. The big new house on a bluff over the bay looked like an expensive toy. He wouldn't want to swim, but he didn't think they were three miles from shore, either. "Then this is the place. What's the depth finder say?"

"Three hundred feet."

"Perfect." He peered into the sapphire blue of deep water. "I'm ready if you are."

"This is a good place, I think." Lara put the engines into neutral.

Ken climbed down from the helm and gave the seasick man a pat on the shoulder. "You'll feel better when you get in the water." He handed out snorkels and masks. "Put on a lot of sunscreen, because you're going to be so enthralled you won't realize when you're medium rare."

The passengers tittered nervously. "You sure a shark can't bite through that?" One of the travel agents gestured to the big cage hanging off the boat's stern.

"Absolutely."

"Can one jump into it?" someone else asked.

"No way," Ken answered. "There will be about two feet of Plexiglas and steel above the surface of the water. That baby is custom-made and professionally tested."

Lara turned off the motor. Birds and water slapping the hull were the only sounds. The boat rocked with the swells, and the sick man slumped in his seat, swallowing repeatedly.

Ken gently lowered the big aluminum and Plexiglas cage into the water and tied it securely to a set of aft cleats. Once the passengers were inside, Lara would push the cage away from stern and keep it in place with flexible poles. Tubular floats kept the top edge out of the water.

Ken put on a mask and snorkel and demonstrated how to get in and out of the cage. Soon he and the five passengers were in place, with their faces in the water. Every now and then, one of them would raise his or her head and point with excitement as the powerful sharks began to arrive.

Lara allowed a smile of relief to cross her face. As her fishermen friends had told her, the sharks had been conditioned by the sound of the boat's engine to expect food. Several weeks' work was paying off. The travel agents loved it, except for the poor seasick guy, but that wasn't her fault. He should have taken his Dramamine; Ken had warned everyone before they left the harbor. The reporter, to her delight, looked enthralled.

A half dozen sandbar sharks already circled the cage. They were usually the first to arrive and ranged from four to six feet. Impressive, and about the same size as the three Whitetip reef sharks, which were easy to identify from the white tips on their first and second dorsal fins. Whitetips were fairly common; her scary encounter on Thursday had been with a Whitetip. They were far from that particular shark's territory, so he (or she) wouldn't be part of this group.

Lara sat up a little straighter, and a thrill went through her. Two Galapagos sharks had appeared. These guys would seal the deal. How could people resist this kind of experience? Eight to ten feet long and three or four hundred pounds, the dusky brown-grey bodies of solid muscle slid through the water as pure and easy as sex.

Fifteen or twenty minutes passed, and Lara relaxed enough to look toward land and gently reposition the boat. It took a shrill whistle from Ken to get her attention. "Bring the cage in. Steve is tired."

Oh yeah. Steve was the sick guy. Lara pulled the cage to the stern and reached out to him. He splashed frantically toward her.

"Easy, I'll get you," she said. "Any one else want to take a break?"

"Hell, no," yelled the reporter, who raised his face just long enough to utter two words. None of the other guests wanted to leave, either.

"Hold on," Lara said to Steve, whose clammy grip had slipped from her hand. "Keep your mask on," she added, but he'd already taken it off and was waving it around. Sure enough, it slipped from his grasp and plopped into a gap between the boat's transom and the cage.

"Leave it," Lara said, but he plunged both arms in to try and catch it before it sank. She grabbed at his upper arm. "Let it go," she shouted. "It's okay."

Idiot, Lara thought. She watched the mask sink, while Steve fished around with the effectiveness of a tea strainer in an ocean. He looked helplessly up at her, his face a pasty white.

"Sorry."

But Lara was no longer looking at him. A dark shadow had passed under them. Huge. It looked as long as the boat. Water magnified objects, but it was twenty feet, at least. A Tiger or Great White. Jesus.

She lunged at Steve, whose hand still dangled in the water. Surprised at her strength, he slid out of the cage and plopped onto the deck of the dive boat like a hooked *mahi*.

"Thanks," he said, and crawled off to a bench.

The other five heads were staring at her, the whites of their eyes like stampeding horses. "What the fuck was that?" one of the travel agents said.

"I'm ready to come in," said the reporter.

"You sure?" shouted Ken. He would have jumped up and down if he could. "This is the sighting of a lifetime."

"Thanks, but I'll watch from deck," yelled another travel agent, and lunged for the side of the cage facing the boat. She'd removed her mask and waved it in one hand, while the other hand gripped the cage so hard it looked like a claw.

"No problem," Lara said, and tied the cage securely to the aft cleats. "Though you're quite safe."

She kept her voice calm and level. But inside, she rejoiced. The *manō*, her *'aumakua*, was on her side.

Chapter Twenty

Neither Ryan nor his father spoke on the way back to the elder Tagama's residence. When Ryan pulled into the port chochère of his father's luxurious Wailea condominium, he stopped the car.

"We have to talk."

Tagama grunted.

"Now." Ryan steeled himself. He couldn't ignore Obake's comments about his father and the hooker. In fact, whether or not his dad communicated would predict their relationship. The uncertain gelato business was better than lies and manipulation.

"Dad, if we are going to work together, we need to tell each other about past mistakes."

Tagama met his son's eyes. "My past isn't good."

"I need to know about it."

Tagama nodded. "Fair enough."

The concurrence surprised Ryan enough that his foot slipped off the brake pedal. The car drifted about a foot before he fumbled to a stop.

Tagama didn't smile, but Ryan felt a lightening in his father's mood. "Let's park," the old man said.

Ryan drove to guest parking and the men rode the elevator in silence to the fifteenth floor. Now that he'd asked for truth, Ryan wasn't sure he wanted to hear it. He wondered how his father felt.

It had been a couple of years since Ryan had been to his father's home. Lara and he had invited his old man to their place for dinner twice, and Tagama had taken the two of them to nice restaurants on occasion. Ryan remembered his father's apartment as having a great view to the ocean, but no soul. No family pictures, no magazines, papers, notes on the refrigerator door. Spotless glass, leather, and cold marble.

There were only two apartments on the fifteenth floor, both opulent and large. Ryan was surprised to see two pairs of his father's shoes outside the door. The other apartment had a pile of shoes, small ones among them. Taking off shoes before entering the home was an island custom, but Tagama not only wouldn't leave personal belongings in public view, he wouldn't abide the untidiness.

And there sat his somewhat muddy, custom-made golf shoes. One lay on its side, next to some rubber slippers. Ryan had never even seen his dad in flip-flops. Or a swim suit, for that matter.

Tagama opened the door without explanation, and kicked off the shoes he was wearing. Ryan shed his also, too surprised to say anything about his father's change of habit.

Inside, glorious light reflected from the beach and brilliant turquoise of the ocean, filled the apartment. The room, however, looked different to Ryan. Same glass and marble coffee table, but it was strewn with the morning's *Honolulu Star Bulletin*, *New York Times*, and the *Hawaii Hochi*, a Japanese language paper. Two teacups and a plate, empty except for a scattering of crumbs, sat next to the paper. A couple of magazines were stacked at one end of the sofa—not the rigid black leather and stainless sling that Ryan remembered, but a cushy saddle-colored one. With throw pillows. He stared. The scene momentarily eclipsed Obake's nasty accusations.

Tagama misinterpreted Ryan's surprise. "Er, the maid is running late."

"No, it looks good. I like the new couch." Ryan couldn't say any more, though, because he'd caught sight of something else he'd never expect to see in his father's living room. He could only point. "That's a—"

"My *obutsudan*?"

"Yeah." Ryan blinked. "A Buddhist shrine?"

"I'm trying to change some things." Tagama cleared his throat.

"Right."

"Excuse me a minute." Tagama picked up the cups and plate from the coffee table and took them to the kitchen. Some food items—a loaf of bread, a hand of bananas, an open package of English muffins, and a crumb-strewn toaster—were still on the countertop.

"Dad, are you seeing someone?" Only a woman could make this much of a difference.

Tagama didn't answer, and a moment later, Ryan heard the refrigerator door close. His dad came out of the kitchen with a pitcher of orange juice, a bottle of Grey Goose, and two glasses. "You want vodka with this? We have a lot of talking to do."

Without waiting for an answer, he pushed the newspapers aside and set the bottle, glasses, and juice on the coffee table. He poured juice without liquor, then walked across the room to the shrine.

Ryan had still not taken a seat, and he stared after his father as the older man placed the glass of juice and sections of a peeled orange on a small offering stand.

Tagama sensed his son's scrutiny and looked over his shoulder. "An extra offering to Guan-Gong. He gives protection. Before he became the god of martial arts and war in the afterlife, he was a general in the Chinese Army."

"Chinese?" Ryan sputtered.

"Chinese, Japanese, I figure we're all the same in the afterlife."

"Where did you learn this?" Ryan gestured toward the neat, lacquered red box, which smelled faintly of incense. A glowering statue with flowing beard and warrior's armor presided over the orange pieces. If his father had told him the figure was samurai, Ryan would have believed him. But Chinese? Tagama had always struck him as a Japanese nationalist, patriotic to the point of xenophobia.

"We'll talk about that later. We have enough to discuss." Tagama came back to the sofa, sat down, and poured two glasses of orange juice.

Ryan took a grateful gulp. It was fresh and delicious. His father didn't squeeze oranges, either.

His throat not quite as tight and dry, Ryan forced out the question that had tormented him since leaving Obake's club. "What rape was he talking about?"

"When you were young, I did some things I'm not proud of."

Ryan sat back on the couch. He'd still been hoping his father would tell him Obake had lied.

"It was a big mistake," Tagama said.

Ryan's stomach rolled. Obake had told the truth? His father was a rapist? Ryan swallowed his nausea with effort. He felt poisoned.

"I managed a club."

Ryan didn't respond, and Tagama went on. "We had a tour business, mostly Japanese businessmen. Very expensive, very exclusive. A week's vacation on Maui at a fine hotel. I won't tell you the name of the hotel. We sold it ten years ago. Evenings at the club—"

Ryan interrupted. "We?"

"You know this part. Obake was a partner in those days."

"Is this the money we're investing now?" Ryan's words were bitter rinds of loathing. "The money I'm taking home to Lara? The money I'm saving for my own son one day?"

Tagama held up a hand. "Please, let me finish." His tone was so calm and sad that Ryan sucked back his acid tirade.

"I hadn't learned that money doesn't civilize a person, or give him humanity. I didn't know how people use money to hide their atrocities."

He fumbled with his juice glass. "Not only did my ego and ambition blind me, I was a coward." He mumbled the last words, and Ryan saw him glance at the vodka bottle.

"But I must regard my failures with clear eyes. It is a way of life I am late in adopting."

"What about the rape?"

"It was during a party with a group of *sokaiya*."

"Just tell me in English," Ryan snapped.

"Yakuza posing as a company's shareholders. They own a few shares, but they mostly get dirt on the company's officers and threaten to reveal it at a shareholder's meeting." He looked at his son.

"Extortion," Ryan said.

"Yes, though I thought they were regular businessmen, just one of our vacation packages. As always, we'd set up a few nights with girls, who were well paid."

Ryan interrupted. "Who was the pimp?"

Tagama sighed. "I don't know. I closed my eyes to that part of the preparations."

Ryan's stomach still clenched, but the nausea had passed. He listened with the same sick voyeurism he felt when he saw a bad traffic accident. "What happened?"

"Obake was host of this group."

"What business was targeted?"

"Just a small local group. Nothing big, some people who wanted to buy a local restaurant. But you asked about the women."

Tagama looked at his son, and Ryan sat up a little straighter. He watched his father's hands, which were curled around his untouched orange juice glass. The skin over Tagama's heavy knuckles was shiny with tension.

"Go on."

"We had a suite at the hotel. I was with about twenty men, drinking at the bar in the big sitting room. There was a kitchen, too, and a couple of bedrooms. Obake told me to go first, with a pretty blonde. She was young, and I think a little scared, but she whispered in my ear when I went to embrace her in front of the other men. She told me I had to make it look rough."

He shook his head at the memory. "I drew back." He glanced at Ryan, who couldn't meet his eyes. "This is true, son. It took me a minute to realize she'd been paid extra to act out a role."

Tagama sighed. "But she was afraid, and when she acted like she was sucking on my ear, she whispered that if we didn't play the part, it would be bad for both of us."

Ryan felt as if he'd swallowed a golf ball. Tagama went on.

"I gave her a shove, which made her stumble. She caught herself, though, and I made like I was pushing her down the hallway. She was a good actress, too, she even lost a shoe on the way. The men laughed."

"Where was Obake?"

Tagama looked at the floor. "He had another girl. He and some other guys went in the kitchen. They were doing one-armed push-ups, showing off their muscles before they—"

"*Guys?* How old were these girls?"

"Fifteen, sixteen." Tagama didn't look up.

"'That was statutory rape." Ryan's voice rasped in his dry throat.

"No, Hawai'i has the lowest age of consent in the United States. A child fourteen or older can have consensual sex."

"That's awful."

"Yes, it is." Those three words sounded as if they'd been dragged from Tagama's soul.

"It makes it easier for the Yakuza to force little girls into prostitution."

Tagama just nodded.

"So Obake was with other men, and in the kitchen with the other lucky girl. Where were you?"

"A bedroom."

"And you fucked?" Ryan's words were lifeless.

"I gave her a large tip."

"Great." Ryan fell back into the sofa and stared at the ceiling.

Tagama didn't talk for several minutes. Ryan felt as if his father had opened his jugular and filled him with lead.

"I didn't rape her." Tagama brought his glass to his lips, and Ryan noticed that his father's hand trembled.

"But that shove, it gave a couple of the other guys ideas." Tagama sighed deeply. "She came out a few minutes after I did, and one of the men grabbed at her. She pulled away, and he hit her in the face. Broke her nose and knocked a couple of her front teeth out. She spit them at him."

Ryan stared, numb.

"Everyone laughed. Obake was busy with the other girl, so I grabbed her arm and got her out the front door and to a doctor."

Both men sat in silence for a while. Years ago in California, Ryan had been at a fraternity party with hookers. He hadn't had enough money to share in the fun, but he'd been curious. He didn't know what he'd have done if someone had told him to go first, that it had been paid for. He might have gone for it. Now he wondered how the girls felt. He'd never considered it.

Tagama might have misinterpreted his silence, for he spoke in a voice so low Ryan only caught a few words. "…can ask her."

"Huh?" Ryan said, and stared at his father. Ryan was reeling from his father's story and his own memories of the fraternity party. How different was he than his father?

The elder Tagama's words sank in. Ask her?

This woman would be ten to fifteen years younger than his own father and mother. Tagama had said she was blonde, and someone had punched her in the face and knocked out a couple of her teeth.

He tore at his hair and moaned. "Oh, Dad."

Her teeth had been repaired. A smile with a glint of gold came to him. He knew who she was.

Chapter Twenty-one

Stella stared out the windshield with glassy, unseeing eyes for at least ten miles. Storm's mind whirled on the implications of Keiko and Carmen together. Stella was the first to break the silence.

"Can Keiko be arrested for kidnapping?"

"Possibly. She's going to need a lawyer."

"Will you take the job?" Stella asked.

Storm pulled a sigh from the bottoms of her feet. What the hell was she getting into? "I have to talk to her."

"I can pay you."

"We'll discuss that," Storm said. "Right now, let's find her."

"She has cash and could get a hotel room somewhere." Stella thought for a minute. "I didn't check to see if any of our camping gear was missing. That's another option."

"Does she have any friends?"

"Not really. She isn't very outgoing."

"Does she trust any of your friends?"

Conversation was returning some color to Stella's face. "Maybe Pauline Harding. We call her Auntie Piko."

"The one with the jewelry store?"

Stella was surprised. "You know her?"

"No, I just heard she sold her store."

"Lara offered her a good price and it was good timing. She was tired of the drive."

"But the Tagamas own the shopping center, right?"

"Pauline wouldn't sell to the Tagamas. She doesn't trust them." Stella was firm.

That was odd. Manny of Manny's Deli and Louise the waitress told Storm that Pauline *had* sold to the Tagamas. "Do you trust them?" she asked.

Stella squinted into the sun. "I have history with Ichiru Tagama. He's okay." She added an afterthought. "As long as he's not being pressured by some of his partners."

"Who are his partners?"

"I'm not sure these days."

Storm gave Stella a hard look, but she didn't notice. The older woman seemed to be pondering how much to reveal, and Storm decided to let her spill it on her own.

It was interesting how the woman with the most property— and the most to lose—was Lara. And Lara wasn't nearly as inclined to protect her interests as Storm wanted her to be.

"Do you trust Ryan?" Storm asked.

"He's a nice boy." For the first time since Stella got into the car, a flash of amusement brightened her face. "I introduced them."

They traveled the next ten minutes in silence. No one spoke until Storm stopped at the Pi'ilani Highway cutoff.

"Where does Pauline live?" Storm glanced over at her passenger.

"Upcountry, in Makawao."

They were nearly in Kihei. If Stella hadn't needed to get to work, Storm would have suggested making a u-turn and going to see Pauline. She wanted to talk to Aunty Piko about a number of things. It would be interesting to hear Pauline's version of why she'd sold the shop. Storm also wanted to know her history, and how she came to be close to Keiko and Stella.

"Would you mind calling her?" Storm asked. "See if Keiko's been in touch."

Stella pulled out her mobile phone and dialed a number. "Hi Pauline, this is Stella again. You seen Keiko yet?" She listened to Pauline for a couple of minutes, then responded. "You're right.

She's probably running some errands. Um, have her call me if you see her?"

Frowning, Stella disconnected. "Not there."

"You called her earlier?"

"Yes, and she said the same thing."

"What's wrong?"

"She's becoming annoyed." Stella sighed.

"She'll forgive you." Storm kept her tone light. "Say, did Lara get along well with her father?"

"Sure, why are you asking?"

"We were talking about our fathers the other day, and she told me about the restaurant he wanted to buy."

"Lara is convinced that restaurant mess was the final straw. She thinks it gave him the heart attack."

"She said he was betrayed."

"You could put it that way." Stella glanced at Storm. "But to answer your question, she worshipped her father."

"He was good to his family?"

"When he wasn't drinking." Stella rushed to complete her thought. "You see, Angela was his baby. He hit the bottle for a while after she left home."

Storm gripped the steering wheel in surprise. It was the first time she'd made the connection that Stella's goddaughter, who'd died from an overdose, was Lara's sister.

"How old was Angela when she left?" Storm asked.

"Eighteen. Right before her high school graduation."

"Was Barb about the same age when she left school?"

Stella looked out the window, away from Storm. "Barb was younger." Her voice sounded as if it traveled from the past. "Angela had some conflicts with her mother. I always told Barb it was just teenage stuff. She needed to relax."

"Did Lara have difficulties with her mother, too?"

"Not like Angela's."

"Did the sisters get along?"

"There was some sibling rivalry, but nothing unusual. When the girls were young, Lara was a little jealous. Angela was a great swimmer. But Angela quit, and it wasn't long before she felt she couldn't measure up to Lara."

"Did Lara make her feel that way?"

Stella thought for a minute. "No, though Lara could be a bit selfish. Competitive, you know? But she always loved her sister." Stella resumed twisting her hands. "I always told Angela she was beautiful and had her own talents."

They rode in silence for a few minutes, and then Stella spoke as if there had been no pause. "She always looked to men for approval. She didn't do things for herself, you know?"

"Who did? Angela?"

Stella looked over at Storm. "I was thinking about Barb, but yeah, Angela did it too."

"What do you mean?"

"They both were smart, but didn't care much for school. Barb believed her looks were the most important quality she had, but she only felt beautiful when men verified it."

"Verified it in a sexual way?"

"I suppose so. We don't think through these things when we're teenagers, do we?"

"No, I guess not," Storm said. "How about after she married Michael?"

"She relied on him."

"For everything?" Storm asked.

"Totally."

"That must have been hard on him, too."

"You know he got Barb away from the water trade, right?"

"He did?"

"Yeah." Stella smiled at the memory. "Barb always talked about how he rescued her. He was very loving and strong in those days."

"He changed?"

Stella looked uncertain. "Life changes people. Michael got laid off, then got a job as a bartender, and he started drinking. The owner eased him out and helped him start a restaurant supply business. He was doing good until Angela left."

"He went back to the bottle?"

"For a while, but he pulled it together." She considered this thought, then continued. "It seemed to me when Barb got weak, Michael got stronger. It was the way of their marriage. And Barb was at wit's end when Angela left."

She looked over at Storm. "You can understand why, right? She knew firsthand what her baby was getting into. Hell, she was running to it. Almost like she wanted to punish her mother." The lines of fatigue in Stella's face deepened with the memory.

"You tried to stop her."

"Of course, and so did Michael. Lara's right about the restaurant. He thought Angela would come back and run the place with her sister."

Not if Angela felt unworthy, Storm thought, but she didn't say the words aloud. With a wave of sadness, she related to Michael Farrell's hopes. Years ago, her father had hoped that a change of lifestyle would improve his wife's depression, so he'd bought land around Hamakua and planned to farm macadamia nut trees or coffee. But Eme Kayama's suicide had gutted the dreams. Part of him died with her; the rest tagged along four years later.

More than twenty years passed, and the land was in Storm's name, but the dreams were her father's. Her life was on O'ahu. The property required minimal maintenance and taxes were still low. Land costs weren't going down, and she was gaining equity, but she felt the prick of her father's wasted hopes. One day she'd go back and do something with it.

"When did Angela die?" Storm asked.

"Five years ago. She was twenty-three."

That was when Lara stopped windsurfing. "That must have been awful."

"You have no idea."

Storm did have an idea, though people had different perspectives. Sad family stories were like old fishing nets. Lines were cut, frayed, retied, and interwoven. One opinion couldn't reveal truth; ten viewpoints just might begin to shed light on the knot of betrayal, heartache, and bad decisions. A knot that led to disaster.

Stella's mind was still unraveling the Farrell family story. "Angela's death finished off Michael. Barb, too, for that matter."

"Lara thinks Michael's death was due to his restaurant falling through. She said he died a week after some friends betrayed him on that deal."

"Maybe, who knows?" Stella sighed. "Though Angela was gone, he still saw it as a means of success and independence. Plus, Lara was interested. She wanted her father's approval."

"Seeking a father's approval is normal, isn't it?" The hint of emotion in her own voice surprised Storm.

"It's difficult when your younger sister is the one who gets noticed. Negative attention sucks up a lot of parental energy, and Angela was their baby. In the family, Lara was known as the dependable one."

Hamlin's family history was similar, Storm realized. The recollection sent a strong pang of longing through her. Hamlin would understand the friction between the good sibling and the rebel. He was the responsible one; his older brother had run away from home when he was in his teens. The brother had died in early adulthood, too, and Hamlin missed him deeply. He also admitted to feeling both love and resentment for that brother, a lost soul who'd put their mother through hell.

Thinking of Hamlin's secrets, Storm missed him with a tenderness she'd been afraid to feel for a long while. Had she told him the emotional burden of her land near Hamakua? She didn't think so.

Everyone has childhood scars, and people go on. They grow up to one degree or another. But it helps to share. Learning to trust and share is part of loving another person. Hamlin knew her mother's suicide left a scar. But had she ever admitted that her father's more subtle departure left a vacuum? It made her wonder about her own abilities to love and confide.

Storm pulled into the parking lot adjacent to Lara's dive shop. Stella turned to her. "Thanks for going out of your way. I appreciate it." She still looked pale and disturbed.

"We'll find Keiko. I'm going to talk to a policeman I know."

"No." Stella's hand flew to her mouth. "No cops. They won't help."

"This is a nice cop. He's a young guy, with kids of his own."

"No, you can't trust cops. Them and the liquor commission guys. Too much money at stake." She looked even paler, and Storm could see doubt in her eyes.

"Okay, I won't tell him. Don't worry."

"Thank you."

Storm began to put the car in gear, and thought of another question. "Stella?" Stella stopped and looked back, though wariness darkened her face.

"What's the name of the guy who owns the club? The one that sells spring."

Stella stepped to the passenger window and leaned in to whisper. "The Red Light. It's in Lahaina."

That was the bar she'd seen the Tagamas come out of. "The owner's name?"

Stella looked around the parking lot, uneasy. "Obake. That's all I know." She practically ran into the shop.

Storm watched her flee. She knew elders who believed in ghost stories and didn't want to mutter the word *obake*, for fear of conjuring the faceless ghost of local legend who sat on the chest of a sleeping person and sucked the life from her. But Stella didn't seem the type. No, Stella was nervous about the man, whoever he was.

Chapter Twenty-two

Ryan and his father sat in silence for some time. Ryan slumped on the soft leather couch and felt as if his own stuffing had been knocked out of him. Tagama looked pale and ten years older than he had when Ryan had picked him up that morning.

"Who called you when we were driving to the meeting with Obake?"

Instead of answering, Tagama lumbered across the room to the neat little shrine. From a nearby cabinet, Tagama withdrew a bottle Ryan recognized as sake, and poured a few ounces into a small cup. He placed the cup carefully near the warrior god Guan-Gong and muttered some quiet words. He then bowed twice, clapped twice, and bowed once more before he turned and limped back to the couch.

"That was Yasuko," he said.

"Obake's madam? You're still involved in prostitution?"

"No." Tagama's eyes widened. "That stopped with the story I told you."

Too many questions ran through Ryan's mind, and he missed the chance to question the risk Yasuko was taking. Instead, he returned to concerns about his father's activities.

"Why does Obake let you do business here? Hell, why does he let you live?"

"His real name is Akira Kudo. He's high in the organization, but he isn't *oyabun*. He's not the top man."

"That means someone's protecting you. You're still connected."

Tagama sighed. "No, but it's complicated."

"Really?" Ryan sneered.

"Yes." Tagama glared at his son. "I've made bad decisions in the past, but I'm doing the right thing now."

Ryan broke eye contact first. Doubt frayed his thoughts. His head felt like a bowl of overcooked noodles, a sticky blob. For the first time in years, he felt like calling his mother for advice, but she only knew the past, and she wasn't particularly charitable toward Tagama. The present was his predicament alone.

Ryan took a few moments to reflect. "How did you meet Yasuko?"

"She knows the woman I told you about. Yasuko knows we are friends."

Ryan stifled a snort of derision. Friends, indeed. "The blonde?"

Tagama ignored his attitude. "Yasuko first contacted me because of another young woman." His eyes rose to meet his son's. "You know about Angela."

Ryan swallowed. "Yes, it took a long time, but Lara told me."

"Yasuko tried to save her, but failed. She had to inform Stella about her."

His father had finally called Stella by name, which made Ryan feel marginally better. "That wouldn't go over well. Stella is very protective."

"It was awful for everyone," Tagama said in a soft voice.

The men sat in silence for several minutes. Ryan was the first to speak. "I need to think."

Tagama lowered his chin in acknowledgement. "I understand." He stood, straighter than he had before. "I am proud of you, son. You're one of the things I've done right."

Tagama walked him to the door and either ignored or didn't see Ryan's bleak glance.

"I have some loose ends to tie up," Tagama said. "Will you and Lara have dinner with me tonight? At seven-thirty? I'll make reservations for four."

The word four registered in the elevator when Ryan was halfway to the lobby. He also missed seeing his father hurry to the phone once he'd seen his son out. Nor did Ryan see Tagama, when no one answered, rush to the shrine to make another offering.

After that, Tagama dialed a different number and murmured into the phone as if he were afraid someone would overhear.

◇◇◇

Storm backed carefully out of the dive shop's parking lot. Lara's Corvette wasn't there, and though Damon's truck was sitting in the hot sun, she would see him in a few hours. If she left right then, she might make it to Makawao and back in time for dinner, but it was no guarantee. She considered her options at a red light. No, she'd talk to Auntie Piko tomorrow morning. Right now she needed to do some work for paying clients.

First, Storm checked her phone for messages. Grace had called with an office update, and Hamlin had sent a text message. He'd be on a three o'clock flight tomorrow. That was good news, which actually made her next thought more tolerable.

Her phone had Internet access, but it was slow and reception was spotty. She'd be better off finding an internet café. What a headache. If she ever found the *kekeface* who'd stolen her lap top and her handbag, he'd better move like a mongoose crossing the freeway, because she wanted to crush him.

Two blocks from Lara's dive shop was another cluster of shops, among them a coffee shop with computer access. They wanted twenty cents a minute, but the café smelled of rich, dark coffee and its frigid air conditioning promised to cool her simmering temper. A cappuccino would also help soothe the evil thoughts that were aimed at the guy who broke into her room. Storm settled into the most remote terminal, where she communicated with a handful of clients, emailed the O'ahu Family Court on behalf of a child, sent a message to her secretary, and set up appointments for next week.

She took a contemplative sip of her cappuccino. It was delicious, and reminded her of an old friend, a technical whiz. Last time she'd spoken with Mark Suzuki had been over lunch as a bribe, er, thank you, for getting information from the state Department of Health. She hoped his personal email hadn't changed. Shadowman@hawaii.rr.com was an easy one to remember.

Despite efforts to the contrary, her mind returned to Stella's sad story, Keiko's and Carmen's disappearance, and the theft of her purse and laptop. She hoped her computer's password held up. Meanwhile, the assholes who'd taken her stuff had only made her more determined.

Mark Suzuki, true to form, was plugged in. "Where are you?" he responded a half second after Storm hit "send."

"Maui," Storm typed. "How 'bout you?"

"New job. Advanced Medical Systems, a software company. Two blocks from the old job. You going to buy me lunch?"

"Dinner, if you can help me. What's your cell number?"

"Got my interest, girl. 808-224-0176."

Storm caught the eye of the guy running the shop and pointed to the restroom sign. He nodded his understanding, and she left her cappuccino to reserve her computer terminal.

Inside the little one room lavatory, Storm called him.

"You on your cell?" Mark asked.

"Yes."

"Our high school reunion isn't for another five months. Why don't you call me later?"

"Crap, Mark." But he'd hung up.

When Storm exited the rest room, the manager was busy with his own phone call. She walked out of the café and scanned the street for a public phone booth, which she found on the side of a pharmacy two doors down. This was costing twenty cents a minute just for the computer terminal, dammit.

"Mark, both of these calls will be on your cell. And you emailed me the number."

"I relay my calls through other numbers, and I change the number every week or two."

"What the hell are you doing these days?"

"Selling software." His voice oozed innocence.

"Yeah, sure."

"Why'd you call me then?"

"Okay, okay." Storm considered the information she needed. "Can you get me phone records?"

Mark wheezed.

"Are you laughing?" She wondered about his health, mental and otherwise.

"Storm, my beauty, you crack me up. Whaddya need?"

"The Red Light, in Lahaina. Ichiru Tagama, his son Ryan, Lara Farrell, and this one." She read off the number her cell phone had saved from Stella's call that morning. "And Pauline Harding," she added as an afterthought.

"That's a lot of dinner, sweetheart."

"Was that your Sam Spade imitation, or a rusty hinge?"

Mark coughed. It sounded wet and gravelly. "Over what period of time do you want this?"

"Start with last Tuesday."

He paused. "Wasn't there an explosion in Kahului on Wednesday?"

"Yeah, there was."

"You're gonna owe me lobster and a bottle of wine, my choice."

"Mark, it'll be my pleasure." Though she'd be doing him a better favor if she took him to Natural Health Café, which served tofu lobster. Probably flavored with tilapia.

"I'm holding you to it." The warning in his voice cut through the rasp. "Watch your back."

"Thanks," Storm said, but the line was dead.

She went back to the internet coffee joint, downed the rest of the now tepid cappuccino, and responded to a few more emails. Eight minutes later, the computer timed out and her phone vibrated with a text message.

"Reunion confirmed for August 30. Call for your class assignment."

Storm went back to the pay phone on the side of the pharmacy.

"I should have asked for two dinners." He sounded impressed.

"Why?" It was her turn to exude innocence.

"Some high rollers on that list of yours."

"You didn't have to identify the numbers." She didn't know whether to be annoyed or grateful.

"You were going to do a reverse number search?" He wheezed. "From a pay phone?"

She'd planned to call a police friend in Honolulu. He was her best friend's fiancé, and Storm trusted him with her life, which he'd saved on more than one occasion. But Lieutenant Chang played by the book, and he would have demanded a lot more information than Mark Suzuki before he did what he might see as dodgy research. Mark's initiative had saved her some effort, not that she'd ever admit it. "I have my methods."

"Yeah, right. Well, you need to find a fax. A safe one."

"I'll call you back."

Forty-five minutes later, Storm found a pay phone and a fax at the public library. She'd taken the extra precaution of making a few stops to make sure she wasn't being followed. Mark's paranoia was catching.

"That will be $2.75," the librarian said, and lined up the edges of Storm's eleven faxed pages.

A bargain, Storm thought, and handed over the money. Back in her sweltering car, Storm looked over the sheets of paper. This was going to take some work, and she needed a cool, private place to cross reference and compare. Her hotel room was probably the best place, as long as she didn't use the hotel phone.

Just as she started the car, a text message came through on her cell phone. It was from Mark, and it said, "This # no longer in svc."

Storm grimaced. The guy was a nut case.

Chapter Twenty-three

A half hour after sitting on her bed and looking through Mark Suzuki's information, Storm knew she had to get to another computer terminal. This brought another surge of annoyance at the *kukae*-eating low life who'd stolen her lap top, but it was tempered by a wave of excitement.

Though she expected calls among family members and friends such as Stella, Lara, Ryan, and Ichiru Tagama, there were a couple of surprises on Mark's fax. Ichiru Tagama appeared to have a girlfriend. There were calls at least twice a day to a mobile phone owned by Yasuko Matsui. There were two calls between Stella and Pauline Harding, but that wasn't as interesting as the two made from The Red Light to Stella's phone. Even more intriguing was Mark's note, handwritten next to a call from Pauline to a number that was no longer in service. Mark had printed *Akira Kudo changes phones more often than I do.*

He'd also starred two calls from the same discontinued number to Ichiru Tagama's phone. The calls were barely a minute long, and they went one way. Kudo called Tagama, not vice versa.

Shortly after sending the fax, Mark ditched his old phone. Storm would lay odds that he'd burned the film in his fax machine, too. Hell, maybe he'd changed fax machines. Which was why Storm had to get access to the Internet. Who was Akira Kudo, anyway?

It was already after four, and Storm had planned to meet Damon in Lahaina at six. She changed into a dress and sandals, applied a bit of mascara and some lip gloss, checked that she had what she needed, and headed for her car.

At the first traffic light, she dialed Stella's mobile number. The shaky anxiety in Stella's voice gave Storm the answer before she asked the question, but she asked anyway.

"Any news from Keiko?"

"I called Pauline again. I also called the hospital and some other friends, but no one's seen her."

"Is Lara around?"

"Uh, let me see." Stella must have put her hand over the phone, because her shouts were muffled. After a few attempts, she came back. "I guess she left. She's upset about Keiko, too."

Storm hung up and focused on driving the spectacular, winding road to Lahaina. About halfway through town, she found an internet café. Soon she was logged on to her email account. The first message she sent was to Mark Suzuki. "I'll bring the beer. How many people are you expecting?"

He got right back to her. "I'm checking. Can you get to your previous phone number?"

"No." She wasn't about make the long drive back to Kihei and the pharmacy pay phone.

After a minute of staring at her inbox, she gave up on waiting for a response. She opened another window and went to Google, where she plugged in the name Akira Kudo. A link to Wikipedia opened, which listed Kudo as a member of the Yakuza, but after that tidbit, Wikipedia asked for facts, records, and a bio, if available. The guy was a ghost. That thought hit Storm with a jolt. Like his moniker, *obake*.

There was another link to a newspaper article dated four years ago, and Storm clicked on it. The site came up with, "The page you requested is no longer available. Please check the URL and try again."

She did, and it still didn't work, but it gave her an idea and she tried the websites of several Hawai'i newspapers. Nothing came up on Akira Kudo. She went back to Google, and typed *prostitution in Hawai'i*. That brought up several pages of links, most of them about AIDS or controversial prostitution laws. *Prostitution rings in Hawai'i* elicited several articles, and one in particular caught Storm's attention. It was dated a year ago, and revealed that a large prostitution ring involving Hawai'i and a list of big mainland cities was being investigated for trafficking in underage girls. The article mentioned specific federal judges and investigators, but not one of the twelve persons charged with kidnapping, offering children for sexual purposes, child pornography, and money laundering was identified. Some of the girls were as young as eleven years old. All twelve suspects remained at large.

Storm was appalled. She still didn't have any information about Akira Kudo, though. A quick glance at her watch and she marveled, not for the first time, at what a sinkhole of time the Internet could be. She'd been at the computer for over an hour, and she had only a few more minutes before she had to leave.

One more idea came to her. In the article about the interstate child prostitution ring, an investigator named Stephen McPherson was mentioned twice. She Googled him, and found an interview in a Detroit newspaper. McPherson mentioned how he had worked with Terry Wu of the U.S. Attorney's office, Hawai'i Division.

Five more minutes Storm told herself, and plugged in the U.S. Attorney's Office, District of Hawai'i. Terry Wu wasn't mentioned, but there was a Honolulu phone number. Storm paid her Internet fee and left the café. Outside, she dialed the number and asked for Terry Wu, who actually answered when the operator transferred the call.

Storm explained that she was a local lawyer with a client on Maui, and that she'd read a newspaper article about the child prostitution ring he'd once worked on.

"I can't talk about it," Wu said. Storm thought she caught a note of frustration in his voice. If the case was still pending, he couldn't discuss it. Storm agreed; whether or not his spineless slugs were the same as hers, she wanted them nailed.

"I understand. But perhaps you can answer a question or two for me. If you can't say, just tell me."

"Okay." Wu drew the word out. Both of them knew that she would get a good deal of information from whether or not he answered the questions.

"Did the child prostitution trafficking include the island of Maui?"

Wu paused. "That's public knowledge. Yes, it was on Maui and a couple other islands. Mainland cities, too." Anger clipped his words.

"Do you recognize the name Akira Kudo?"

Wu made an odd choking noise. "I can't answer that question."

"Okay," Storm said. "Have you ever heard the name Obake in connection with this ring?"

"Can't answer that, either." After a long pause, Wu cleared his throat. "I have some advice."

"Yes?"

"Whatever you're doing, stop." She could hear papers rattle before he spoke again. "And come back to O'ahu. I don't want to read about you in the papers."

The hard edges of his words chilled her.

"Right, thanks."

Storm slowly lowered her phone, only to have it ring. She half-expected it to be Terry Wu reiterating his warning, but it was Mark, calling from area code 415, which she knew was in San Francisco. She'd have to ask him how he did that.

"We need beer and wine. Call me back and we'll talk quantities."

The restaurant should have a public phone. "Fifteen minutes," Storm said.

She was at The Fiddler Crab five minutes early, but Damon was already sitting at the bar with a beer. He waved her over. "What can I order you?"

"Whatever you're having," she said. "I'll be right back."

The pay phone was next to the men's room. It was a busy place.

A guy with one hand on his fly sidled up to her. "Hey babe, you're wasting your time. I'm right here." Odors of beer and urine trailed after him.

Storm turned her face to the wall. "Mark, this is a really big hassle. You have no idea."

"Neither do you, sweetheart. I'm putting myself out on a limb. I want this number off your cell phone. It's there from the last call. At least get a new memory card."

The drunk came back. "Whoever you're talking to, I'm better." His hand was still on his fly.

"Who's that?" Mark asked.

"Just a minute." Storm looked at the drunk, glad that she'd worn sandals with heels. She was taller. "Hey, you. My parole officer wants to talk."

The greaseball's Adam's apple bobbed. "No shit?"

She handed the phone over and watched the drunk's face change. In a few seconds, he dropped the phone like it had turned into a piranha. He slunk off, and Storm caught the swinging receiver.

"What did you tell him?"

"Never mind. You need to come home."

"Tomorrow."

"Change phones. Hell, change your name."

"Take it easy. Are Akira Kudo and Obake the same person?"

"Yes. Now get home." He hung up.

On the way back to the bar, Storm passed the drunk, who whispered something to a friend. Both men watched her, and if their eyes hadn't been bloodshot, the whites would have been showing.

◇◇◇

Ichiru Tagama scribbled a note and left it on the kitchen counter. He double-checked the lock on the front door and took the elevator to the parking garage, where he collected his car. He liked it better when Ryan drove, but his son had a lot to think about, and Tagama was old and wise enough to know that he needed to leave Ryan alone to sort through what he'd been told.

Before leaving the apartment, Tagama had visited the shrine once more, and he'd muttered a prayer for both Yasuko's and Ryan's safety. He also prayed that his son would understand Tagama's regrets and forgive. Of all the ups and downs in Tagama's life, Ryan was his biggest source of pride. Nevertheless, it was neither safe nor prudent for Tagama to reveal all of his secrets.

He drove across the island to Wailuku. The sun was already setting, and he was confident the man from the U.S. Attorney's office would be on time. But his mind strayed from the meeting with Dave O'Dell. Where was Yasuko? Even if she missed a call, she always got back to him within a half hour, but an hour and a half had passed since his first call.

Throughout his life, Tagama had faced fear, but it had usually been for himself. Though he'd monitored Ryan's young days and let his ex know he was watching, he'd never revealed how glad he was that his son lived in California, far enough away to escape the attention of his unscrupulous associates.

Now he was frightened. His hands, cold as fish, slid on the plastic of the steering wheel. Though he tried calming breaths, a meditative technique that had served him for years, it wasn't working now. Why hadn't Yasuko answered?

She believed in him. She'd done so much for his *ki*, his spirit, every aspect of his life. And despite the fact that she worked for his worst enemy, he trusted her. She'd proven herself.

In Wailuku, there was one spot left in the restaurant parking lot and Tagama required three tries to get into it. He banged the door of the car next to him, and nearly forgot to lock his own car.

Once inside the crowded sushi bar, he forced himself to slow down. Snatches of laughter and conversation grabbed at him as he wove through the tables of businessmen, families, and over-laden waitresses. A wave of relief passed through him when he saw Dave O'Dell in the corner, his cell phone at one ear, a forefinger plugging the other. O'Dell was shouting, but he put the phone down when Tagama got to the table.

"That was Terry Wu. He thinks the top's going to blow off this whole scene. Some lawyer called him today with questions about Akira Kudo."

Tagama's eyes narrowed. "Storm Kayama?"

"Yeah, you know her?"

"I know she has a reputation for being a tough cookie."

"Wu's on his way over. He's afraid she'll look under a rock and scare someone out prematurely. He doesn't want her getting in the sights of whoever set that bomb."

Tagama forced himself to sit down and take a deep breath. "Does he know who set the bomb?"

"He's got some ideas." O'Dell looked around for a waitress. "Hope you don't mind, but I ordered the same sake we had last time."

"Who's he suspect?" The waitress arrived and set down their drinks. Tagama removed the overflowing sake glass from its graceful box and took a generous swallow. The warmth barely reached the tightening knot in his stomach. He dumped the remaining sake from the lacquered *masu* into his glass.

"He isn't saying much."

Tagama's phone vibrated on his belt, and he just about shot out of his chair, but when he checked the call number, the light in his eyes faded. "Lara, it's nice of you to call."

Like O'Dell had done, he stuck a finger in his ear to block out the buzz of conversation in the crowded room. "You're where?"

"Your apartment." Lara raised her voice, too. She could undoubtedly hear the background noise. "Where are you?"

"At a meeting in Wailuku."

"Ryan asked me to call you. You'd better get here."

"Why are you at my apartment?"

"Ryan wants to see you."

"Can I talk to him?"

"Tagama-san, he's talking to the police. You need to come home."

Chapter Twenty-four

Despite the hapless drunks' efforts, Storm walked away lost in thought. Since picking up Stella six hours ago, she'd come across so much information she wanted to make an outline just to sort through it. To think that a day ago, she'd told herself to let the police handle Hiroki Yoshinaka's suicide and his connection to Paradise Consortium. Now she was up to her ears in the mess, mostly because of Carmen and Keiko.

Despite her non-committal response when Stella asked her to be Keiko's lawyer, Storm couldn't turn her back on Keiko after what she'd been through, let alone Carmen, who was not only too young to understand what danger she was in, she was too injured to resist.

In addition to what she'd just learned, the hotel break-in had Storm worried. The guy not only had connections, he was a master of stealth. The fact that he'd been right next to her was downright creepy.

She was certain the thieves wanted information stored on her computer. Thing was, she wasn't certain whether they wanted to know what she'd discovered, or whether they wanted to deprive her of the records. Or both. Whatever it was, it was tied into the twisted knot that began with a bomb-related death and included Keiko, Carmen and her family, Stella, Lara, the Tagamas, and the dive shop. It was all connected.

Add the theft to the warnings she'd received from a savvy techno-geek and an Assistant U.S. Attorney, who were both reacting to questions she'd asked *after* the break-in. No, she was swimming in it. She just hoped she wasn't over her head.

Storm dropped onto the barstool next to Damon. He shoved a beer and a shot at her. "This is what I'm having," he said.

Getting hammered on boilermakers wasn't on tonight's agenda. It might make her forget her troubles, but she couldn't afford that. She gave him a sidelong glance. "What round is this?"

"Only the second. Hey, it's Saturday night," he said, and downed his shot, probably Jameson's or Wild Turkey.

"Why don't you slow down? It's still early." She wanted him to be coherent for a while longer.

"Early, that's what I was thinking. The night is young." He faced her with a big grin.

Storm was glad the hostess appeared to show them to their seats for dinner.

"Does this have to be all business?" Damon asked. He'd shaved; there was a dab of foam inside his ear.

"Business over a nice dinner," Storm said. "Say, speaking of dinners, Lara told me she's thinking of buying a restaurant."

"She did?"

"Why do you say that?"

"She said not to tell anyone until she'd signed the papers." Relief lightened Damon's face. "Oh, she wants you to handle the legal aspects."

Storm shrugged as if she couldn't betray Lara's confidence. "What do you think of the plan?"

"I dunno, seems like she's pretty busy with the dive shop."

"Have you done some other work for her?"

"I'm helping her with a remodel…" He stopped. "But you probably know all that."

"She mentioned it," Storm lied. "How's it going?"

He appraised her, not so drunk after all. "I'll let her tell you."

Storm changed the conversation topic to his daughters and when he would be seeing them. It was a good tactic; he could talk about them for hours. She shared how much fun she found her best friend's twelve-year-old son. "I can understand how you miss your girls. I miss Robbie, and he's not even my child."

"You like kids, don't you?" Damon asked.

"Yeah, I do. Though I was never one of those people who went gaga over babies. I guess I didn't know what to do with them."

"Once you have them, you know."

"I can believe that," Storm said.

"You should do it."

Storm couldn't help but laugh. "Have a baby?" Like baking a cake.

"Well," and Damon had the grace to blush, "you know, settle down. Like that."

Easy for you to say, Storm thought. "Maybe some day. Meanwhile, I have friends with kids." She leaned toward him and dropped her voice. "Have you heard anything about Carmen?"

"Uh," he picked up his beer, avoiding her eyes. "I heard she's doing okay."

"Who told you?"

"Lara did. I think she talked to Stella."

Storm doubted that. "Poor kid. I heard Hiroki Yoshinaka had a gambling problem."

"Yeah," Damon rearranged the sodden coaster under his beer bottle.

"Did you hear about that? Were some guys after him?"

"Look, I couldn't do anything."

Storm sat back. "What do you mean?"

"I'm tapped out. I don't have that much cash lying around."

"He asked you for money?"

"Yeah." Damon's hand trembled. "I wish I had, you know? But I didn't know how bad it was."

"How much did he ask for?"

"Twenty."

"Twenty thousand?"

"Yeah." He peeled the label from his beer bottle, anything to avoid looking at her.

Storm thought about the numbers she'd seen, the ones Sergeant Moana had mentioned. Yoshinaka had asked Damon for a little more than his debt. He rounded up, probably for other expenses, like food and clothes for the girls.

Damon's eyes glowed with moisture. "I didn't know."

"No, how could you?" Storm said. "No one would expect such an extreme reaction. Not for twenty thousand."

"I didn't have it in cash, but I did have some saved for my daughters' education. Twenty thou wasn't worth his life or Crystal's."

"Of course not." She reached a gentle hand to his arm.

"I feel awful about this." The emotion in his voice carried to nearby diners, and some turned to see what was happening.

"I believe you."

"I made a bad decision, and I'd take it back in a minute if I could."

"What did he tell you when he asked you for the money?"

"His English wasn't so good, and my Japanese is worse." Damon took a shaky breath. "He said something about 'for the girls.' I just didn't get it."

"No one would have."

His Adam's apple bobbed, trying to force down a gobbet of remorse. "Yeah, it's like politics." His lips attempted a smile. "You can't tell what's going on behind the scenes."

"Yeah, what do you think people who voted for W feel like?"

He stared at her. "I voted for him."

"Oh. Never mind."

"Yeah, well, I didn't know." He downed the rest of his beer.

"Let's get something to eat," Storm said, and waved the waitress over. They placed their orders, and when the waitress left, Damon's mood had ascended from black to merely blue.

"I feel like shit."

"It's the fault of the guys who threatened him, not yours." She lowered her voice. "You need to believe that."

"I could have helped."

"Do you know where he gambled?"

"No." The answer came too fast.

"Damon, you can't protect him any longer. Anyway, I've heard some things."

"Stay out of it, Storm." A bit of steel that hadn't been there before showed in his voice.

She eyed him. "Let me ask you a question, then."

He didn't respond. Still scraping for shreds of self-esteem.

"How did he gamble? Pachinko?"

"I think so. At least, partly."

"Sports betting?"

"Maybe a little." He breathed out heavily through his nose. "Heck, we all do that."

"Cards?"

Damon frowned. "I doubt if his English was good enough."

"I thought poker was international."

"Maybe. I don't know." That sounded honest.

"Where do these games take place?"

"Lots of places. We take bets at work, in bars—anyplace there's a TV with a game on."

"What bars?"

He turned in his chair and pointed at the bar TV set, which was tuned to a baseball game.

"What bars have Pachinko machines?"

"Why do you want to know about Pachinko?"

Uncle Miles used to tell her not to trust a person who answers a question with a question. "Come on, where did Yoshinaka gamble?"

Damon looked around for the waitress, took time to catch her eye and gesture for another beer. "Why do you want to know?"

Another question. How much should she tell him? Maybe another little shock was what he needed. "Yoshinaka might have been threatened with his daughters' welfare. Prostitution goes on in a lot of those places."

"Fuck." The waitress put the fresh beer in front of him, but he didn't look up. He just wagged his head from side to side as if he wanted to deny the thoughts that dwelled in his mind.

Their meals arrived right after the drink, and Storm was glad for the interruption. Damon wasn't responding to her questions; discussing the Yoshinaka family seemed to drive him further away.

She'd missed lunch and was starved. Her lamb chops were delicious, but Damon poked at his steak.

"That can't be. They're too young," he said finally. "They're my daughters' ages."

Storm tried to imagine how Hamlin would react to a menace of this magnitude toward children he knew. It seemed to her he'd show a lot more revulsion than Damon. Hamlin might erupt with something on the order of, "Fucking maggots, how could they?"

Not Damon. He acted like he'd already heard a rumor and was in denial.

"How old's Keiko?" she asked.

Damon's head came up. "A lot older than the Yoshinaka girls."

Storm glared at him. "You knew she worked in one of the bars."

He moved garlic mashed potatoes around on his plate. "She's twenty-something, and Lara's trying to help her out. Stella, too."

"Stella's helping Keiko or Lara's helping Stella?"

"All of them, I don't know. You know how women are." He stabbed at his food as if he wanted to use the fork on someone. Her, probably.

Storm concentrated on her meal, which was delicious. "How are those mashed potatoes?"

He took a bite. "Good. And garlicky—I like that." He put a big chunk of steak in his mouth and chewed.

Storm stayed on safe conversational subjects all the way through dessert. She ordered a warm apple galette with ice cream, he got the hot fudge brownie sundae, and they shared.

"How many jobs have you done for Lara?" she asked.

"This is my third."

"The remodel was the first?" Storm reached her fork across the table for a bite of his brownie and pushed her plate toward him. "That was an apartment, right?"

"Yeah, I think she was testing me for the house, which was her big project. Has she shown you that? She's got two rich investors bidding on it, and she's going to make a bundle."

Storm remembered the day the shark had chased Lara, and how well Lara had known the Makena locale. She'd also recognized the construction guys coming from work on projects in the area.

"Is that the one on the bluff down by Makena?"

"It's on the ocean side of the street, and better hidden than that place. Private, yet right on the beach." Damon took a bite of the apple tart.

"She's a smart woman."

"Yes, she is." His voice was thoughtful.

"I'm a bit worried about how much she's taking on at one time."

"That's crossed my mind, too," he said.

"Is her mother's health worrying her?"

Damon finished off the last of his brownie and pushed back from the table. "She won't be leaving that rest home. That would worry anyone."

"Yes, it would."

They left the parking lot together and said good-bye standing on the gravel next to their cars. "Thanks for dinner," Damon said.

"I'm leaving tomorrow, so I might not see you for a while. Call me if you visit O'ahu," Storm said.

"I thought you were meeting Lara tomorrow morning."

"You'll be at the shop? On Sunday?"

"We're in a rush, remember? The final push for the grand opening."

Damon left the parking lot first, and Storm followed. She faced a half-hour drive on a winding road, so she was glad she'd merely sipped at the second glass of wine.

Five minutes down the dark highway, Damon's brake lights gleamed. Ahead, the flashing blue beacons of several police cars pierced the night. Storm followed Damon into the small, crowded parking lot bordering one of the many little beach parks that dotted the coastline. The headlights of the police cruisers streamed from the cars toward the vastness of the ocean, only to dissipate feebly into a pillow of inky night. There were no people in the cars, but down by the lapping waves, flashlight beams converged in one area, where they flitted like agitated fairies, united against the dense night.

Chapter Twenty-five

Damon pulled to a stop next to a white Corvette. Lara's car.

He was out of the truck before Storm found a place she could park without blocking everyone else.

"Lara," he shouted, and rushed toward a small group of people facing a line of police.

Storm got out of her car more slowly. Lara and two men stood under a grove of trees whose graceful canopies sheltered the flat shapes of picnic tables and the faint glow of an emergency call box. The trio looked lonely and frightened. In the dim light, Lara wrung her hands.

Storm hung back for a few moments, but Damon ran toward Lara and the men. A group of four patrolmen approached from the other direction, probably to keep Lara's group from getting closer to the beach. Their manner was gentle, even sympathetic. One of police was Carl Moana.

Lara held the older man's elbow. Ryan stood on the other side of his father, his strained white face reflecting the search lights. He looked more shocked than the older man.

Damon touched Lara's shoulder. "What happened? Why are you out here?"

Lara glanced at Storm, who'd caught up to Damon. Her eyes glistened in the dim light. "What are you guys doing here?"

"We saw the police, and your car," Storm said. "Can we help with anything?"

Lara gestured to one of the policeman, who answered Storm's question. "There's nothing to do right now."

Storm caught Moana's eye and saw the discreet shake of his head. No one was giving out information.

Lara saw it, too. "Let's keep our appointment tomorrow morning, and we can talk then."

"You've got my number if you need me," Storm said.

On the way back to her car, she slowed to observe the officials who were coming and going with resolve, but without urgency. The engines to the cars and the ambulance were off. One of the cars was unmarked and had the plates of a county vehicle. Storm would bet it belonged to the Medical Examiner's office. A woman in tailored business clothes softly closed the door to a police cruiser. In her hands was a big roll of yellow crime-scene tape.

Footsteps crunched in the gravel, and she turned to see Damon. "Do you know who's on the beach?" she asked.

"No, but Ryan looks more upset than anyone. I wonder if it's one of his friends."

"Maybe," Storm said. "His dad looked grim, too. Almost wooden."

"Lara doesn't deserve any more heartache."

"No, she doesn't." And there was nothing else to say or do. They got into their separate vehicles and eased onto the road.

Passing cars had slowed down to see why the police were gathering. Some had even pulled onto the side of the road, along with two vans from television stations. As Storm joined the crawling line of traffic, a couple of automobiles pulled from the shoulder. Others took the open spaces. Whoever had died wouldn't stay secret for long.

By the time Damon turned off the main road, the line of cars had thinned to normal traffic. When Storm got into Kihei, she remembered she needed some deodorant, and while she was at it, some bottled water and juices for the room. She'd seen a supermarket on South Kihei Road a mile or so from the hotel. This required leaving Pi'ilani Highway before the cut-off to her hotel, and she wasn't sure which cross streets would go all the way to the smaller, parallel road. At ten-thirty, she didn't want to loop around a residential neighborhood, setting all the dogs barking.

She chose a street with a traffic light and made her turn. Behind her, the high, bright lights of some shiny-grilled SUV reflected from her rear-view mirror. Another car trailed behind it, all heading to the hotels and businesses along the ocean road.

Storm stopped at the store, got her supplies, and headed in the direction of her hotel. Two or three blocks down the road, she came upon a black Land Rover, which was inching away from a green light. When she braked, the lights of the car behind her lit the inside of her car. Her own lights lit the inside of the Rover.

With a flicker of apprehension, she wondered if the Rover had been the SUV behind her when she turned off Piʻilani Highway. At first, she'd assumed the driver was creeping along because he was on the phone. But she could see the back of his head, and there was no phone at his ear. Bluetooth? Maybe. But then she saw the flash of what appeared to be sunglasses in his rear view mirror.

Suzuki's and the assistant U.S. Attorney's paranoia had rubbed off. Who wore dark glasses at night? Was that guy watching her? There were few other cars on the road, but she was sandwiched between two of them.

About fifty yards ahead, an old, decal-covered car with surf racks waited to exit a restaurant parking lot. Storm slowed and motioned for the driver to move out. When he did, and shot a happy shaka from his side window, she waved and returned the gesture.

The SUV, which now led a line of four vehicles, slowed again. The surfer put on his brakes, probably assuming the SUV driver was lost. Storm jerked her wheel hard, veering into the parking lot the surfer had just left. She was going a little too fast for the turn, and her tires squeaked in protest.

The car behind her slammed on his brakes. So did the SUV, and the surfer's car swerved, squealed, and came to a smoking stop after thunking into the SUV's rear bumper. The surfer hadn't been going fast, but his car was old and rust-pocked, and its hood humped into a rusty accordion. Water hissed from the radiator. The SUV stopped at the impact, but appeared to be unmarred.

"Hey, assholes," the surfer screamed, and jumped from his car. "You did that on purpose."

Storm, phone in hand, dialed 911. They did do it on purpose, but not for the reasons the hapless surfer thought. In the little time she'd had to come up with an escape plan, she'd only hoped her pursuers would decide not to make a scene in front of witnesses. She hadn't meant to set the surfer up for a wreck, poor guy.

A big muscular guy climbed down from the SUV. His dark glasses glinted. A smaller guy got out of a sedan. The big guy approached the surfer, who was half his body mass.

The surfer was undaunted. He shouted, pointed, and stamped his rubber slippers. Storm thought she might fall in love. Meanwhile, the cringe factor of crunching metal and breaking glass had lured others to the scene, and people emerged from nearby restaurants and shops.

For a moment, Storm considered taking off, but the thugs already knew who she was. What good would running do? So when the police cruiser arrived, Storm approached the patrolman.

"I saw the whole thing," she said. "The SUV braked suddenly for no reason. It looked like a setup." She gave the officer her name as a witness and left.

But now she had to go somewhere. These guys recognized her car. They probably even knew where she was staying.

The first person Storm thought of calling was Stella, but Storm needed someone with a car, and Keiko had it.

Storm phoned Damon, who sounded sleepy. "Sorry to bother you so late."

"S'okay. I was watching the tube."

"Do you have a car I could borrow? I mean, other than your truck?"

"You have an accident?"

"No, but I need to change cars. I think someone's following me."

"I've got old station wagon. It's my ex's. The battery's probably dead, but I can get it going. You seen the news?"

"No, what happened?"

"I'll tell you when you get here. Why is someone following you?"

"I'll tell you when I get there."

◇◇◇

Ryan and Lara drove Tagama to their place. His apartment was part of the crime scene. The police were certain by the mayhem in Tagama's condominium that Yasuko had been attacked there and taken from the premises.

It was bad enough, Ryan thought, that Yasuko had been killed. But the fact that Yasuko's and Tagama's shared place was the place of her final struggle made him even sadder. For the first time in his life, Ryan knew that his father had a home he cared about. And it had been destroyed, along with Yasuko.

Ryan walked from the car with a heavy sorrow that slowed his steps to the pace of his father's. The old man hadn't said a word since he'd identified her. Tagama had slipped one of the crushed gardenias from the tangle of her hair, and now that they were out of the crime scene tech's view, he took it out of his pocket. The way he caressed the ruined flower nearly broke Ryan's heart.

Right before they'd left the scene, one of the detectives had rushed up to them. He was doing his best to show Tagama a kindness when he promised, "We'll find who did this, sir." He'd then turned to an ID tech and said, "Bag her hands. Looks like she put up a fight."

Lara had made a choking sound and Ryan had cringed, but he'd been watching his father. Tagama's only reaction was to blink twice. It would have been better if he'd made a noise.

On the way home, Tagama's cell phone rang, but he let it go. He'd been like a statue in the back seat of the car. When bumps in the road caused him to lean, he'd come to rest upright against the door.

Ryan got his father settled in their guest room. Tagama murmured a thank-you, closed the door, turned off the lights, and sat on the bed. For nearly a half hour, he stared out of the window. The moon was a sliver and the night was dark. He couldn't see stars from the room, but he knew they were there, and he wondered if Yasuko was among them.

"I'll get him, angel," he whispered.

In the dark, Tagama pulled off his pants and felt the weight of his phone in the pocket. It reminded him of the call he'd received. Sure enough, his aide had left a message.

"Tagama-san, she caused an accident. She saw either me or the Land Rover, I don't know. When the police asked me what happened, she drove away. She didn't go to the hotel. I lost her."

Tagama tossed the phone onto the bedside table, folded his slacks and shirt on the back of the chair in the room, and climbed into the single bed. He turned on his side and looked out the window, into the night sky.

◇◇◇

Damon's directions to his home were easy to follow, and Storm arrived about twenty minutes after calling him.

He answered the door in sweat pants and a T-shirt, probably what he slept in. "The dead person was on the news. She was a Lahaina bar maid. I don't know why Lara was there."

"What's the woman's name?" Storm asked.

"Yasuko Matsui. You ever heard of her?"

"Just recently. I think she was a friend of Ryan's father. Did they mention the bar she worked in?"

"The Red Light." He scrutinized Storm's face. "You think Ryan and Lara know her, too?"

"Ryan's dad was involved with her."

"You sure?" He looked confused. "That's a hostess bar. Lara wouldn't have anything to do with one of those."

Like she'd suspected, Damon did know more about hostess bars than he'd let on. "Because of Stella and Keiko?"

"Partly." He dropped onto the sofa, then remembered his manners. "Have a seat. Can I get you something to drink?" He pointed to the beer he'd been drinking. "A nightcap?"

"No, thanks. What were you saying?"

"Lara tried to help women. She wouldn't do anything to support a place like that."

"Stella told me some things," Storm said.

"Really?" Damon picked at a hangnail for a long moment, then seemed to come to a decision. "You need to know something about Stella. She's had a hard life, and one of the results of it is that she exaggerates. Oh hell, she lies."

"What does she lie about?"

"You know, how bad her life was."

"What about Lara's sister?"

"She died of an overdose. Angela was a cocaine freak, then she got into crystal meth."

"Why'd she use drugs?"

"She couldn't live up to Lara's standards."

"Did anyone in their family make her feel she couldn't?"

Damon threw himself back in his chair. "No, it wasn't like that. Well, maybe Barb was a little hard on her, but Angela had it coming."

"What happened to Barb? Why's she in the rest home?"

"When Michael died, she went to pieces. She just couldn't go on. Lara takes care of her."

Storm nodded. "It's really sad."

"No shit. I hate to see anything else happen to Lara."

"Yeah, I understand."

Storm looked at Damon, who was frowning into his bottle. "Have you ever heard of a guy named Obake?"

His raised his eyes slowly to hers. They were bloodshot and tired. "No, who's that?"

"I don't know." Storm stood up. "I'd better let you get some rest. Thanks for letting me use your car."

"I already jumped it. It's been running, so you should be okay. If it doesn't start in the morning, give me a call. Your hotel isn't that far from Lara's shop."

"I'm going to stay around here," Storm said.

He looked surprised. "Hey, I've got an extra room."

She was grateful for the offer, but staying in his place didn't feel right. "Thanks, but I'll be okay."

"Where are you going?"

"Not far, believe me."

He blinked a few times. "'Kay then. Call me if you change your mind."

The Subaru Legacy station wagon was dusty, but in decent shape. Storm waved her thanks and started down the road. Even if she'd looked, she wouldn't have seen Damon watching her. He stood in the shadow of a big monkey pod tree a few doors down from his house, checking to see if she turned right or left at the stop sign at the junction of Honoapiʻilani Highway.

A few miles away, near the turn at the beginning of Front Street, Storm saw a modest, two-story motel with a lighted welcome sign. Twenty minutes later, she was in a room, comfortable in the knowledge that no one knew where she was, at least for a few restful hours. She settled into bed, thinking about what Damon had told her that night about Lara's Makena house.

Makena was the new hot spot for investors, and Lara had prime ocean front property. The house could make the young woman millions in profit.

Lara was working to cement her financial independence in a way that couldn't be threatened. It made sense, especially in light of her family and their problems. It also explained Lara's evasiveness on the ownership of the strip mall where the dive shop was located. If Lara bought it, the terms of incorporation would be changed. What would Ryan's role in the shop be? And what did he know about her plans to buy the land from Mālua LLC?

Storm decided she'd have to raise the subject when she met Lara in the morning. She could do it tactfully, mention that she'd heard about the Makena house, and compliment Lara on her real estate acumen. Their appointment was at ten-thirty. If she got up in time, she could drive to Makawao, pump Auntie Piko for information on Paradise Consortium and Mālua LLC, and be back in plenty of time to meet Lara.

Chapter Twenty-six

Storm couldn't get comfortable. The bed was hard; there was a lump in the center of the mattress. She was hot, she was cold. She should have adjusted the motel's air conditioner better when she went to bed, but now she couldn't muster the energy to get up and do it. It hummed and made rattling noises. She drifted into deeper sleep.

An elegant woman touched her shoulder, but Storm couldn't rouse herself. The woman leaned over her, and Storm shivered. Now the air conditioner was on too high; it was inconsistent. She'd have to tell the management about it.

She was freezing. Not enough blankets. The woman loomed before Storm's face, but Storm knew it was a dream because somehow she knew her eyes were closed. If she were awake, she'd get up and put on another blanket.

The woman was Japanese, middle-aged, with expressive almond eyes and perfect, rosebud red lips. She wore an elegant suit with a silk flower on the lapel. At some level, Storm knew her mind was unraveling the trauma of last night, when she'd observed the wooden stoicism on the older Tagama's face.

Storm had never seen Yasuko, but she knew she was the lovely woman in her dream. Storm wondered what Yasuko had really looked like, but she liked the vision she'd imagined. Ryan and Lara were there now, too. Lara's face so white, it glowed like the light behind her. Ryan's eyes were wet.

No, no, on the beach, Lara's eyes had been wet and Ryan's face was white. But this was a dream, so it didn't have to make sense.

When a ray of sunlight worked its way through the drapes and scraped against her burning eyelids, Storm felt as if she'd worked all night. It was six-thirty; she was as tired as if she'd had two hours sleep instead of seven. A shower helped a bit, and she was grateful for the motel's little bottle of shampoo. When she'd bought deodorant the night before, some guardian angel had whispered in her ear that her old toothbrush looked like it had been flattened with a steam iron and her toothpaste tube was nearly as bad. So she was set for the basic morning ablutions, but she'd have to put on the same clothes that she'd worn to dinner. Jeans and a sweatshirt would have been her choice for a trip upcountry, but the dress and sandals would have to do.

Storm knew it could take an hour or more to get to Makawao, which was across the island to Kahului and another eight or ten miles up Haleakala Highway. She had to be back at Lara's Aquatic Adventures in Kihei by ten-thirty.

She got a large coffee at a Starbucks in Kihei, near the northbound road to Kahului. In Kahului, she pulled into a little mall and picked up another travel cup of Bad Ass coffee. It was the inspiration she was seeking. She was beginning to feel like herself.

She also filled the tank in Damon's ex's station wagon, which was running like a dream. A few loose papers—they looked like soccer-signup sheets—fluttered around the back seat, which made Storm feel right at home.

The weather in Kahului was clear and sunny, with trade winds blowing about ten to fifteen knots, and *mauka* showers. Mauka, in this case, was exactly where Storm was headed: up the mountain called Haleakala, House of the Sun. This was where the Hawaiian god, Māui, had lassoed the sun. After using his grandmother's magic rope to catch Kalā, Māui then tied him to the roots of the wiliwili tree and chopped off some of his legs with a sacred adze.

Violent tales, Storm reflected as she drove upward, into the clouds. Mist clouded the windshield. A brutal legacy, those Hawaiian tales, like so many other cultures' birthrights. A shiver passed through her, and Storm felt vulnerable in her sleeveless dress and sandals. Not the clothes for a confrontation, certainly, and she reconsidered her purpose for this drive, which was twofold: to see how Pauline felt about the sale of her shop to Mālua LLC and Paradise Consortium, and to see if Pauline had heard from Keiko and Carmen. The second reason overshadowed the first at this point.

Storm had grown up in small towns like Makawao, and she found the local grocery without any trouble. Inside, she breathed in the aromas of fresh baked goods and the earthy smells of produce. It took her five minutes to fill a small basket with four papayas, limes, a jar of passion fruit butter, and a loaf of fresh Moloka'i bread.

The clerk rang it up and added a few home-grown mangoes to the bag. "My tree," she said.

"Thanks, I love them," Storm said, and sniffed at the sweet fruit. "Do you know Pauline Harding?"

"Where you from?"

"O'ahu. I'm here for the weekend, doing some work and visiting friends."

"She lives about a mile from here. Real pretty place with a great view. I heard her son bought it for her." The clerk gave Storm directions, and even threw in two more mangoes. "Here, she'll like these. Someone told me she's got some friends visiting."

"I'll tell her they're from you," Storm said, and wondered about those visitors. Back in the car, she called Stella's number. Stella must be sitting on the phone, because it didn't have time to ring.

"Any word from Keiko?" Storm asked.

"No." The woman's voice was ragged. "I don't know what to do."

"Call the cops."

"I have to, don't I?"

"Yes, and do it now. Have you talked to Pauline since noon yesterday?"

"I called her again last night."

"What did she say?"

"She said she already told me she'd call if she saw them." Stella sounded embarrassed. "She told me I'm bugging her."

"Really," Storm said. Some friend.

It was easy to follow the clerk's directions, and Storm marveled at the homes on the mountainside. Elevation was around fourteen hundred feet, and many of the homes had views across miles of velvet green foliage to the sparkling sapphire of the Pacific. They might not be as expensive as ocean front estates, but people paid for vistas like these.

Pauline's address was easy to find by the number on a lava rock post by the street, but the driveway was long and tree-lined, and anyone watching from the house would see her coming for a quarter of a mile. Storm didn't want to give Pauline that much time to prepare for a visitor.

When Storm saw the Rainbow Bed and Breakfast only three properties from Pauline's place, she allowed herself a big smile. To make things better, across the street from the B & B was a turnout. Storm pulled into it, looked around at a scattering of cigarette butts, and surmised that she wouldn't be the first to stop and enjoy the scenery.

A low lava rock wall ran between Pauline's property and her neighbor's, and Storm stayed on the neighbor's side of it. She walked along and thought up excuses for taking this route if someone asked, but there was a narrow path and she figured she wasn't the only one to have used the trail. Eucalyptus trees and ironwood provided shade, while Pauline's side had only a few plumeria trees and some flowering shrubs.

Storm wished she wore sneakers instead of sandals, and she now questioned the wisdom of stopping at the store for omiyage. It was an island tradition to take a host or hostess small gifts when visiting, but Storm had a nagging feeling Pauline wasn't going to greet her with open arms, especially since Stella said she was annoyed.

As Storm grew parallel to the house, she saw steps incorporated into the wall. They led to a path across Pauline's lawn. Storm set down the gift bag and climbed over. She picked the bag up again. It gave her a degree of legitimacy.

The view was outstanding, and a wide lanai encircled the house, whose front window panes looked out onto the wide green lawn, flowering plants, and wisps of clouds. The house itself gave off a feeling of self-imposed isolation. It took a minute for Storm to realize that the reason for this was that all the windows were closed. If this were her house, she'd have them all open to the cool, eucalyptus-scented air.

Maybe Pauline had taken her guests to another island or to Hana, a long drive from upcountry Makawao, for a day or two. The quiet, closed house could be entirely innocent.

Storm walked around to the front, climbed the steps to the lanai, and called out. "Hello?"

No answer. She thought she heard a noise from within, but it could have been something in the yard, a branch or a nearby bird. "Hello? Pauline?"

Not a sound this time, so Storm walked toward the carport, which was to her immediate right, on the far side of the house from where she'd climbed the wall. The driveway widened around the structure to include a parking area. Like many of the homes in the area, the carport had walls, but no door. Inside was a late model BMW sedan.

Storm's feet crunched on the gravel of the drive. "Hello?"

She could see a car parked on the other side of the house, pulled off the gravel of the drive onto the lawn, where it sat in the shelter of a Plumeria tree.

It was a blue Toyota sedan with a dull finish, a few rust spots, and a Save the Whales bumper sticker. It was Stella's.

Chapter Twenty-seven

Storm's heart raced. Pauline had lied to Stella. Unless Keiko had hidden Carmen without telling Stella—a possibility—Storm had to assume the worst. The girls were being held against their will in Pauline's house.

Storm fought the urge to drop her gift right there on the grass and tear across the yard to safety on the other side of the rock wall. Her arms trembled, and she tightened them around the bag. But no footsteps sounded, no voice called out, no window shade trembled. The house stood mute.

Storm tiptoed down the steps and forced herself to saunter back to the wall as if she were a disappointed caller. She climbed over and set the bag down.

Either no one had seen her or there wasn't anyone home. So get a grip. No dogs, no running guards, no warning shouts. The only sound was the wind soughing through the soft needles of the ironwood trees.

Except for the thumping noise she'd heard, and the memory troubled her. It was the kind of thud a falling branch would make, or the sound of an elbow or head striking a wall.

Storm slipped into a copse of ironwood trees where she could lean against a broad trunk and observe Pauline's house. Graceful grey-green needles on drooping boughs acted as a screen, a reassuring partition that allowed her to catch her breath, slow her heart rate, and gather her wits.

Five minutes went by, and nothing moved in the house or garden next door. Storm tried to make a call on her cell, but couldn't get a signal. While she stood there, she thought about Carmen, helpless, and Keiko, who looked terrified sitting at comfortable restaurants in Kihei.

What had she promised Carmen? "I'll be back. I'll bring you your kitty."

And when the little girl asked, "Will you help me go home?" Storm said yes.

She stared at the curtained windows of the house. It was broad daylight and once she stepped out of the trees and crossed the wall, anyone who looked out would see her. There was no point in running across the lawn, as it would only make her look more furtive.

Storm picked two mangoes out of her bag and marched back across the lush grass. If someone stopped her, she would say her tree was dropping mangoes and she was offering them to neighbors, a common activity for islanders whose trees had bounty crops. She hoped Pauline didn't recognize her neighbors.

Storm got to the side of the house without hearing or seeing anything suspicious and paused between two closed and curtained windows to decide what to do next. Now she had to choose among the plans she'd rejected on approach.

It didn't take her long to decide to head in the direction the sound had come from, and she rounded the corner toward the back of the house. Shrubbery and flower beds bordered the outside walls, but most of them hadn't filled out to the point where could use them as cover.

If she crept behind them, she'd make more noise than if she walked on the lush grass, so she strolled as if she hadn't a care in the world. Or so she hoped.

Not far from the back door, she stopped again, nervous. They're not here, she thought. Keiko is protecting Carmen and Pauline took them for a drive. Sure, the BMW was there, but Pauline could have another car. The problem was, she couldn't deny Stella's car and how Keiko had disappeared without a word to Stella.

No, chicken shit, you've got to do something. Bang on the door, check to see if it's open.

Storm had her hand on the doorknob, and a child's voice rang out. "It hurts," the thin voice cried.

A second voice said something, but Storm couldn't hear the words. Then a third voice carried through the house. "I'm sick of your crying. Dammit, I didn't ask for this job." And a door slammed.

A whimper floated to Storm's straining ears, then no other noise.

Storm shrank against the side of the house and crouched between two mock orange shrubs.

The grumpy woman's voice moved closer, and spoke to someone else. "The kid looks sick. I don't want them here anymore, you hear me?"

Storm couldn't hear an answer, which strengthened her hunch that Grumpy was on the phone. She put her ear up to the wall. When the back door slammed, it practically deafened her. It also scared her so much she froze, which was a good thing, because a heavy woman in a loose dress and dyed red hair stormed out of the house, twenty feet from where Storm crouched between the two inadequate shrubs.

The woman stomped in the opposite direction of Storm's hiding place, along a cement walk toward the carport, her rubber slippers slapping at cracked heels. She muttered to herself as she disappeared around the corner. A moment later, a throaty engine growled from the carport, followed by the crunch of tires on gravel.

Storm waited until the crunching stopped, the car changed gears, and the powerful engine hummed away. The back door was locked, of course. She went to the car port. There, arranged along on the wall, were the yard tools she'd hoped to find. She grabbed a hedge clipper, a shovel, and a pair of work gloves.

Wearing the gloves, she returned to the back door and used the handle of the shovel to break out one of the panes of glass. She knocked away all the jagged edges. Then, she stood to the side of the door with the face of the shovel raised like a bat in case anyone came running to check out the noise.

No one came. No one made a noise, either. Keiko and Carmen were probably too frightened.

After a few long moments, she reached through the hole and fumbled with the door knob. The bulky gloves made the job difficult, but she got the door opened and stepped inside.

Her sandals crunched over the glass on the floor. "Keiko?" she called in a soft voice.

"Hello?" A young woman's muffled voice came to Storm from above. "Who's there?"

"It's Storm." She pounded up the staircase, which was off the living room area. "Keep talking. Where are you?"

"Here," Keiko called again.

"Help," a weaker voice echoed.

"I'm in the hall," Storm said.

"We're in a bedroom." Keiko's words were muffled. "In the closet."

The master bedroom had a great view, but the bed was unmade and the room smelled of unwashed clothes. "Talk to me."

"Back here," two voices said together, and Storm flung open the only other door leading off the room.

It was a big, walk-in closet, packed to the ceiling with boxes and assorted paraphernalia. A Stair Master was jammed against one end, though the clothes strewn over it would have kept anyone from using it to exercise. It was an effective restraint, though. A length of chain, the kind used to tether big dogs, was looped through handcuffs that held Keiko's arms behind her back. She could sit and stand, but that was it.

Carmen's hands were tied in front of her, but the ropes that held her must have been agonizing to the injured shoulder. Her face was the color of the pale beige carpet and she smelled of urine.

Storm knelt before the little girl. She positioned the hedge clippers and snipped carefully at the clothesline around the girl's wrists.

"How long have you been tied up?"

Keiko answered. "She untied us at night, but we slept in here. She tied us up right after she gave us some tea and toast."

"Was it light out?"

"No," Keiko said. "I tried to tell the time of day when she opened the door."

Poor injured Carmen, kept two days in this scruffy suburban prison. The little girl gasped at the sudden jerk when her arms fell free, then wrapped the injured one in the good one and rocked back and forth. She shivered, and Storm pulled a sweater off a nearby hanger and wrapped the girl in it.

"Carmen, you're going to be all right. We're going to take care of you."

Storm had to take a calming breath before she lifted her hedge clippers to Keiko. "I think I can cut that chain, but we'll have to take the handcuffs off later."

"As long as we get out of here," Keiko said. "I want to get Carmen to the doctor."

Storm looked at the young woman. This wasn't the same self-destructive waif she'd seen a couple of days ago. And that wasn't the statement of a suicidal victim. Keiko was angry, and it was a good thing.

The hedge clippers worked well on the chain. "Do you have your car keys?" Storm asked.

"No, Pauline took them."

"I parked down on the main road. We'll have to walk a bit." She bent down to Carmen, whose color looked better. "You think you can do this? Keiko and I will help you."

Carmen nodded and got to her feet. Her legs wobbled, but she walked. The three of them exited the closet, and Keiko stopped next to the bed.

"Wait a minute," she said, and slid her cuffed hands down the back of her legs. She bent over at the same time, and stepped over her hands.

Storm marveled at her agility.

"It's easier than it looks. She caught me trying it. That's why she chained me to the exercise machine."

She took a cold look around the room. "Hey, her cell phone's plugged in. They don't work up here." Her face, thin and pale, transformed with a grin. She went to the dresser, pulled the phone out of the wall and slid it into her jeans pocket.

"Let me see those clippers."

Storm handed them over, and watched her skip to a land line on the bedside table and snip the wire to the wall. She managed despite the handcuffs.

Keiko dashed from the room and down the hall. Storm and Carmen were slower, and they heard the door of one room slam open, then another. Keiko took a little longer in that room, while Storm and Carmen headed down the stairs.

While Storm took Carmen to the kitchen to scrounge for something to eat, Keiko made her rounds. With each clipped wire, she looked happier. Carmen's eyes were taking on a shine, too.

"How 'bout the electrical wires?" the little girl asked.

Storm had gathered two apples and a couple of bagels. "Forget it. Let's get out of here."

Keiko was already out the kitchen door and into the back yard. Storm and Carmen could track her movement by the jangle of the handcuffs. Storm handed Carmen one of the apples and the two followed. Carmen munched the apple and Storm looked in the direction Keiko had gone.

She'd disappeared around the corner toward the car port, the opposite direction from the lava rock wall and the path down to the main road. Storm wanted to get the girls as far away from Pauline's house as fast as she could.

"Keiko? C'mon, let's go."

No response. Then, a crashing thud and a yelp of pain interrupted the peace.

Storm bolted in the direction of the noise. Around the corner of the house sprawled Keiko, half on the gravel drive, half under a hedge. Beside her was a large, overturned plastic flower pot. The hedge clippers dangled from a thick wire that led up the side of the house. Sparks flew from the blades, still embedded in the wire's insulation.

"Keiko," Storm shouted, and ran to her. "Talk to me."

The sparks gave a final burst, the hedge clippers dropped to the ground, and Keiko sat up. She took a couple of deep breaths. "It knocked me off the flower pot."

"That flower pot saved your life." Storm gaped at the cable. "Are you all right?"

Keiko grinned. "You think I stopped the electricity?"

"I'd say so." Storm stuck out a hand and pulled Keiko to her feet. Keiko winced, but looked happy. "Can we go?" Storm asked.

It took about ten minutes to get down the hill to Damon's car and another half hour to get to the hospital in Wailuku. When her mobile picked up a signal, Storm called Stella.

"Did you call the police about Keiko?"

"Yes, right after I talked to you."

"I've got her. And Carmen."

"Thank God." Stella's voice trembled with relief. "Where were they?"

"I'll tell you later. They're okay, but they need food and rest. I'm taking them to the hospital."

"I'll come. I'll call a cab."

"No, sit tight. Don't tell anyone yet."

"Lara will want to know."

"Not yet. I have a meeting with her in," Storm looked at her watch, "a little over an hour."

"But—"

"Please, Stella, it's important."

"Okay."

Storm handed the phone to Keiko, who reassured Stella that she and Carmen were fine. Storm noticed that she didn't tell Stella where they'd been, either.

Chapter Twenty-eight

Hospital personnel recognized Carmen and whisked her into an examination room. One of the security guards produced a key and removed the handcuffs from Keiko. He exclaimed at the burn on her hand, an open sore an inch wide that traversed her palm. An ER doctor soon arrived to take a look at it. Before Keiko went off with him, she handed a cell phone to Storm. Pauline's phone.

Another security guard pulled Storm aside. "Have you called the police about this?"

"I came directly here."

"We need to report the kidnapping and their injuries."

Storm agreed. "I'll do it now. I know the officer who's handling the case involving Carmen's father."

Gloom crossed the security guard's face. "Sad situation, isn't it? Say, do you need medical attention?"

"No, I'm fine. Tell Carmen and Keiko I'll check in with them later."

Back in the car, Storm turned on Pauline's phone. Once she handed the phone over to the police, she wouldn't see it again. She went to the menu to check both incoming and outgoing phone calls over the past several days. There were a lot, particularly in the last two days.

With an old ball point pen retrieved from Damon's glove box and one of the soccer flyers on the back seat, she went back five days. It didn't take her long because Pauline called the same people over and over. She had a few different incoming calls, but not many. Storm saw Stella's number three times, and jotted down the dates and times of the calls. With a skip of her heart, she recognized one number as Akira Kudo's. The most frequent calls were to and from Wayne, who was in Pauline's address book. Wayne was also on speed-dial.

Storm finished, then called the police station number Moana had given her and got a recording, which told callers to use 911. The lack of response reminded her that it was nine-fifteen on Sunday morning. Except for coffee, she hadn't had anything to eat yet. Storm parked near the hospital and walked to a sandwich shop down the street.

On the way, she walked past the bombed-out shell of Blue Marine, the ruined restaurant. A lone police officer paced the cracked and rutted sidewalk, and directed the infrequent Sunday pedestrian to the other side of the street.

Carl Moana looked glad to see her. Patrolling construction sites was either overtime or scut work, and Moana was probably bored.

"Are you still on Hiroki Yoshinaka's case?" Storm asked him.

He shrugged. "Senior level detectives took it over. The woman that died last night in Lahaina worked at the bar where Yoshinaka gambled. The Red Light."

That was the information Storm wanted from Damon. She'd asked him in at least three different ways. She'd even bought him dinner and drinks. Lots of drinks.

"I heard that place has Yakuza ties. Some guy named Obake owns it."

Moana frowned. "How'd you hear that?"

"I heard from someone else about Obake."

"Who?"

"It's a small island, remember?"

He looked at her carefully. "He's bad news. Don't get involved with him."

"How did the woman die?"

"Looks like she was beaten, knocked unconscious, and dumped in the ocean. An isolated beach, and no one saw her."

"Do you think there's a connection between her and Yoshinaka?"

"No indication of it. But we do know there's a connection between her and gambling, and Yoshinaka and gambling. It's tempting to connect dots, but they could be the wrong dots, you know?" He shoved his hands in his pocket and kicked a pebble on the sidewalk.

He knows about the prostitution, Storm thought. "Is Obake a suspect in her death?"

Moana laughed without humor. "You should hear him. He's a victim of a murder attempt, and she was a wonderful person and a lifelong friend. He claims it's the same person who set the bomb." Moana gestured toward the ruined restaurant.

"Does he have alibis?"

"Of course. With people who corroborate all his claims."

"That figures," Storm said. "You knew about Carmen leaving the hospital?"

He wheeled to face her. "Yes, have you heard anything?"

"I found her and Keiko." Storm told him about Pauline Harding's house, and how Harding had telephone contact with a man named Akira Kudo.

Moana's hands fell out of his pockets. "How'd you get that information?"

"Keiko stole her cell phone."

"Could I have it?"

"Yes, but it's in my car." She pointed. "I'm parked down the street."

Moana walked with her. "I owe you."

"A guy like Obake is connected."

"I know." He looked uneasy. "I thought of that. I'm going to check the phone log carefully."

"Good," she said. "Will you call me after you see Keiko and Carmen? I've got a meeting in Kihei." She handed him a business card, which had her cell phone number. He reciprocated.

Chapter Twenty-nine

Ichiru Tagama sat with Ryan at the breakfast table. Lara had left and Ryan was having a giant cup of coffee, but he'd made his father green tea.

Tagama gave his son a grateful look. The boy was the best thing he'd ever done. He'd told Yasuko, and she agreed, though she hadn't had the opportunity to get to know him. Tagama was about to start that process last night.

"Can you meet our clients in Wailuku?" he asked Ryan.

"Dad, we can cancel. They'll understand."

"I don't want to cancel. These are important investors." Tagama sipped from his tea. "Give them my apologies."

Tagama could feel his son's scrutiny, but he was also certain that Ryan would listen. For one thing, the boy was sensitive. And Tagama wanted time alone; Ryan would know that.

"Eat something," Ryan said.

Tagama knew he'd won this round. He nodded, but stared at the steaming surface of his tea.

Ryan toasted English muffins, buttered the halves, and set them in front of the old man. "If I'm going to be on time, I'd better get going. I'll call you after the meeting."

"Thank you, son."

Tagama sent a prayer after the boy, nibbled on the crunchy edges of the muffins for long enough to let his son get on the road, and then left the apartment. He knew that the digital nature of cellular phones made them hard to tap, but he didn't trust a conversation in Ryan's place. Obake's people were likely to have a bug in place, or a directional microphone set up in an adjacent apartment.

Tagama strolled into town, found a park bench next to a playground full of boisterous elementary school students, and dialed a number on his cell phone.

"Maui Police Department, Major Lekziew's office."

"Good morning, is the Major in? This is Stan Driver calling."

"Mr. Driver, he's in a meeting. May I take a message?"

"Sure, tell him Green Sands Golf Club has moved our tee time up. It's for 4:30 instead of five."

Tagama sat on the bench and watched the children play. If he had it to do over, he'd have had another child or two. Hell, he'd have done a lot differently. Ten minutes passed, and his phone rang.

"Ichiru, I'm sorry for your loss." Lek Lekziew's voice was private, compassionate.

"Thank you."

"We don't have much yet."

"What do you know?"

"A witness has retracted a statement. Says he made a mistake because he wasn't wearing his glasses."

"What did he see before he forgot he wasn't wearing glasses?"

"A black Land Rover."

"Ah."

"There are other black Land Rovers. They're fairly common."

"Okay. How about the tissue samples under her nails?"

"No matches." Lek exhaled slowly. "We're looking at the FBI's CODIS, but if they haven't shown up in the local database, they're not going to show up nationally."

"This is going to be tough," Lek said. "They're going to be hard to identify."

"Let me see what I can do."

Tagama disconnected. He sat for a while longer. The first group of students went inside—recess over—and a second group blasted out the double doors. He turned his face toward the warm sun and smiled at the children's unrestrained delight.

A few minutes later, he walked back to the apartment, went to the living room, and sat on the most-used piece of furniture, a comfortable sofa situated before the TV set. For several minutes, he sat and considered his timing. Then he speed-dialed a number on his mobile phone.

"Ramirez, I need you to meet me."

"Now?" asked Ramirez.

"Olowalu Wharf in a half hour."

"You sure?"

"I'm sure."

"Okay, Boss."

Tagama disconnected and stood up as if his knees hurt. He looked around the apartment slowly and gave the room a sad smile, though no one could see it. It was a smile of reminiscence.

He walked out the front door and didn't look back. At the front door he asked a security guard to call a taxi for him and went outside to sit down. When he was sure he was alone, he hit the same speed dial button.

"Where is Storm now?" Tagama asked.

"She got Keiko and the kid. They're at the hospital in Wailuku, and Storm just left."

"She's in a rush to make her appointment with Lara."

"Looks that way."

"Obake's at home?"

"Waiting for another call from Japan." Ramirez chuckled. "My man tells me he's wearing a towel, pacing back and forth."

"Good. When's the next call from Japan?"

"About an hour."

"Excellent. I'll see you soon."

Chapter Thirty

Lara had a half hour before her appointment with Storm. She paced the floor of the dive shop, and tried to shut out the pounding and sawing coming from the back office. Just as one problem was solved, others arose.

The Makena house brought a price higher than she'd dared hope for. Not only had the bidding war been brilliant—she had her realtor to thank for that idea—the buyer's financing had come through. And the right buyer had won; she and the realtor had manipulated that situation a bit, but no one would ever suspect.

She had a closing date, six weeks hence, and her real estate agent had already made an offer on the little strip mall in which Lara's Aquatic Adventures was located. It was a safer deal than waiting to see if Ryan's dad would make a wedding present out of the space. Plus, it would be in her name.

With the resolution of one problem, others arose. Yasuko's death was a terrible blow. Ryan took it very hard, and Tagama's reaction was even worse. He'd insisted on seeing Yasuko's body, and before she was loaded into the Medical Examiner's vehicle, the police had allowed it.

Though Ryan hadn't said anything about it, his father's state of mind had to weigh heavily on him. It was so sad, just as they were all getting to know one another. Even she saw redeeming qualities in the old man, and Ryan had promised to tell her a secret that he promised would make her feel better about Tagama.

Now that Yasuko was dead, it was probably a moot point. Though Ryan and his father had blocked her view, she'd caught a glimpse of Yasuko on the gurney. A cluster of drooping white flowers stood out against her wet hair. Tagama had caressed the gardenias with excruciating tenderness. The gesture squeezed her heart.

Wasn't it an odd coincidence that Yasuko had gardenias in her hair? Even broken and bruised, they were similar to the ones she'd taken to the nursing home yesterday, the blooms she'd cut from the potted plant to pin in her mother's hair.

Lara thought about the flowers. It was ten o'clock, and the nursing staff at the home would have finished with Barb's morning bath. She dialed the extension on her mother's floor and was delighted to reach a caretaker she recognized.

"Elisabeth, would you mind watering that gardenia plant for my mother? She won't remember."

"Oh." Elisabeth sounded surprised. "She told me about it."

"That's good," Lara said.

"Yes, I'm glad to hear it's real." Elisabeth thought for a second. "She probably put it someplace safe. She'll do that from time to time."

"What do you mean? You didn't see it?"

"Don't worry, we'll find it."

It was a coincidence. How could he suspect? The realtor and she were the only ones who knew.

"Lara, are you there?" Elisabeth asked.

"Sure, I'm here. How about the orchid Stella brought? Did she, uh, hide that?"

"No, it's on the table. She had one of the flowers in her hair."

Lara bit her lower lip. "Thanks, Elisabeth. I'll visit this afternoon."

It was a message; she'd known the minute she'd seen the flowers in Yasuko's hair. He knew she'd be on the beach when the body was found, too. He was playing them all.

Lara set the receiver down and paced back and forth a half-dozen times. She picked up the phone and dialed another number. She got her realtor's voice mail and left a message to call her back. Probably showing some property; Sundays were busy days for realtors.

She made another call. "Ken, are you keeping an eye on him?"

"Sure, just like you asked."

Lara could hear the sound of waves in the background. "What's he doing?"

"Nothing. Well, he's walking back and forth in his living room. Wearing a towel and looking pissed."

"Good. Get back to the boat and meet me here a little before noon."

"You sure you want to do this?"

"I'm okay."

◇◇◇

Storm had little time before her meeting with Lara, but she was itching to cross-check Mark Suzuki's information with numbers she'd pulled off Pauline's phone log. Five minutes away from Lara's shop, she pulled to the side of the road.

Not wanting to leave any documents in the hotel room, she'd been carrying around all the paperwork she'd collected over the past two days, and she flipped through the file she'd begun until she found the paper she wanted. Pauline had several calls to and from numbers Storm didn't recognize, but there were also two from Lara's cell phone and one from Pauline to the dive shop.

Storm's first thought was that Lara was helping Stella look for the missing girls. But the calls were made yesterday morning, all between seven-thirty and eight. Stella had told Storm that Keiko left around nine.

None of the calls on Stella's phone were made to a number designated as Keiko's, so Storm had to assume for the time being that Keiko didn't have a cell phone. She hadn't had one in that closet, that's for sure. Maybe she and Stella shared.

But Mark had noted a call from Pauline to Stella's apartment on Saturday morning at eight-thirteen. She'd ask Stella if she remembered that call. If not, then chances were that Keiko'd picked up. The call took four minutes, too long for an answering machine or a hang-up. Long enough to exchange information.

It was time to go to her meeting. She'd review the list later, perhaps make another call to Mark for the unidentified numbers. If Akira Kudo changed phones often, maybe one of them was his. Or one of his bodyguard's. Kudo would have other people doing the work of kidnapping young women and raiding hotel rooms. Or driving a black Range Rover.

At the dive shop, Storm watched Lara fumble with the lock at the front door. "I didn't want anyone wandering in yet. People walk right in unless the door's locked."

"Are you open today?" Storm asked.

"We've got a dive group going out this afternoon." Lara turned to lead Storm into the back office. Damon stopped hammering.

"Good morning," he mumbled to Storm. He picked up his tools and left the room.

Lara watched him leave with a quizzical expression. She looked like she was about to ask Storm a question, but he'd left too quickly.

"No time off?" Storm asked. "I'm sorry to hear about your friend."

"It's sad for Ryan and his father. I didn't know her, to be honest."

Storm saw emotion—was it fear or grief?—pull at her features. What was the connection between Yasuko and these women? Stella had told Storm about the young women, but Stella hadn't mentioned Yasuko, who worked at The Red Light, and had for a long time. Stella would know her, and if Stella's story was true, Lara knew her too—and not just through the Tagamas.

"I heard she worked at The Red Light," Storm said. "Stella told me about that place."

Lara's head whipped around. "Don't listen to Stella. She's got her facts all mixed up."

"She seems to care about you."

"I care about her, too. I gave her a job, didn't I?"

"Keiko, too."

"Yes, and Keiko's a mess. You've seen her." Lara pointed to a chair in front of a desk. "Let's get to the insurance questions. As I remember, I'm paying you for that job."

Storm sat down and laid her folder on the table. "Okay, I'll start the clock."

Lara sighed and took a seat behind the desk. "I'm sorry, it's been a very long night. Hell, it's been a long week."

"I understand. We only have a few details to cover."

"Where's your briefcase?" Lara asked.

"It got stolen."

"Shit," Lara whispered.

"Don't worry, no one can get into my work data. The files are encrypted."

"You sure?"

"Absolutely. I have a very good tech person. Laptops are stolen too often for me to risk having cases exposed." Another of Suzuki's talents, for which Storm was highly appreciative.

Storm opened the folder. "And I back everything up."

"No one could find out what we talked about?" Lara's tan had faded.

"No, but think about it. We talked about insurance for the dive shop, a logical conversation for a new business owner. Believe me, it would take weeks to hack into my files, and even if it happened, yours wouldn't reveal any vulnerability."

"Yeah, I guess not." Lara sighed. She leaned forward in her chair. "I'm going to buy the shopping center." She tapped on the desk with her index finger. "The deal is finally coming together. Sorry I didn't mention it earlier, but I thought it would be *bachi*. You know, bad luck."

"I'm glad to hear it," Storm said. "This changes your insurance policy, but it'll benefit you in the long run."

"I hope."

"How are you handling the real estate transaction?" Storm asked.

"I've got a realtor taking care of that."

"Good. I'll make the changes in Honolulu and fax you the papers."

"When are you going back?"

"I'm going to the airport soon." Storm didn't mention Hamlin's arrival. He might want to spend the night, but that was none of Lara's business.

"Thank you for your help. Your understanding, too," Lara said.

"You're welcome."

Lara walked Storm through the shop to the front door, where they shook hands. Damon's tools were piled in a corner, but he was staying out of the way.

Lara watched Storm walk out the door and disappear around the corner. When she could no longer see Storm, she rushed to answer her cell phone, which was ringing in the office. She recognized the number as her realtor's office, and assumed Mary Robbins was returning her call. But when she got through and listened for a moment to the sobbing voice on the other end, she collapsed into her desk chair.

With a shaking voice and hands that trembled so that she could hardly hold onto the phone, Lara asked, "Where did the accident happen?"

"Honoapiʻilani Highway. She was on the way to Kapalua."

"How…how bad is she hurt?" Lara's voice wavered.

The woman on the line broke down again. "She's dead."

Chapter Thirty-one

Ichiru Tagama took the taxi as close as he could get to Olowalu Wharf. The driver didn't want to leave him on the deteriorating road, but he also didn't want to take out the undercarriage of his aging sedan.

Tagama reassured the cabbie that he wanted to stop there, and he didn't need to wait. Tagama knew the driver would remember him. A polite, elderly Japanese local in nice loafers and a long-sleeved Barong Tagalog in a fine Pina fabric, like he was going to a wedding. Or a funeral. A bit dressy for a meeting at Olowalu Wharf.

As he'd planned, Tagama arrived about twenty minutes ahead of his scout. Ramirez was a good man, and he was punctual. He also had nine grandchildren. Tagama didn't want him coming too early.

Tagama was counting on the isolation of the place, though it was known among history buffs and people who wanted to get away from the better known hiking trails. There were a few cars in the parking area, among them a black Range Rover. The other five cars were either generic rentals or rust-spotted locals.

Hopefully the drivers of the rentals were checking out the nearby petroglyphs or the site of the 1790 Olowalu Massacre, when American merchant Simon Metcalf slaughtered a hundred Hawaiian villagers because someone stole his boat. Only the keel of the boat was returned, along with the stripped thigh bones of the watchman. Times had changed, but human nature hadn't.

Now he was at the site, Tagama wondered if he hadn't made a mistake by not pinpointing a specific meeting spot. The area was bigger than he remembered, and the trees were large and provided excellent shelter. It had been years since he'd been down here. But then he heard the rumble of men's voices, and knew he'd found his prey. Or his predators.

Tagama swallowed hard. His hands had become icy and his knees weak. Remember that strength is not always measured in muscle. They don't know that you knew Ryan's apartment would be bugged. And remember what these thugs did to Yasuko. You are old, and you can do this. It is right.

He whispered a prayer to Guan-Gong, Chinese general and god of martial arts and war in the afterlife. Yasuko had been Chinese by birth, brought into the water trade so long ago she thought she was Japanese until she was in her twenties. But Guan-Gong would help her. And, in seeking justice, Tagama himself.

He walked silently along the path, glad now for his loafers, which had soft, man-made soles. When he passed around the branches of a big Norfolk pine, he encountered the two big bodyguards. One had his back to Tagama, but Steven Kudo's eyes narrowed at Tagama's approach and the other guy turned.

Tagama allowed himself a small recoil. It wasn't difficult; his legs were nearly boneless with apprehension. "What—" he exclaimed, and watched Kudo's cruel smile.

When outnumbered, take out the biggest or the leader, Tagama remembered from his long-ago fighting days. Kudo would be first, he thought.

"Hello, Mr. Tagama," said the other guy, and gave Kudo a smug look.

"Well, hello. Have we met?"

The bodyguards snickered. "Have we met?" Kudo repeated.

"I've got no issue with you fellows," Tagama said. It didn't take much effort to sound uncertain.

"Of course not." Kudo reached into his jacket for a gun, and the other man followed. Kudo carried a Glock G20, the other guy a big Heckler & Koch. Compensating for something, Tagama surmised. He'd still take out Kudo first.

Tagama raised his hands. "I don't carry a gun."

"Stupid you," said Kudo.

Tagama felt the flush of anger, a good feeling. He needed it.

The men lined up so that the three of them formed a triangle, with sides of ten feet. Tagama took a couple of steps closer. "What do you want from me? I told you I'm not carrying."

Like he'd hoped, the men backed up. But they backed up on a parallel path, so that the three of them formed a line rather than a triangle. Excellent, Tagama thought. If they fire, they'll shoot each other, too. The fact that neither of them had corrected the awkward geometry of the situation told him that they weren't planning to kill him here. Either they preferred to take him to Obake, or they'd seen people in the vicinity before he'd arrived. He didn't care.

"I'm going to put my hands straight out, okay?"

"Keep 'em away from your body," said the thug.

"Of course," Tagama said.

No way would he be able to hide a gun in the pockets of his slacks, and the men knew it. Tagama wasn't wearing a jacket, and he knew Kudo and his sidekick had eyed his shirt tail for a bulge. He'd let them have a good look at his back when he raised his arms.

As he'd hoped, they relaxed. They didn't consider that his long sleeves were for anything other than an old man's chill.

Neither of them saw Tagama slide the light, stainless steel throwing knife into his hand where he kept it pinched between his thumb and forefinger, hidden by his relaxed fingers and his palm. By the time he smoothly raised and snapped his wrist, the two men had just begun to react.

The scalpel-like blade found its target in Kudo's neck before their guns were raised. Kudo, startled by the slight impact, did what most people would do. He blinked and put a hand to his neck. Startled to find a handle poking out of his throat, he pulled it out. The three-sixteenths inch thick blade had done its work, though, and a gout of blood followed. It pulsed with the beat of his heart and sent a spray across Tagama and past Kudo's sidekick, an arc of nearly twenty feet. It was an unsettling sight.

Tagama, though, was prepared for it. When the other thug's mouth fell open with alarm, Tagama launched another knife. Another neck shot, and the guy did exactly what Kudo had done. He pulled the knife out. That instinct was too strong, and Tagama knew it. A fountain of blood followed.

But Tagama had to hand it to Kudo for his next reaction. Despite a hand clamped against the pulsing spray that jetted through his fingers, the man raised his gun with the other hand, aimed, and fired.

Tagama crumpled like he'd been hit by a car. He might have had a better chance against a car, he thought, as he went down. He landed on his back with one leg twisted under him, but didn't have the strength to straighten it. He smelled the warm, damp earth mixed with the needles of ironwood and Norfolk pine, a pleasant aroma, and didn't fight the little convulsion that shook him. It was hard to breathe, and the gurgling noises he made frightened him a bit. But he'd suffered worse pain.

As the blackness crept from the sides of his vision, Tagama whispered to Yasuko. "They won't make it as far as their car, my sweetheart. And their DNA is all over the place, so the police can tie up loose ends." Some of the last words were spoken in his mind, but that was okay. She'd understand.

Chapter Thirty-two

Questions tumbled through Storm's head. Why had Damon's greeting been so reserved? Why was Lara touchy and preoccupied, and why did she claim not to know Yasuko?

She had questions for Pauline Harding, too. Out in the parking lot, she unlocked Damon's car, opened the door, and felt a blast of heat like a kiln. She rolled down the windows and leaned up against the back fender.

Pauline answered the phone with a smoker's rumble, then reacted to Storm with a phlegmy grunt. "What do you want?"

"Have the police talked to you?"

"Of course. They don't have shit." There was the hiss of a match, an inhalation.

That was interesting, considering there would be evidence all over her house. What had Keiko told the police? Or not told them?

"I want to talk to you," Storm said.

"Fuck you," Pauline said, and hung up.

Okay, that went well. Plan B, Storm thought, and called Stella's apartment. No one answered, so she called Stella's cell phone. No one answered. She called the hospital next. Carmen had been admitted for observation, but Keiko had been released after the burn on her hand was treated. No one knew how she left.

"Did someone pick her up?" Storm asked.

"I have access to who's been admitted, but I don't know how people leave," said the person on the other end of the line. "Patients aren't supposed to drive," she added.

Storm stood for a moment, thinking about what to do next. She called the mobile number Sergeant Moana had given her and got his voice mail. Where was everybody? Maybe people charged their cell phones on Sunday.

A noise distracted her, and Storm turned to watch a painter enter the shop by the side door. She waved him down.

"Will you see Damon?" she asked.

"Probably," he said.

"Would you ask him to give me a call, please? I'm—"

"You're the lady lawyer," the painter said. "I'll tell him."

Storm took stock of her situation. The dress she'd worn to dinner the night before had a food spot in the middle of her chest and drooped from her shoulder in tired folds. Her heeled sandals felt like tightening rubber bands on swelling feet.

She would go back to the hotel. It was hard to imagine that it would be dangerous in the middle of a bright, sunny day. Goons like the guys in the black Range Rover liked to work in the dark.

In the hotel lobby, happy families and affectionate couples debunked any lingering anxieties. But a short elevator ride later, she found her room freezing cold with the air conditioning turned on high. She hadn't done that. Nor had she dumped her suitcase on the floor and trampled her clothes.

Storm went back into the corridor and called the front desk. "I need security."

"Room 322? Again?" said the operator.

Storm waited in the hall. Security arrived within two minutes, and she was glad to see a different man than the defensive fellow she'd had the last time her room was burgled.

"We're going to move you to a different room," he said. "Have you looked to see what's missing?"

"I'm checking out. And I thought you should see it before I started to clean up."

"Did you call the police?" he asked.

Their arrival answered his question. One of the officers was the same short, lean man who'd come before. "A little over twenty-four hours and it happened again?" He looked around the room. "I guess so."

The other office, a woman whose uniform embroidery said B. Dillis, eyed the overturned suitcase. "When did it happen?"

"I don't know." Storm told her how she'd been frightened enough last night to get another hotel room. They both ignored the huffing noises made by the security man.

Dillis nodded. "Good move." She had eyes so black the pupils were indistinguishable from the iris. They fastened on Storm like tractor beams. "Why is someone following you?"

"Good question. I'm here on business. My client is opening a dive shop."

"Lara Farrell," said B. Dillis.

"Yes," Storm said. She let the silence build. Cops used the same technique she did, so Storm knew better than to fill the awkward void. The four people stood looking at each other for a few long moments. It was the security guy who broke.

"So," he said, "You think it's the same person who did it Friday night?"

Storm and the two police looked at him.

"Don't know yet," said the short, lean officer.

B. Dillis made her way to the bathroom and flicked on the light with the end of her pen. "Same thing in here. Dumped out all your toiletries." She looked at Storm. "If I were you, I'd buy new ones."

"I don't have anything anyone would want. They've already got my laptop."

"Hope it's got a password other than your birthday," Dillis said.

"It's pretty secure. This is a scare tactic. They want me running."

"That's my guess, too," the male cop said. "After the note he left you."

"We'll dust, but chances are we won't get prints we can use," said Dillis.

"Like before," said the security man. Everyone looked at him. "What's wrong?" he asked. "I mean, the room's covered with prints."

"Right," said Dillis.

On the way out the door, B. Dillis looked back at Storm. "Smart of you to avoid staying in this hotel. But I'm curious. We know you're working with Lara Farrell. Is there anything else you've done that could have rattled someone enough to send you such a hostile message? Someone wants you gone."

Storm swallowed, then told Dillis about visiting both Carmen Yoshinaka and the storage facility. "I've talked to Sergeant Moana about this, also."

"Carmen Yoshinaka, little girl whose dad shot her and her sister?" B. Dillis hooked her thumbs in her wide leather belt and frowned at Storm. A few seconds passed. "What led you to her?"

Storm leaned against the open door. "Carmen's father worked at the dive shop." She told Dillis how she and Damon had gone to the Yoshinaka's house the night of the murder/suicide.

"So you went to see her in the hospital? Most people wouldn't do that." Dillis' dark eyes were probing, waiting.

"My parents died young," said Storm. "The kid's situation got to me."

A spark of compassion flared in Dillis' eyes, and she seemed to accept Storm's explanation. "When are you going back to O'ahu?"

"Either this evening or tomorrow."

The cop arched an eyebrow, then reached in her pocket and handed Storm a card. "Call me if you need help."

Storm watched her walk to the elevator. At least Dillis hadn't asked Storm to leave now, or given her any dire warnings. She hoped that was because the cop knew something about the case that Storm didn't. It also made Storm want to talk to Sgt. Moana, who might be inclined to reveal a fact or two since she'd turned over Pauline's phone to him.

Storm closed the door and began to clean up the mess. She shook out her clothes and repacked her suitcase, then did the same in the bathroom. This was a malicious message, loud and clear. The thief didn't even take anything. He just wanted Storm to know he could get to her any time he wanted.

Anything that went in her mouth or eyes, like some of her makeup, went into the wastebasket. Just playing it safe—or succumbing to paranoia, she wasn't sure.

When she finished packing, she changed into a bathing suit, sneakers, and jogging shorts. A run would help her sort out her thoughts. Hamlin's plane wouldn't arrive for another three hours. There was plenty of time, and she could shower and change in the restrooms on the public beach.

At the front desk, she settled her bill with the account her secretary had set up.

"You want the rest of the cash, or should we credit your account?" the receptionist asked in a soft voice, after checking to make sure no guests were in earshot. Storm figured she was the only one with the problem; no one else was in danger, so she obliged the employee's desire for discretion.

Storm took the cash—she might need it—and rolled her suitcase out the front door to the hotel parking lot and Damon's car. Before she got out of the parking lot, her phone rang.

"You called?" said Sergeant Moana.

"I wondered what Keiko and Carmen told you."

"Some of my colleagues think you advised Keiko not to talk. So she wouldn't be charged with kidnapping."

"I didn't," Storm said. "Why would your colleagues think that?"

"Keiko told us Pauline was a good friend, who'd asked her and Carmen to visit."

"Shit."

"I think so, too. You think Keiko was threatened?"

"Did you look at the phone I gave you?"

Moana lost some of his attitude. "Yeah. It's why I stuck up for you. There are some questionable calls."

"Questionable timing, too," Storm said.

"Keiko wouldn't tell us, but the little girl did. She said they were tied up in the closet. She's got rope burns to show for it."

"I cut her free."

"Yeah, I figured. We've got a guard outside her hospital room."

"Where did Keiko go?"

"She said she had a ride."

"I can't find her. I can't find Stella, either."

He didn't answer, and in the silence Storm heard sirens. "It's been a busy morning," he said, and the sirens grew louder, then stopped abruptly. "There's been a fatal car crash out by Kapalua, and there was some kind of revenge killing for that woman that died last night. Must be a full moon or something." He sounded tired. "I'll get some people looking for them."

"What revenge killing?" Storm asked. "Who died?"

But Moana had hung up.

Storm climbed into the car and turned on the radio. After scanning up and down the dial, she finally found a report that three people had been found dead near Olowalu Wharf in an apparent gang war, but identification was being withheld.

She tried the dive shop, but no one answered. Lara had probably left, and if Damon was still there, he was wearing his ear protectors.

Storm drove to the public beach access. She locked the car and began a slow jog toward Makena Beach. She needed to think, alone, without any interruptions.

When Dillis had asked her if Carmen Yoshioka was linked to the dive shop, Storm was flooded with ideas, most of which were too tenuous to share, especially to a cop who needed solid evidence, not filaments of innuendo.

Dillis knew the obvious connections, but her instincts were telling her there were more. Good instincts, Storm thought. She wished she had a coherent explanation. It bothered her that Paradise Consortium owned the house Yoshinaka rented and had part ownership of the strip mall Lara was trying to buy. But she didn't have anything concrete.

When Stella explained the water trade, some details fell into place. Though The Red Light didn't have an obvious link to

Paradise Consortium, Yoshinaka had a relationship with both establishments. So did Lara's family members.

On a related train of thought, the elder Tagama sat on the board of Paradise Consortium, which also owned a portion of the shopping center under Lara's shop. Tagama father and son ran Mālua LLC. Were the Tagama men setting Lara up in a business they could control? A dive shop would be an effective place to launder cash. If so, perhaps that was why Lara was scrambling to buy the place.

Obake, aka Akira Kudo, was the thread that ran through the whole mess. She'd knew from her conversation with Terry Wu, the assistant U.S. Attorney, that Obake was on their watch list. From her friend Mark Suzuki, who was connected to God knew what, she knew he was notorious for evasion and secrecy. Both men implied that he was dangerous.

Damon wouldn't even talk about The Red Light. He'd tell her Lara's secrets about real estate deals, but wouldn't tell her where Yoshinaka gambled. Why not? It wasn't just because she was Lara's lawyer. He'd left the beach park in a big hurry the night Yoshiko's body was found, as if he knew more than he wanted to reveal.

Both Damon and Lara had spoken of a Makena Beach property she was selling for a large sum, more than she'd expected to make. How does someone escalate the value of a property? Lara was, among other things, a savvy and proactive business woman.

What did she do? Start a bidding war? Storm almost stumbled at the thought. It was ruthless, but possible. Makena was a unique and limited slice of paradise. Only a few lots of developable oceanfront land existed, and Lara's was prime.

She'd had a real estate agent handle the transaction. Storm was certain the purchaser and sale price wouldn't yet be public knowledge. Not if the bid had been accepted within the last day or two.

Storm slowed her jog to a walk around a sharp curve in the road. High on her left, overlooking the winding road where

Storm stood panting, an opulent new estate with immature landscaping sat high on a bluff and looked out to the ocean. Just ahead, to her right, a gravel drive disappeared into a copse of ironwood trees that fronted the ocean. Through the shield of trees, she could see the glint of glass.

Storm turned into the drive, stepped over a heavy chain, and followed the winding drive until she saw wide glass windows on a modern house that nestled among lava rock and natural ground cover. It was private to the point of secret, and overlooked a small, secluded beach.

Storm walked back to the road. Next to the drive, a for sale sign swayed in the gentle breeze, though the diagonal red sold banner blocked out most of the information. She peered behind the banner.

She didn't have anything to write on, but she'd remember. All the way back to the car, her footsteps pounded Mary Robbins, 367-5409, Mary Robbins, 367-5409. Maybe Mary could tell her if Lara had been the owner—maybe, in her delight to share the big sale, she'd talk about how they got their record-setting price. Heck, maybe Storm could hope for more pieces to fit the puzzle that had her head spinning.

One thing Storm knew was that Obake was a bad customer. He was the author of death and misery among people that had no chance against his organization, money, and amoral brutality. Obake, Lara, and the Tagamas were all linked by history, family, money, or a combination of all three. Throw in Stella, Keiko, Lara's mother and sister, the murdered Yasuko, and the Yoshinaka family as victims of the Yakuza boss, and she had a festering brew of desperate greed.

Chapter Thirty-three

Back at the car, Storm extracted a beach towel and a change of clothing. She headed for the beach, dived into the ocean, and swam along the shore for several minutes. Long enough to refresh her flushed skin as only a swim in the ocean can do. A fresh water shower revived her even further. She then ducked into the public restroom to strip out of her wet clothes, and put on a fluttery, cool silk skirt in a blue tropical print and a cap-sleeved white T-shirt.

She wanted to look good when she met Hamlin in a couple of hours. Speaking of Hamlin, she might be able to catch him before he left Honolulu. If she remembered correctly, he had about an hour before catching the short flight to Maui.

He picked up on the first ring. "Hey, I was hoping you'd call."

"I was hoping you'd answer."

"Where are you?"

"A beach near Makena."

"The nude beach?" The words carried a grin and a promise.

"Not without you." A memory brought a flush over her, and Storm was glad no one could see her.

"Good, I don't want you getting sunburned."

"I don't sunburn."

"We'll see," he said. "Where shall I meet you?"

"I'll be at the airport."

"I can't wait," he said, and Storm could hear the loudspeaker announcement for his boarding.

"Me either," she said.

She beamed all the way through Wailea, Kihei, and halfway to Lahaina. It wasn't until she got close to Damon's house that the sparkle faded, and that was only because the thought of picking up her own car reminded her of the guys in the black Range Rover.

Screw 'em, she thought. I'll exchange it at the airport before I pick up Hamlin. After that, there will be two of us to intimidate.

Damon's truck was in his carport, and the engine ticked and pinged. He hadn't been home long. She didn't see any suspicious cars in the area. A black Range Rover would have been conspicuous. The streets of the middle-class neighborhood were lined with nice, safe American and Japanese cars.

Storm knocked on the front door. She wanted to hand over the keys and thank him again for loaning it to her. She stood there for a few long moments and listened for footsteps. Only a muffled thump, which would make sense if he was in the shower or bath, but Storm wasn't certain if it came from Damon's house. Children's voices carried from the house on the right, along with the clatter of play.

Still, it reminded her of the thump she'd heard at Pauline's house, and the memory erased the warmth of the sun that stroked her shoulders. She looked around the yard. An air conditioner hummed in one of his windows. From what she remembered from the night she'd picked up the car, it was the living room.

She knocked again. "Damon?"

A neighbor went by, walking the dog. He gave her a friendly nod. The dog stopped to pee on Damon's grass.

Storm looked at her surroundings again. The kids had apparently turned on a television set, because their voices were absent, but explosions and shouts, the same noises in any adventure show, emanated from next door.

The house had a for sale sign, which reminded Storm of the property near Makena. Mary Robbins, 367-5409. Storm decided to give Damon a few minutes while she called.

"Paradise Properties," said a woman's voice. Realtors could usually be counted on to work Sundays.

"Mary Robbins?" asked Storm.

"No, it's not. Why are you calling?" The woman's voice had a confrontational note. What was with that? Didn't she want another client?

"I wanted to ask about a property Mary has listed in the Makena area."

"Oh." The woman drew a deep breath. "That place."

"I thought it looked nice."

"It is. I've got to get in touch with the seller. The closing may be delayed now."

"Is this one of Mary's colleagues?" Storm asked.

"Yes, this is Rose."

"Rose, could I speak to Mary?"

"Mary died." A quiver appeared in Rose's voice.

"Mary died?" Storm nearly shouted; she couldn't believe it. The dog walker did a double take.

Rose swallowed audibly. "Car accident, just this morning, out near Kapalua."

"Shit," Storm breathed, and disconnected. She flopped down on the front step, and her handbag bumped against the door. "Shit," she repeated.

Damon's voice came from somewhere toward the back of house. "Come in."

The dog-walker had moved on, and Storm tried the doorknob. It opened, and she stepped into the cool entry hall. Conscious of the air-conditioner's efforts to ward off the afternoon heat, she closed it behind herself.

"Damon? I can leave the keys on the coffee table. I filled up the tank—"

Someone, a very large someone, simultaneously jerked Storm's legs out from under her and slammed her to the floor. It was an expert move, by a person who'd done it before. It was swift and silent, except for the truncated bleat of shock Storm uttered as she hit the hard floor.

Her staccato yelp ended when the wind was punched out of her. While she fought panic and her convulsing diaphragm, the assailant tied her hands behind her back and dropped a dark cloth over her head and shoulders. The whole procedure took a second or less. Storm gasped, terrified by the claustrophobic darkness.

Breathe, she told herself. That's the first thing you have to get control over. This is really bad, her inner voice blathered. Shut up, she told it, and struggled to draw a complete breath. It was an ineffectual series of gasps. Again. Do it again, her survival voice told her. The scared one emitted a sob. She got more air with fewer spasms the second try, and she did it again.

Whatever he'd put over her head smelled of diesel fuel, and she battled a wave of nausea. It was hot, and it was black. She couldn't see anything, not even a glimmer of light between the threads of fabric. It stank, and she gagged. Not good. She could not—absolutely not—vomit in this bag.

She drew another deep breath, and to distract herself from the odor, she forced herself to think. The person who hit her was big, undoubtedly male. He hadn't made a sound, which meant he'd been standing behind the door when she opened it. He'd also done it easily, as if he'd practiced the move many times.

When Damon had called out, it sounded like he was in back of the house. She'd assumed he was in the shower, which would explain why he hadn't heard her knock at first. How could he have made it so quickly to the front of the house? She didn't think he did, but he had to have known someone was waiting to ambush her.

"Damon?" she said. "Why?" She hated that she sounded like a whimpering child.

No one answered her, but there was a sudden noise. It sounded like a scuffle, then a striking of something solid and meaty. As if someone got slugged. Then there was no other sound, as if the person had been lifted out of place. Zapped, or immobilized.

Storm strained to listen through the heavy material that insulated her from sensation. She lay on the floor with the roughness of the door mat chafing her thighs and knees, which had suffered rug burns in the take-down. Her skirt was rolled to her waist and she couldn't even pull it down. Strange how that indignity crossed her mind and infuriated her, not that she could do a damned thing about it.

But the anger sharpened her senses, and she had the clear impression she was being observed by more than one person. She tried to get a feeling for how many people stood around her, but it was impossible.

Dread numbed her. She'd been warned, hadn't she? Two wise and experienced people (at least) had told her to distance herself from anything Obake might be involved in. In fact, anything he might notice. Suzuki had told her to ditch her phone to protect his new number. Which she hadn't done, and a pang of regret ran through her so fiercely that one of her legs jerked.

Damon had betrayed her. She'd assumed they were friends, or at least amicable. They were definitely drinking buddies, and had witnessed a tragedy together. But Stella implied that Obake could pressure anyone. His threats had forced Hiroki Yoshinaga to shoot his own daughters, for God's sake. A weak-assed wimp like Damon would cave at first contact.

And here she was, trussed like a terrorist's hostage. Or terrorist, depending on where you stood. It didn't matter, though, did it? Fucking Damon had given her up. They'd threatened him with something: his daughters' welfare, his custody arrangement, maybe his drinking or gambling habits, his employment prospects. Did it matter?

She turned on her side, hoping to expand an air pocket in the bag over her head. Maybe work her skirt down over the pretty lace underwear she'd put on after her swim. How dumb was that idea? She'd done it for Hamlin, who would be stuck at the airport, high and dry.

Someone sat on her feet, immobilizing her legs and grinding her chafed knees into the rough carpet. "I'll lie still," she shouted, but in a too-short second, she knew that immobility wasn't her captor's primary motive.

The sharp sting of a needle pierced a vein at her ankle and jerked her wits back to her dilemma as handily as a leash on a mutt. She yelped with surprise and shock. The jab was followed immediately by the burn of a dissipating drug. It felt like someone had dribbled hot water all the way up her leg, along her thigh, and let it ooze into her body and brain.

This time, panic did seize her, and sweat rolled off her scalp and face. It stung her tearing eyes, ran into her open and gasping mouth. "Damon," she roared inside the dark, cloying sack.

Then she shut up. She knew her fear facilitated the effect of the drug, but she couldn't control fear. She could manage her mouth, but her heart felt like it would burst from her chest with each pounding contraction. Stay calm, she told herself, but the rough fabric of the bag over her head stuck to the perspiration on her forehead and cheeks. It puffed in and out with her shallow, frightened breaths.

"I'm sorry, Hamlin," she moaned. And before the drug stupefied her besieged brain cells, she pictured him, and thought of how they'd almost made it. Their reconciliation was a sure thing; they loved each other. She was going to share, to open up, and to ask for understanding, too. He had to meet her halfway, but he was giving every indication he would do more than that.

Until she'd blown it again, that is. He hated how she waltzed into trouble. This time, he'd never know how careful she'd been. Switching hotel rooms, borrowing a car. Who would have thought retrieving the car would be her downfall?

Chapter Thirty-four

Hamlin took a seat at the Aloha Airline gate, and caught the glance of a neatly dressed man in his thirties. Another lawyer, he thought. Where have I met that guy?

The plane was crowded with a tour group and what appeared to be a local high school swim team. Teenagers in matching green warm-ups were having a great time. The only seats left were in row sixteen, at the emergency exit hatches. That was okay with Hamlin. He took the aisle; the man from the lounge smiled at him from the window seat.

"I think we've met," the man said. "It was during the mayor's campaign. I'm Terry Wu."

Hamlin put out his hand and gave his name. "You're with the U.S. Attorney's office, aren't you?"

Wu nodded and smiled. "Getting away for the rest of the weekend?"

"Yes, I'm meeting my girlfriend."

"The beautiful woman who was with you at the mayor's dinner?"

"Yes," said Hamlin. Wu had a good memory, a trait Hamlin worked to cultivate. He recalled meeting Wu, but couldn't remember if he had been with a date, or even with a colleague.

"What's her name again?" Wu asked. "I know she's a member of the profession."

"Storm Kayama. She's got a few clients on Maui," Hamlin said, and wondered if he'd imagined the shadow that had fluttered through Wu's eyes.

Wu's smile didn't falter, though, and a second later Hamlin assumed that some idea unrelated to their conversation had distracted Wu for a brief moment. Maybe he forgot to make a call before the announcement to turn off their mobile phones.

"She takes on some women's causes, doesn't she?" Wu asked.

"Yes, that's Storm," Hamlin said.

"She's got a good reputation."

"I agree."

It was a short half-hour flight from Honolulu to Kahului, and Wu dug into his briefcase for some reading material. Hamlin broke out the local paper, to catch up on whether 'Iolani or Punahou School was leading in the track season. Hamlin had run track in high school and college, and he still liked to follow the meets. Event times were much faster now; the fact simultaneously thrilled him and made him feel old.

When the plane landed, both Hamlin and Wu gathered their carry-on luggage from the overhead bins, exchanged good-byes, and went their own ways. Hamlin went out front, where drivers waited for disembarking passengers. He'd forgotten to ask Storm what kind of car she had, and he scrutinized every rental sedan that passed. None stopped for him.

After fifteen minutes, he figured she'd been held up in a meeting or traffic, and he called her mobile, but got no answer. He sat down to finish the paper. Fifteen minutes after that, he began to pace. She still didn't answer her phone. He was one-quarter angry, and three-quarters anxious. He squelched the anger. No, she said she would be here. Something was wrong.

A dark red Chevy Monte Carlo pulled to the curb and Hamlin dashed across the walkway and grabbed the passenger door handle, only to see Terry Wu through the window.

"You need a ride?" Wu asked.

"That would be great. My ride hasn't come." Hamlin got into the passenger seat. "Would you mind giving me a ride to the rental car desks?"

"No problem, they're five minutes away."

Hamlin was pondering why Wu had driven around the airport loop when Wu's cell phone, which was attached to his belt, rang.

In the quiet of the air-conditioned car, Hamlin caught a few of the caller's words. "Trying…voice mail."

"My phone was off during the flight," Wu explained. The caller must have spoken his next statement more quietly, because Hamlin couldn't hear his voice, though Wu's solemn expression drew his attention.

"Where?" Wu said. "When?" A pause. "I'm leaving the airport now. Should take me about twenty minutes."

"Problems?" Hamlin asked. "You can let me out here."

"It's okay, we're nearly at the rental lot."

"There's a quicker exit from the lot than driving by the passenger pickup," Hamlin said, and pointed to a sign that gave directions to the highway.

"I know," Wu said. "I wanted to talk to you." He pulled between the Budget and Avis huts, then slowly put the car in park before he handed Hamlin his card. "Your friend Storm called me about a case I'm involved in. They're bad people. Do me a favor and call me when you find her."

Hamlin stared at him. "Does this have anything to do with the phone call you just got?" His throat was so dry he could barely utter the words.

"No. That was about something else." Hamlin believed him, but Wu's concern and the grim set of his mouth chilled him.

"I will."

Hamlin leaped from Wu's car. He jogged into the Budget hut, which looked less crowded than the others. In less than ten minutes, he had a car and sat, drumming his fingers on the steering wheel at a red light on the road to Kahului. He didn't know where to begin looking for Storm.

◇◇◇

Ryan unlocked the door to his apartment and walked in. "Dad?" He called out, though all senses told him that the place was empty. He walked through the apartment and called again, though the bathroom door was open, Tagama's bed was made and his overnight bag, neatly packed, sat on the taut covers. His dad had reverted to old, disciplined ways. His breakfast plate was washed and in the dish drainer, though when Ryan peered into the rubbish bin, he found the English muffin he'd toasted that morning.

Naturally, Tagama didn't answer his cell phone. But the minute Ryan disconnected, his own rang.

"Where are you?" a man's deep voice asked.

"Who's this?" Ryan didn't bother to conceal his impatience.

"I'm a friend of your father's. Please go outside to the street and I'll call you back."

Ryan snapped his mobile phone closed, and as he did, he caught sight of a white business-sized envelop on the kitchen counter. His name was written in his father's hand. A chill of dread came over Ryan, and he jammed the envelope in his pocket. He didn't want to look. He'd talk to his father's friend first. Maybe the friend could help stop whatever his father had gone to do.

As soon as Ryan was outside, the man called back. "I'm Major Lekziew with MPD. Your father and I have known each other for years. I'd like to talk to you."

"Where's Dad? Is he all right?"

"We'll talk when we meet. I'm driving a green Ford Taurus."

Despite the doorman's offer of a seat in the lobby, Ryan went outside and paced the curb of the busy street. Lekziew drove up within minutes, and Ryan climbed into his car.

"He's dead, isn't he?" Ryan sagged against the passenger door.

Though he'd used denial to get himself out the door that morning, he'd known when Tagama had sent him to meet their clients alone. Yet he couldn't deny his father, nor could he have shared his fears with him.

When he'd found the apartment empty, his last shreds of hope began to disperse like a battered flag in the wind. Now even his strength left him, and he was alone.

Lekziew couldn't help him. Nor did he want Lara, oddly enough. Somehow, he had to survive the next few hours, then tomorrow and the day after. He had to face that Tagama had known his path since he received the phone call last night, and they'd gone to the beach to find Yasuko. He'd joined Guan-Gong.

"I'm so sorry, Ryan," Lekziew said.

Chapter Thirty-five

Unless she was having the out-of-body experience reported by near-drowning or heart attack victims, Storm knew she wasn't dead. For one thing, she felt awful. Her eyelids were glued together, her head pounded, her mouth felt like and tasted like roofing tar, and nausea roiled somewhere beneath the film that wrapped her consciousness. It was like being under water, so she'd give in and succumb to the sticky darkness, which partially buffered her from queasiness and pain.

The other clue that life persisted was the same attractive Asian woman with the gardenia in her hair whom she'd seen in a dream at some point before—when had that been?—came to visit again. The woman's pale, powdered face wore an expression of kindness and concern, and her carmine lips moved to communicate a message that Storm couldn't quite understand. Storm knew that she and the woman didn't exist in the same realm, and the woman was trying to give Storm an important message.

In the real world, which was still out of reach, Storm felt tossed and pitched, rolled from one side to another. It wasn't helping the nausea one bit. Her brain hummed and voices murmured, though Storm couldn't tell if those were the sounds of the geisha-woman attempting to get through to her or if there were other people around her.

As if the static lifted, Storm understood the woman's words. "Help Damon and Stella," she said, and gestured behind Storm. "You can trust Yuan Ling." Then she held up what looked like a long shepherd's crook, a modern one made of pale blue aluminum. It made no sense whatsoever.

Who would help that rat Damon, and what the hell was a Yuan Ling? Then her sticky eyelids came apart. The first thing she saw was Keiko, who was swabbing her face with a damp rag. The smell of vomit and diesel fuel gagged her, and Storm closed her eyes against the nauseating dizziness that washed over her in waves.

Keiko moved a bucket across the floor with her foot. "If you're sick, can you lean over?" she asked in a soft voice.

A crack in Storm's consciousness opened and shed some light on her memory. Yuan Ling was Keiko. Obake or one of his agents named her Keiko after they purchased her from her parents. With as much consideration as they would have for a rubber doll, or a pricey spittoon. Certainly less than a car, which would cost ten times as much.

Vertigo inverted Storm's stomach and she barely got her head over the bucket in time. She knew how insensate she was when she went to wipe her mouth and found her hands tied behind her back. Whatever held them bit painfully into her skin.

Keiko's wrists were tied with some kind of heavy duty plastic tie, and Storm surmised her hands must be secured in a similar manner. Keiko, with her hands in front, had enough mobility to blot Storm's mouth, though her skin was broken and bleeding in places. Storm remembered how Keiko got her hands in front of her at Pauline's house. She was young.

Storm laid her head down gently so as not to bring on another session of vomiting and moved her eyes slowly around the small, enclosed space. Stella was there, too. She sat opposite Storm on a separate bunk, pale as the walls and stiff as a mannequin. The bed swayed, and Storm knew it wasn't just her vertigo, because Stella cringed in pain. Her arms, too, were behind her and Storm knew they hurt like hell.

The room rolled again, and the movement brought on another bout of vertigo, but at least she knew why their space tilted and swayed. It wasn't due to her drug-induced delirium or dizziness. They were in the tiny forward cabin of a boat, and the hum that had added to the confusion in Storm's dream was an engine. A diesel engine, by the odor. Storm hated that smell. Even without the drugs, the smell of diesel made her queasy. Underlying the diesel was a fishy scent, combined with the stink of urine. Storm gulped back nausea again.

With effort, she began to examine the room, which was V-shaped, the contour of the prow. The bunk on which she lay and the one on which Stella sat met at the point of the V. Between the bunks was a small floor space, where Keiko could just about stand upright. Storm, who at five-eight was a couple of inches taller, would have to stoop a bit.

There were narrow horizontal windows above the bunks, too small to climb through, and they were open a few inches. Thank God, or the women would have baked. Hot wind drifted through the side on which the sun shone, which was Stella's side of the cabin. Stella's face was glossy with sweat, and her color was grayer than Storm had ever seen it. She didn't look good.

Storm struggled to a sitting position, which caused pain to shoot from her deadened hands to her cramping shoulders. It was why Stella was trying not to move, though the bouncing boat made that effort impossible.

The boat wasn't moving fast, just steadily, and the ocean had to be clean and glassy, or they would have been tossed around like corn in a popper. As it was, they were subjected to a good deal of swaying with an occasional hard thump. The downside of a clean and glassy ocean was that there was virtually no breeze. Hence, the stifling heat.

Storm looked up at the ceiling. Topside, it would be the forward deck of the boat. As she'd expected, there was a good-sized hatch.

"You've tried the hatch?" she asked, knowing the answer.

"Yeah." Stella said.

The only other space big enough to get through was the door to the cabin, and Storm didn't bother to ask if they'd tried it. There had been some pounding in her drug-induced stupor, and she surmised that this had been Stella and Keiko's work. She'd have done the same.

Next to the cabin door was a smaller door. "What's in there?" Storm asked.

"A toilet," said Keiko, who sat next to Stella on the bunk.

"Anybody on the boat used it?"

"No," said Stella. "But Keiko checked it out."

"No windows?" Storm asked, and the other two women just shook their heads.

"Figures."

The boat crashed over a swell, and Storm nearly tipped over. Stella did, with a cry of pain.

"Who's driving? Do you know?"

"We don't know," said Keiko, "But it's the *Quest*, one of Lara's boats. They must have Lara tied up somewhere else."

"Have you seen her?"

"No, but we think she's topside. The only other cabin is the galley and salon," said Keiko. "They're open to stern of the boat."

"There's another head. They could have her locked in there."

Ugh, thought Storm.

"We heard her voice. She yelled," Keiko said.

"She was scared." Lines etched sadness onto Stella's face. "I didn't protect Angela, and now Lara's in trouble."

"It's not your fault," Keiko said. "What could you do?"

"How did you get here?" Storm interrupted. "Were you both drugged, too?"

Keiko helped Stella sit up. "I called Stella to tell her Carmen and I were okay, but Pauline answered the phone."

"She'd come to get me," Stella said.

"On whose orders?"

"Obake." Keiko spat the word. "Her son is working with him."

"Wayne made her do it." Stella appeared stricken, as if she still couldn't fathom the betrayal. "She was my friend, the only person who knew the vow I made to Barb to protect her daughters." Stella's voice broke. "Pauline knew how I felt about Angela's death."

"Pauline is not a friend," Keiko said.

"Keiko, what did Pauline tell you on the phone?" Storm asked.

"To wait in front of the hospital, or they'd hurt Stella."

"Who's they?" asked Storm.

"Two men in a van. The ones who picked me up."

"Not a black SUV?" Storm asked.

"No," Keiko said. "I know who you mean, but not them."

"What happened after they picked you up?" Storm asked Keiko.

"They took me home, to our apartment. But Pauline opened the door, and she told me to get inside or someone would hurt Stella."

"And then what?"

"Someone big threw a blanket over me. He knocked me down."

"I was already tied up by the time Keiko got there," Stella said. "Pauline could have helped, but she let them take us away."

"How did they surprise you?" Storm asked Stella.

"Pauline called and told me she knew where Keiko was, but she said she had to talk to me in person. She was alone at the door, but someone else came in the bathroom window."

Storm thought for a minute. "Pauline works for Obake?"

"Yes, her son got her involved," said Keiko. Stella nodded.

"I heard he bought that nice house for her," Storm said.

"The BMW, too," Keiko said.

"But she sold her shop to the Tagamas. Do you think Tagama works with Obake?"

"Yes," said Keiko.

"No," said Stella, at the same time.

Storm looked back and forth between them. Stella was the first to speak. "I can't believe that. Tagama helped me. He got me out of the business."

"But he could be threatened. He wouldn't risk his son's safety, not even for you." Keiko spoke without spite.

Stella didn't want to believe it. "He was smart. He'd know how to get around Obake."

Keiko didn't respond; she simply gazed at her bound wrists.

"We'll figure that out later," Storm said. "Right now, let's get ourselves out of here."

She got to her feet and nearly fell over. Not only was the floor heaving with the sea, but she was still weak and shaky. She leaned against the bulkhead next to the bathroom and crouched into a near-sitting position. Then she tried to slide her tethered hands down the back of her thighs.

Shit, that hurt. She was bent at the waist like a paper clip with her hands at the level of the back of her knees while the sharp plastic edges of the ties gouged her wrists, which were sticky and raw. Nor was her flared silk skirt the ideal outfit for contortionism. It hung off one hip and bunched up at the other, creating more bulk for her aching arms to bypass. But the big problem was the curve of her hips. Why had she eaten dessert last night? Or the night before?

Keiko stood up, reached out, and grabbed the drooping side of Storm's skirt. She gave it a sharp jerk. The wadded skirt pulled smooth on one side. "Hold on," Keiko said, and pulled some more.

Storm yelped with the tug on her strained upper arms and shoulders and almost fell onto the bunk.

"No, stay on your feet," Keiko said. "It's easier to move. Now lean back." Keiko still had hold of the hem of Storm's skirt. At least the fullness of the garment let it be pulled free—a straight skirt would have made the job harder.

"One leg at a time," Keiko said, and held Storm steady. The plastic bands cut deeper, but Storm kept going. She could do this; she was limber enough.

When Storm got her hands to the back of her ankles, she knew she was almost there. She was also appalled to see the deep cuts in the sides and backs of her wrists. Blood ran down the backs of her hands toward her fingers and dripped onto the floor. A wave of dizziness hit her.

"Another inch," Keiko said. She put a hand firmly on Storm's back to steady her. "Easy now, put one foot at a time through."

Storm did it, one bare foot, then the other. Successful but sore, she flopped onto the bunk. "Do we have any water?"

Chapter Thirty-six

Storm sipped from the water bottle Stella gave her. She hoped the water would alleviate the drug-induced headache that throbbed behind her eyes. She also waited for the searing pain in her wrists to subside. A fantasy of pounding the shit out of whoever drugged her, tied them up, and imprisoned them in this stuffy, stomach-churning little cabin kept her alert. Pounding in a figurative sense, of course; she remembered the heft of the person who'd hit her from behind.

"Stella, did you know Yasuko?" Storm asked.

Stella looked startled. "Sure, I know her."

Storm wrestled herself into a sitting position and hung her legs over the edge of the bunk. "She's dead."

Both Stella and Keiko gaped at her. Keiko's mouth dropped open, and her eyes filled.

"I'm sorry," Storm said softly.

"She helped me," Keiko whispered.

"She helped Angela, too," Stella said. "Or she tried to."

"You didn't tell me about Yasuko," Storm said to Stella.

"That day when you drove me," Stella said, "I was just getting started. It's not a short, simple story."

"I gathered," Storm said. "We've got time now. Why don't you fill me in?"

"How'd she die?"

"I'm not sure yet. All I know is that she was found at a beach park."

"Obake," breathed Keiko. She sniffled softly, wiped at her eyes. Her hand trembled. "It's my fault."

"Why do you say that?" asked Storm.

"I went to see her after Hiroki Yoshioka shot himself. I wanted to know if Carmen was safe." She looked at Stella, then Storm. "My father had debts, too. I knew what Obake wanted."

"When did you do this?" Stella asked.

"When you were visiting Barb."

Stella's mouth opened, closed, and opened. When the words came, they were low and urgent. "Obake won't let you get away with it."

"I don't care anymore. I had to stop him." Tears flowed down Keiko's face. "But it was selfish, and it got Yasuko killed."

"You were saving yourself," Storm said. She'd realized this when she'd found the girls at Pauline's house. Keiko was furious, and she acted out her anger with power, a trait she'd been denied her entire life.

"I guess so. I have some catching up to do."

"I'm proud of you," said Stella.

Keiko shook her head. "It was worth risking my own safety, but it wasn't fair of me to risk anyone else's."

"Don't say that," said Stella. Now her eyes brimmed with tears.

"You did the right thing," Storm said. "How old were you when Obake brought you into the water trade?"

"Thirteen."

"Not much older than Carmen," said Storm.

"I was smaller," Keiko said with a smile. "They took me to a doctor when I got here. I weighed thirty-five kilos, about seventy-eight pounds. Carmen's going to be taller and healthier. She's already five-one." Keiko sounded like a proud mother.

"And Yasuko told you that Obake was planning to kidnap Carmen?"

"Yes. His men were going to take her from the hospital."

Obake would know Yasuko had told Keiko, Storm thought. Still, Yasuko had done it for the little girl. Probably for Keiko, too.

Keiko, Storm, and Stella sat quietly for several minutes. All three women recognized the sacrifice Yasuko had made.

"Obake is responsible for Yasuko's death, not you," Storm said. She felt a surge of anger on the woman's behalf. "What was she like?"

"She was kind," said Keiko.

"Yes," said Stella thoughtfully. "She was also confused. Um, there's a term. Conflicted. She was conflicted."

"About men?" Storm asked, and felt Keiko's sharp eyes scrutinizing their faces. She looked to her and Stella as authorities, Storm realized. It wasn't the time to tell the young woman she still had to figure out both men and family relationships.

"She was of Chinese ancestry, and born in the Philippines," said Stella. "I think her parents sold her before she was ten."

"How old is she now? I mean—"

"Forty-something. About my age, but it wasn't something we talked about. She kept herself up very well." Stella paused. "She had to, if she wanted to stay as Obake's hostess. It was a matter of survival."

"She'd been with Obake for more than thirty years?" Storm said. The exploitation of another human being to such a degree was hard for her to believe.

"She was his mistress for at least a decade," Stella said. "When I was there, she was his primary consort."

Storm had a vision of the woman she'd seen in her dream. "Did she look like a geisha?"

Keiko laughed.

"Not so fast," Stella said to Keiko. "A modern one, perhaps. White skin, red lipstick, but Western clothing. She often wore a silk flower on her lapel of her designer suit."

Storm remembered the flowers in her dream. "How about flowers in her hair? Gardenias?"

Stella frowned. "I never saw her with flowers in her hair."

"Me either," Keiko said.

"When she was Obake's mistress, did he protect her from other men? Keep her for himself?"

"Yes, but," Stella winced, "it wasn't an easy job. Obake has certain needs." She wouldn't meet Storm's eyes.

"Were you with him?" Storm asked.

"No, I got out before he—"

"I was," Keiko said. "It's when I did this." She rolled up her sleeves and held up her arms. Parallel scars, six or seven inches long, ran the length of both forearms.

"I'm surprised you're here to tell us about it. You're a strong woman," Storm said.

By the look of the cuts, whoever stopped the gush of blood must have known exactly what to do, and how to do it quickly.

"Yasuko," Keiko said.

"She learned about tourniquet pressure points from another suicide," said Stella. "From one she couldn't save."

"Angela?" asked Storm.

Stella shook her head. "Someone else. Angela overdosed."

Storm looked at Keiko. "You knew Angela?"

"Yes," she said quietly.

"Did you know Barb?" Storm asked.

"I met her once. She scares me."

Storm turned to Stella. "Ichiru Tagama rescued you from Obake, but how did Michael Farrell get Barb out?"

"A week or two after Tagama took me away, Michael negotiated a business deal with Obake."

"Michael loved her," Keiko said.

"He traded a successful restaurant, didn't he?" Storm asked.

"Yes."

"And years later, he tried to open another one."

"He didn't know the deal was forever. Obake lets people go, but they owe him, and once they do, they owe him forever." Stella's words were bitter.

"Did you trust Yasuko?"

Both Keiko and Stella hesitated. "Yes," they said together.

"You weren't sure."

"No one was ever sure about anyone around Obake. He knows how to get people to do what he wants. He capitalizes on weakness," Stella said.

She looked at Keiko, who wouldn't look up. "He used Pauline and me to lure Keiko. He knew she would come because she cared enough to rescue Carmen."

"But why would Pauline help him?"

"She may have been protecting her son. Wayne wanted his boss' job on the liquor commission. Pauline had seen what Obake would do if people didn't agree to his terms."

"What did he have on you?" Storm directed the question to Stella.

She looked ashamed. "He bought my house. And I was afraid of him. I'd see his car idling outside, that creepy son of his in the driver's seat. They'd watch me." She glanced over at Keiko. "Then I worried about Keiko."

"And what about Tagama?" Storm asked.

"Tagama is the only person I've ever known who kept Obake off balance. I think Obake is a bit afraid of him. Tagama knows the islands better; he has people working for him that Obake can't reach." Stella sat up straighter. "If Obake got to one of Tagama's people, Tagama had others. And he paid very well. Land, family security, kindness—commodities Obake never understood."

"But Tagama loved Yasuko," Keiko said. "How come he couldn't protect her?"

"Maybe he didn't know how bad her trouble was." A shadow crossed Stella's face. "He's been able to protect Ryan."

"Why didn't Yasuko leave years ago, when Obake took another mistress?" Storm asked.

"Fear." Keiko snapped the word.

Stella was more thoughtful. "It wouldn't be easy to get away. But here's where I think she was conflicted. Part of her liked the attention from men. Remember, it's the only love she's known, except from the girls she cared for. As she aged, she stayed because she could help the young women. She got them better health care, better clientele, better pay. It wasn't until she became involved with Tagama that she knew her life could be different."

"What pay?" Keiko spat. "And what good does it do when you are thousands of miles from home, in a different country and culture, and have no place to go? The only family you have is whores."

Stella leaned against Keiko. Storm thought if she'd been able, she'd have put an arm around the young woman.

"How long has Tagama been seeing Yasuko?" Storm asked.

"We just found out," Keiko said. "When I asked about Carmen, Yasuko told me to talk to him if anything happened to her. She didn't put it in words, but I knew they were close."

"They've kept it very quiet," Stella added.

"I wonder how they met," Storm thought out loud.

"I thought about this," Keiko said. "Yasuko called Stella when I…" she held up her arms. "But a man was there, too. I didn't see him, but I heard his gentle voice. They needed to stop the bleeding. Stella was a half-hour from Lahaina."

"You think Yasuko called Tagama first?" Storm asked.

"Either that or he was there when it happened. She would have known him from his meetings with Obake." Keiko made a little choking sound. "I wish I'd known."

"I'm sure they were planning something. Some way of getting Yasuko away safely," Stella said. "If anyone could do it, Tagama could."

"But he didn't," Storm said in a soft voice.

"No," said Stella. She stared at her feet and shifted her weight. "I wonder where he is now."

Chapter Thirty-seven

As Hamlin drove toward Kihei, he tried to remember what Storm had told him about the dive shop. It was near some docks, as the owner, Lara, had a dive boat or two. The woman must be well-funded, Hamlin thought. He had a friend on O'ahu who had scrimped to get a dive boat, which he captained himself. They were expensive, especially if they had the warm showers, racks for scuba tanks, and whatever specialty fittings they came with. Some trawled for fish while they were underway.

Once Hamlin got to Kihei, he stopped at a shave-ice parlor to ask directions to Lara's shop. The owner knew exactly where Lara's Aquatic Adventures was located, and gave Hamlin directions.

Hamlin was starving, so he ordered a large shave-ice to go. While the owner chatted about Lara's dive shop and how hard it was to keep a business going, Hamlin hid his impatience. Once he had his order, he dashed back to the car. He ate it while he drove, and considered the stop a good omen. The owner was informative and the shave ice, with its hidden ice cream and azuki bean, was delicious. Who knew when he'd get the chance to eat again?

Hamlin found the dive shop easily. It was locked, and no one answered his knocks. The front door was made of thick glass, plus the plate glass windows on either side of the door, where scuba gear and idyllic pictures of boats and underwater scenes were displayed, let in enough light that he could see inside. No one was in the front of the store.

He remembered Storm's descriptions of the work going on, and decided to walk around to the back and see if he could find workers whose power tools kept them from hearing him. Not that they'd come running. They weren't there to answer questions, only to finish the renovation.

Back in the parking lot, Hamlin discovered a side entrance, but it, too was locked. He pounded on the solid wood door, but no one answered. There was a folded note addressed to Damon, though, and Hamlin considered it fair game. He probably wouldn't have torn open an envelope, but this was folded and duct-taped to the door. He didn't even have to pull it off; he just peeked inside.

"Noon. Call the Lady Lawyer," it said. It was signed Fred, with a scrawled phone number.

Hamlin called the number, and a man answered. "Fred, I'm looking for the lady lawyer. You know where she is?"

"Who's this?"

"Ian Hamlin. I'm a friend of Storm's from O'ahu. I saw your note on the door of the dive shop. Hope you don't mind."

"S'okay," Fred said. "I don't know where she went after I saw her. That was a while ago."

"Yeah, I figured. You think she went to Damon's?"

"Could be. She had his car."

"You mind giving me his address? I was supposed to meet Storm a couple of hours ago, and I'm getting worried."

"Lemme call Damon and get back to you."

Fred disconnected before Hamlin could respond, and Hamlin sagged against the side of his car. Fred sounded like a laid-back, trusting guy, but if he didn't call back, Hamlin didn't know where to go. He didn't know Damon's last name, though he figured he could canvas the streets and ask who was doing construction on the shop. Kihei was a small town; he'd find out, but it would take more time and effort than he wanted to spend. He was getting more anxious by the minute.

Five minutes later, Fred called back. Hamlin had already started to pace and glance at his watch. He was beginning to sweat, too. He needed to get out of his work clothes.

"He doesn't answer. Probably at the beach. But you're Storm's friend." Fred rattled off a street in Lahaina, and Hamlin wrote it down.

"You have Damon's phone number?"

Fred gave it to him.

"Thanks, man. I really appreciate it." Hamlin had the car heading onto the main road by the time he disconnected. No one answered at the number Fred had given him for Damon, and Hamlin didn't have any other leads.

Budget Rental Cars had given him a map with their contract, but it wasn't very detailed. Hamlin had it open on the passenger's seat to the page with details of Maui's south coast. He was probably going to have to stop and ask, as the map was geared for popular tourist destinations, and he doubted that residential areas would be on it.

Hamlin's rental car hugged the lane of Honoapi'ilani Highway closest to the chiseled cliff. A steel net like hurricane fence kept boulders from falling into passing traffic. Ten feet from the other side of the road, the Pacific Ocean caressed the shore. Shallow coral reefs under the gentle surface imbued the sea with undulating green and turquoise hues. Farther out, where the depth of the sea plummeted between the volcanic mountain tips that comprise the Hawaiian Islands, the ocean glittered sapphire.

The smaller isle of Lanai hulked along this coast; it looked close enough to swim, Hamlin thought, and the calm ocean lured people to try. There was a popular race from Lanai to Maui. But Hamlin knew individuals had died in the attempt. Though the island looked barely a mile away, it was nearly nine, and the channel was patrolled by sharks.

Ordinarily, big sharks are merely glimpsed by people enjoying the crystalline waters, but a couple times each year, a Tiger or Great White attacks someone. One theory is that the predator has confused the human with its usual prey: turtles, seals, birds, fish, dead animals.

Hamlin also knew that this stretch of the highway was notorious for car accidents. Its twists, turns, and tunnel required a focus that was easily drawn astray by the azure sea. So he kept his eyes on the highway, and found his curiosity aroused when he rounded a tree-shaded curve where the road curved inland and saw a line of police cars on the berm of the road.

Hamlin wasn't the only driver to slow in order to see what was happening. A long column of cars threaded through the area at about twenty miles per hour, and all heads were turned toward the woods to see what was going on. Had to be something big; there was a fire truck, an ambulance, at least six blue-and-whites, plus three or four unmarked cars. People came and went from paths among the trees, which were plentiful enough to block any view of the scene. Not even the ocean was visible.

Hamlin, like everyone else, peered at the officials milling around the vehicles. But when he saw Terry Wu standing by his dark red Monte Carlo, Hamlin's heart lurched. The anxiety that was simmering below the surface of his thinning facade bubbled to the surface. Worse yet, his eye caught Wu's, and Wu, who looked miserable, looked away from him.

There was too much traffic to pull over. Hamlin drove a quarter mile up the road, where he found a narrow turnout on the ocean side of the road. It was approximately where the gawking drivers were speeding up again, and no one took any notice of his quick exit from the stream of traffic.

He dug into his overnight bag, found a T-shirt, chinos, and his running shoes, and changed clothes in his car. Then he threw his bag in the trunk, locked up, and jogged back to where he'd seen Wu.

A burly policeman stopped him where the line of official vehicles began, but he asked the cop to find Wu, and the man did it. Wu appeared after five or ten minutes, and didn't look any happier than he had when Hamlin had driven by.

There was sand clinging to a damp spot on one knee of Wu's dark trousers and the tail on his tucked-in aloha shirt poked out on his left side. Since tucking in one's aloha shirt in the first place was considered fastidious, Hamlin surmised that whatever Wu was up to was rattling him.

Wu spoke first. "Have you found Storm?"

"No," Hamlin said, and raised a hand in the direction of the woods. "Does this have anything to do with her?"

"She's not here. Have you heard anything about this?" Wu waved his hand in the direction of the woods.

"No, but it doesn't look like the annual police picnic, either."

Wu ran his hand through his hair. "We're trying to keep the press away as long as we can. Looks like a couple of local thugs had it out with," Wu faltered, "someone."

Someone? Hamlin's heart squeezed with urgency, and he analyzed Wu's words and the way he'd delivered them. Storm wasn't in the woods, and Wu was being truthful. In a way. He hadn't answered Hamlin's question, either.

"I understand the need for keeping whatever this is under wraps," and Hamlin tilted his head toward the protected area, "but I'm worried about Storm. Do you have any idea where she might be?"

Wu shook his head. "I was hoping you'd found her." He sounded sincere.

Hamlin showed Wu the information he'd gotten from Fred. "Do you know where this is? She may have gone to this address."

"It's a few miles up the road, a little subdivision with town-houses and small homes. Take the first left after Front Street."

Hamlin gave Wu a hard look. "Will you call me if you hear anything?"

"Yes, I will," Wu said.

Hamlin jogged back to where he'd left the car. He forced his way into the slow-moving traffic going toward Lahaina, and found himself at Damon's address within fifteen minutes. As Wu had said, it wasn't far.

Wu was also correct in his description of the neighborhood, which was modest and middle class. No sidewalks, and mostly carports instead of closed garages. Damon's house had a new coat of paint, but the yard was dry and needed mowing. The only car in his driveway was a sun-faded Subaru station wagon.

In Hamlin's experience, most contractors drove pickup trucks, but no truck was parked near the house. He banged on the front door. As he'd expected—it was typical of how the day was going—no one was home. On the other hand, it was four-thirty on a sunny Sunday afternoon. Not quite late enough for people to be coming home for dinner, but way too late for Storm, who was supposed to have met him an hour and a half earlier.

Hamlin tamped down his rising panic, balled up his fist and banged again. Someone next door came to see what the racket was, but no one answered at Damon's house. Hamlin walked across the lawn to the neighbor's. A skinny teenager with an incipient moustache and acne was at the door.

"You know where Damon might be?"

"Haven't seen him," the teenager said. "I thought you were someone else."

"Does he have a lot of visitors?"

The kid shrugged. "I guess. His wife left."

"Any women come by lately?" Hamlin described Storm.

The kid shrugged again, rubbed his upper lip as if it might encourage the spotty moustache. "Maybe. Long hair or short?"

"Shoulder length, wavy. Usually in a French braid."

"She looks like a model? Drives a white Corvette?"

"Maybe." Hamlin thought he'd play out this line of questioning. "When did she come by?"

If he shrugged as much as this kid, he'd get a kink in his neck. But at least the boy was friendly. "Like, yesterday?" the kid said.

"Is that Damon's car?" Hamlin pointed to a late-model white Chrysler Sebring sedan parked between Damon's house and the kid's.

"That's one of his lady friend's. That's what my dad said, anyway."

"Your dad around?"

"Nope, he's out fishing."

"Your mom?"

"No."

Hamlin thanked the young man, and went to check the Sebring. No visible stickers or tags, because the rental companies didn't want to draw attention to visitors' cars. Their offices were full of signs warning tourists about burglaries.

Hamlin peered into the passenger window, and held his breath. On the front seat was a little hairbrush, one that he knew Storm kept in her purse.

The last communication he'd had from her was when she'd called from the beach. By that time, she'd checked out of the hotel. Perhaps she'd put other things in the trunk, but the doors were locked, so he had no way of finding out. The hairbrush was enough, though. She'd been here.

Storm had told him about Lara, and Hamlin knew Lara was the driver of the Corvette. He also knew Lara was engaged to a guy named Ryan Tagama, so Hamlin surmised that Lara's visits to Damon's house were probably either social or business contacts.

Maybe some of the other neighbors had seen Storm. A yapping dog drew him across the street, and he knocked on the door. An older gentleman answered, with a reprimand that silenced the dog. Hamlin explained that he was supposed to meet Storm, and began to describe her.

"I know who you mean," the man interrupted. "Buster and I saw her. A real pretty *wahine*. Right, Buster?" The dog sat by his owner's feet and wagged his tail.

"When?"

"Well, we'd had lunch. It was later than usual because Mrs. Dressle came by with tickets to a fundraiser. Let's see…"

Hamlin wanted to jerk open the door and squeeze the answer out of him. Instead, he made himself take deep, even breaths.

"It was around two, I'd say. Maybe two-fifteen."

"What was she doing?"

"Knocking on his door." The man pointed to Damon's house. "He didn't answer, so she talked on the phone. Someone died. She was kind of upset."

"Did she say a name?" Hamlin had difficulty keeping calm. Could Damon have died? His worker, Fred, would have known, wouldn't he?

The man's eyes rolled as if he were examining one bushy eyebrow, then the other. "Yeah. Buster, did she say Mary?"

The dog wagged his tail again.

"Do you know who Mary is?" Hamlin asked.

"No idea."

"Thanks," Hamlin said, already halfway down the front steps.

Two o'clock. Storm stopped here on the way to meet his plane, but her car was sitting stranded, and so was a Subaru station wagon. Hamlin had a strong hunch she didn't leave this place. At least not under her own will. He looked at the closed house. The front curtains were drawn, and it sat still and unforthcoming.

He dashed back to his car and got his phone. "Wu, are you still at that crime scene?"

"I'm leaving, why?"

"I need help."

Chapter Thirty-eight

Storm looked at the pain on Stella's face. Though it was mostly due to hearing about Yasuko's death and her concern over Tagama's welfare, some of it had to be because her hands were still fastened painfully behind her back.

Storm stood up, bent her knees to move with the swaying cabin, and slid her feet along the floorboards. She was at eye level with the outside deck, stooped slightly in the six inch rise the locked hatch provided. Two oval portholes provided what little fresh air there was. The windows were secured from the outside by large screws.

She needed something sharp, an object with enough edge to saw through the heavy plastic ties that bound their hands. One trip around the tiny room at eye level didn't give her anything to work with. There was nothing on or around the bunks, either.

She opened the door to the head. The toilet had a hand pump, and though the shaft was metal, it was smooth and round. The handle was plastic.

But the fire extinguisher was another matter. It was made of red-painted steel, and it had a metal pin and metal handles. It was also bracketed to the wall of the tiny lavatory with slightly corroded metal calipers.

Stella and Keiko had at first assumed she went into the head to use it, but when she hauled the extinguisher off the wall, they began to pay attention. Keiko got to her feet.

"See if there's anything sharp on this," Storm said, and handed the red tank to her. It was fairly heavy and about eighteen inches in length and six or seven inches in diameter. "I'll try the bracket."

Keiko didn't need to be asked twice. She hauled it to one of the bunks and began loosening one of the bands that attached the hose and nozzle to the tank.

The upper edge of one of the wall brackets was rough and narrow, and Storm began to work her wrist restraints back and forth against it. Each tug sent pain shooting up her arms. Blood began to flow again, and Storm gritted her teeth. The plastic was beginning to fray, though, and she kept at it.

Five minutes later, her eyes were squeezed closed against the pain and the sight of her tattered skin. When Keiko tapped her on the shoulder, she was lost in the effort and she jerked with surprise.

"Put your arms out." Keiko held the flat blade of a box cutter in her free hands.

Storm stared. "Where did you find that?"

"Someone slipped it under the door."

"When?"

"I don't know. We just found it."

"You didn't see who did it?"

"Must have been Lara," Keiko said. She attacked the ties at Storm's wrists.

There was a sharp, painful jerk, and Storm's hands dropped free. Stella stood behind Keiko with a first aid kit.

"I found this in a storage compartment under the bunk," she said, and squeezed a tube of Bacitracin ointment along the cuts on Storm's arms. She then took a roll of gauze and covered the abrasions. Both her arms and Keiko's were wrapped, too.

"What a relief," Storm breathed.

Then the three women looked at each other. "Now what?" Keiko asked.

"Did Lara open the door?" Storm asked.

Both women shook their heads.

"You didn't see her? Not even her feet in the crack under the door?"

"No," Stella said. "But who else would it be?"

Storm thought for a moment. "I wonder how many people are on the boat. Lara, a driver, at least one other person to watch Lara. Probably two. "Did anyone look in on you while I was out cold?" Storm asked.

"No," Stella said. "A man shoved us in here, and he loosened our hoods. We waited for him to leave before we worked at getting out of them."

"He didn't want you to see him," Storm said. "I think that's a good sign."

"We thought so, too," Stella said. "But why are we here?"

"Maybe because of Carmen." Panic lit Keiko's eyes. "They're going to kidnap her again."

"Carmen's hospital room has a guard," Storm told her. "The police won't let it happen." She told them about Yoshinaka's gambling debts at The Red Light.

"You're sure this is Lara's boat?" Storm asked.

"Sure, it's called the *Quest*. We've worked on it," Stella said. "Obake must have stolen it."

Storm looked around the cabin from her seat on the bunk. Someone had left water bottles even though their hands were tied behind their backs. It didn't make sense.

Obake so far had been pitiless. Storm would bet he wasn't on the boat. Yet, that is. Perhaps the three of them, four with Lara, were being taken to him. If Obake wanted information, their captors would be told to keep them conscious and coherent.

Storm stood up and went to one of the narrow portholes. The view was out to sea, blue as far as she could see. The dizzying vastness made her slightly panicky, and she darted to the porthole on the other side.

There she could see a sliver of coastline, a wedge of white sand alternating with rough, black boulders along the shore. But the boat was either rounding a point or was heading toward shore, because the limited scope of the window showed only a glimpse of land. The rest of the view was the same expanse of space.

There were no hotels or other buildings. That meant they probably weren't headed toward Kapalua or Honolua Bay. Those areas would be more developed. There would be people, boats, and activity. She would also be able to see either Lanai or Molokai. Unless they were already off the far shore of one of the other islands. That thought brought another jolt of alarm.

She wondered where Obake might want to meet them. Someplace isolated, where no one could observe. It was easy to get rid of people in the ocean. People often disappeared at sea, especially from boats, never to be seen again.

"How long have we been under way?" she asked.

"You woke up not long after we got going," Stella said. "I'd say we've been on the water for about twenty minutes. This boat was docked in Kihei."

At that moment, Storm glimpsed a dive boat off in the distance. It was way off in the distance, too far away to notice them, but just seeing other people gave her some comfort.

The dive boat got Storm thinking about popular dive destinations. There were a lot of prime dive spots on Maui, including the extinct volcanic crater known as Molokini. She put her face as close to the window as she could and strained to peer around the edge of the window frame. If only she could get her face out farther for a wider scope. Impossible, though.

Her eyes ached with the effort of trying to glimpse a view just out of sight, plus the sun was slicing through the window on the open-ocean side of the boat and heating up the cabin.

"What time is it?" she asked. Her own watch was gone, probably lost in her struggle on the floor of Damon's living room. She'd liked that watch; it was a bright turquoise Nixon surfer's watch. Waterproof, naturally. Lot of good that was doing her now.

Stella answered. "Five o'clock."

"Then that's west," Storm said, and pointed out the window where the sun streamed in.

"And we're heading south," Stella said.

The sight of a big house on a bluff overlooking the shoreline validated Storm's theory. They were heading to the Makena area, toward the area around Lara's beach house. It made sense, if that's what Obake had been trying to acquire. That's where the confrontation would be, where he could rub Lara's face in her defenselessness. It would just about drive her over the edge. He had her vulnerability pegged.

Storm looked over her shoulder at Stella and Keiko. "Did you know about Lara's property at Makena?"

Stella nodded. "Her father left it to her. He bought it for a song in the seventies. It had a fishing shack on it. Barb and I used to skinny dip and drink beer there." She smiled at the memory. "We took the girls when they were little. We'd walk the beach, looking for cowry shells and glass balls. Remember those?"

Keiko looked blank, but Storm knew what she was talking about. The blown glass balls, floats for fishing nets, were now collectors' items. Storm had looked for them with her parents, and she felt a pang at the memory. It was a good memory. She wanted to share it with her own children one day. And Hamlin, too.

She turned to Keiko and Stella. "Where's that box cutter?"

Keiko handed it to her, and Storm went to the door, where she put the palms of her hands flat on the door. She could feel the vibration of the engine through the wood, which was constructed of solid planks an inch thick, unlike the common hollow interior doors in modern buildings. The door had a small brass lever instead of a door knob, which moved freely up and down.

"Do you remember what kind of lock is on this door?" she asked.

Chapter Thirty-nine

Storm ran the blade in the thin space between the white-painted door and the bulkhead. The door was such a tight fit that the blade caught on bumps and rough spots in the wood. About two inches above the brass door handle, the blade came to a solid stop.

Neither Keiko nor Stella could remember a lock, and the only part of this cabin with which they had any familiarity was the head. Stella had been out on the boat twice, Keiko once.

Keiko, who had taken up a post at the land-side window, reminded Storm and Stella that she wasn't confident in the water. She was doing all right with the motion of the cabin, though. Better than Storm, who was beginning to feel the headachy lethargy that preceded seasickness. She was no stranger to motion sickness. Headache and lassitude were the first stage; the next would be weakness and nausea. After that, she'd be on her knees at the porcelain bowl. At that point, she'd welcome Obake throwing her into the ocean, no matter how far out they were.

They needed to get out of there. Storm went to the porthole, gasped at the fresh air, and went back to the blade she'd left sticking in the crack of the door. She'd checked the latch in the tiny head, which was a metal hook that slipped into a little round eye. It would a blessing if that were the kind of obstacle that held them in the cabin.

It was doubtful; when she tried to push up on the device, it didn't budge. The barrier felt solid from above and below, and the blade encountered it with a soft metallic click. There were probably many kinds of locks that she didn't know about, but the only other one she could think of was a bar that slid into a pocket or bracket.

So she carved away tiny slivers of paint to give the blade more lateral play. Meanwhile, the close, hot work made her dizzier and more nauseated.

"You don't look so good," Keiko said. "Let me work on it."

Storm lurched to the window, where she let the light breeze ruffle her hair. Then she lay down. Just for a minute.

Next thing she knew, Stella was at her side, tugging on her arm and whispering, "Wake up."

The cabin had cooled, as the sun no longer blasted through the porthole. It was late in the afternoon, still light, but the sun was setting. Storm sat up.

"You got the door open?" she asked softly.

Keiko nodded. "I'm holding it closed. I thought we'd better have a plan."

Storm felt the lowered timbre of the engines. "We've slowed."

Stella handed her a half-empty water bottle. "It's the last one. We saved it for you."

Storm took it gratefully and drank it in one go. She was thirstier than she'd thought. Drugs, heat, seasickness. This sucked. She went to the porthole. "We're a lot closer to land." She peered out the window on the other side. "Looks like a bay."

She looked at Keiko. "Boats are required by law to carry life jackets. If we had to swim, could you do it with a jacket?"

Storm would find it an impediment, but she'd grown up around the water. She watched Keiko's tentative nod.

They'd have to stay together. It would not be a fast or secretive getaway. Last resort, Storm thought. How many alternatives would they have?

"Let's make a plan."

The other two women nodded and gazed at her with expectation in their alert and hopeful eyes.

Shit, thought Storm, and took a deep breath. "There's only one way out of here, so we've got to go together, as quietly as we can." The other two nodded again.

She pointed at the fire extinguisher. "Keiko, you take that. If you discharge it, do it right in his face. Don't hesitate to clobber someone with it. Hard."

Keiko winced, but nodded again. They were starting to remind Storm of windshield hula dancers, the kind with their heads on springs. For a moment, she wished that her only responsibility was herself. Three people meant three times the challenge of staying organized, three times the chance of a fuckup. Three times the likelihood of capture, and not one of the women would leave anyone behind. Which could be good or bad.

"Stella, you take the knife blade. Keep it hidden, if you can."

Stella had a set to her jaw and a glint in her eye, and Storm remembered Keiko cutting the electrical wire to Pauline's house. She'd been blasted off her perch with a shock that could have killed her. Still, she'd scraped herself off the ground looking for a fight. This team was going to have to be good enough.

"Is there a galley?" Storm asked.

"No stove, but there's a sink and a small refrigerator," Stella said.

"How about a salon, or seating area?"

"It's one space. There's a helm there, too, under the canopy."

"Is that where the captain will be?" Storm asked.

"Not necessarily. There's a flying bridge. It's a nice, calm day, so he'll probably be up there. The view is better."

"Is it covered?"

"It has a canvas cover that can be folded up, kind of like a convertible top."

"And a ladder from the salon?"

"Yes, the ladder is about a four-foot climb." Stella frowned. "It'll be hard to sneak up on him."

Storm thought a moment. "How many people surprised you in your apartment?"

"At least two," Keiko said.

Stella agreed. "The person who threw the bag over my head was big and strong. I think he was hiding in the bathroom."

"A man got me, too," Keiko added. "Right after Stella."

"Then there was someone waiting in the van," Stella said.

"And someone was in the back with us," Keiko said.

"You think there are three or four people?" Storm asked.

"I haven't heard any voices other than Lara's," Stella said. "It seems like four people would make some noise."

"Unless they were told to be quiet," Keiko said. "Obake's guys don't talk much."

"Was Lara in the back of the van with you?"

"I don't know," Stella said, and neither did Keiko. "They kept stuff between us."

"What kind of stuff?"

"Tarpaulins, maybe." Stella said. "I smelled paint."

"Does Damon have a van?" Storm asked. "I've only seen him drive a pickup."

"No, but a couple of the workers have vans," Keiko said.

"We need the element of surprise," Stella said.

"Once we're out of here and through the salon, we need to split up," Storm said. "If they capture one of us, at least two more are free."

"If one of us gets captured, sit tight. We'll come back to get you," Keiko said.

"Good idea," said Storm.

The three of them stood for a long moment. Keiko held the door closed.

"I'll go first," said Storm.

Chapter Forty

On her way out, Storm grabbed the canvas bag that had been used in her capture. Now that she could see it, she recognized the rough sack as the type that stored lines and other nautical equipment. It had *Quest* stenciled on the outside.

Stella and Keiko were close behind, and all three women tiptoed through the low door into what passed for a galley. The boat was configured in a typical fashion for a dive boat. Only the forward cabin and the toilets had privacy, and the women now stood under the bridge in a large seating area, which was half in open air, half under cover of the bridge. It was enough space for at least a dozen people to mill around, take off gear, relax on the cushioned banquettes, and mostly stay out of the way of the crew.

To the women's great relief, the space was empty. All three of them had been poised to challenge whatever guard was posted, and no one was there. Someone was steering from the bridge directly overhead, but he couldn't see them, as they stood under him. The reprieve was palpable; someone behind Storm released a long, pent-up breath.

Storm realized she'd anticipated confronting Damon. She wanted to tell him what a traitorous scumbag he'd turned out to be.

So where was he? And where were Obake's people?

If Storm was going to commandeer a boat and take hostages, she'd have had someone posted in the stern, where he or she could watch both the cabin and the helm. Someone else would be fore, and she'd want another person moving around.

The women faced aft, toward a rock outcropping that defined the outer limit of the bay. Waves hit the lava rocks and flowed over their broad, imposing shoulders. Because the boat had recently turned, they were about a quarter mile from the most prominent boulders. The shore itself, part rocky and part sandy, was at least a half mile away.

The women eyed the long, empty banquettes uneasily. "I thought Lara would be out here," Keiko whispered.

One of the bench cushions lay on the deck and another was knocked askew, which gave the impression either someone had been in a big hurry to find something in the storage compartment beneath the seat, or there'd been a scuffle.

"Maybe she's inside the banquette," Stella whispered. Her eyes darted from the dislodged cushion to Storm.

"We can't go out there now, the captain will see us," Keiko said.

Stella nodded. "The others must be forward."

She and Keiko looked pale and scared, but Stella held the knife blade and Keiko carried the fire extinguisher. Both were alert and poised for action.

Storm pulled on a line that had been left on deck. Another sign of either carelessness or a struggle, she thought. A rope like this should be stowed under the banquette, or some place where it wouldn't tangle and no one would trip over it. She wound it into a loose coil and slipped the loop over her shoulder.

The women stood for several minutes, waiting to see if someone would come to check on them. It would be better to ambush someone coming from the forward deck, as this person would be clambering along the narrow starboard or port decks, than to be the one climbing. Vigilant, no one spoke. No one approached, either.

The twin diesels throbbed beneath their feet, and the boat reached the other end of the bay, where the captain reversed its path. Keiko bent her knees and rode the surge caused by the ocean swells behind them. Storm had heard this called the following sea, and knew it could swamp a boat on a rough day. The boat rode it easily, like a cork. Stella put out a hand and braced herself against a small sink. Storm swallowed to get her stomach out of her throat. The vessel turned 180 degrees to head back across the large bay.

The women steadied themselves, and Storm held up a hand. "I'll go up," she whispered softly, and pointed toward the helm. "Once I'm up there, go in different directions."

Stella looked alarmed at the implication that Storm might not be successful, but Keiko gave a grim nod.

Storm had no time to spare. The ladder sat starboard of center, which was, after the last turn, on the ocean side of the boat. If the captain was keeping his eye toward shore, his attention would be away from the ladder. She had to sneak up on him before he made another turn. And once her head rose to the level of the bridge, she had to be fast.

She climbed. The ladder was only five vertical steps, a little more than four feet.

The helmsman heard her. "You came up for the view?" he asked without turning around. He thought she was someone else, cocky bastard.

"Yep," said Storm, and pulled the bag over his head in a smooth motion. At the same time, she leaped to throw her weight against him. Though she'd aimed for his shoulders, he was at least six feet tall, the chair was higher than she'd anticipated, and he outweighed her by more than fifty pounds. She only knocked him half-way.

Startled, he shot sideways, and his shorts slid on the shiny plastic of the high captain's chair. Reflexively, he seized the nearest stationary object, which was the boat's wheel. The *Quest* skewed in a sharp U and the deck tilted suddenly. A shriek of alarm came from below.

Storm hoped no one had fallen overboard, but she didn't have time to stop and look, or even call out. She, too, reeled with surprise. Right before she'd pulled the bag over his head, Ken McClure had turned his head, shock and confusion on his handsome face. Her own expression must have mirrored his.

What was he doing at the wheel? He was probably Lara's most important colleague at the dive shop, her second in command. She had never seen Ken and Damon in conversation, though she had to admit she hadn't spent enough time in the shop to know how the men interacted. Perhaps they'd kept their relationship hidden from Lara, too.

He clung to the wheel with one hand and grappled with the bag over his head with the other. He also screamed bloody murder, or threatened it in a muffled rant, while he kicked out with one muscular, violent leg. He had wrapped the other leg around the chair pedestal with his foot hooked under the circular footrest.

At least he couldn't see where to aim his kicks. Storm body-checked him again, higher and harder.

The slick, waterproof upholstery of the chair seat was a big help. So was the kicking leg, which thrashed to reestablish balance. Storm gave it a push to tip him further.

This final shove accomplished what Storm intended, and the man crashed to the floor with a scream. But when he went down, the foot in the circular footrest was trapped. His ankle snapped with a sound that nearly made Storm gag.

He screamed again, thrashed against the bag over his head. The leg twisted in its aluminum noose. It popped free, bent at an angle that sickened Storm. She could see the sharp edges of bone poking at the skin.

Pain must have overcome him, because he flopped once more and lay still. Storm was relieved, for herself and for him. She straightened him onto his side, bad leg on top.

He didn't respond; the man was out cold. The leg looked awful, the jagged bones ready to pop through. As it was, he had to be bleeding internally. She tied his hands behind his back, but didn't secure him to anything. To do that, she'd have to move him to one of the stanchions that held the canopy, and the thought of dragging that leg into another position made her skin crawl.

Storm glanced one last time at Ken's motionless form, then noticed with a gasp that the boat was only fifty feet or so from the rocky point that defined the bay. Boulders sharp enough to slice through an aluminum hull like diamonds cutting coal hulked below the surface of the water.

She leaped into the captain's chair and jerked the wheel starboard. There was a rock only a few feet from the prow. Storm knew that water distorted distance, but she didn't know how much. Nor did she have any idea of the *Quest's* draw. Five feet? Ten? The black shape looked like she could stand on it and keep her head out of water.

Scuttling the boat might be a good escape strategy, but she couldn't do it until she knew where Keiko and Stella were. They were looking for Lara, and if all three were trapped below, it would be a terrible plan. She had to keep the vessel safe until she knew that everyone was free.

From the flying bridge, Storm had a good view of the sea and the fore and aft decks. The foredeck was empty. So was what she could see of the salon, except she knew how easy it was to hide in the galley area.

Who had cried out when Ken grabbed the wheel? Storm thought it had been a woman's voice, and her eyes swept the water. Where was she?

No people, but something big was under the boat—

Wait, she could see part of a person on the port deck. Behind the rise of the cabin, she could make out the bend of a leg; the rest of the person was hidden. Keiko or Stella? God, she hoped not. She stood up to get a better look, but she also had to watch where she was steering the boat.

Whoever it was hadn't moved. It looked like a man's leg, which pleased her. Maybe Keiko had bashed someone with that fire extinguisher.

She hoped the young woman had tied him up securely. Any of Obake's people could overcome her the same way she'd overwhelmed the helmsman. The boat's starboard side faced land now, but she'd have to turn again, which would make her more vulnerable.

Her best option would be to get the *Quest* in a safe position and leave the helm. The few times she'd helped friends with their boats, anchors were stowed in a forward hold. As she remembered, setting one was a noisy operation. She was wary of attempting it alone, especially when she didn't know where the rest of the crew was. She would be in a bad position if the enemy caught her leaning out over the water with a heavy object in her hands.

They were about a half mile out and there was little wind, though there were small swells, which would eventually carry the boat in. The breeze was off-shore, though, which would counteract the push of the ocean toward shore. Storm wasn't an expert on boats, but she understood swells and currents from surfing. She knew the ocean was unpredictable. Chances were good it would push them onto the rocky shoals.

So how much time would she have if she drove to the middle of the bay and left the helm? She simply didn't know, and Keiko and Stella still weren't visible.

Except for the unconscious Ken and someone's inert leg, no one was evident. Where were Obake's men, and the rest of the crew? Where was Damon, that traitorous scumbag?

Did that motionless form on the port deck belong to Lara? Why hadn't Keiko or Stella helped her?

Storm eyed the rocks on the other side of the bay, and gently turned the wheel. No sudden movements this time. She didn't want to draw attention to the helm. Storm concentrated on the currents and the vessel's rise and fall in the sea. She kept the *Quest* on the course Ken had followed.

The only other people within view were on shore, where a burly man in swim trunks and goggles seemed to be shouting at two tall, thin guys in suits. Though the heavy guy was stomping around and pointing at his watch, the incongruity of suits on the beach was what caught her eye.

Storm looked around for binoculars, but Ken hadn't left a pair nearby. Next, she looked for a boat horn or a radio, but didn't see either. Could she wave at these people for help?

When a woman's urgent voice shouted from behind her, she almost jumped out of the captain's chair.

Chapter Forty-one

"Storm!" Keiko yelled.

Storm spun to see a man struggling in Keiko's grasp. With his arms tied behind his back, he lurched and stumbled across the rolling deck.

Thrashing against Keiko's restraints, he went down hard and swore. Though many of the words were unintelligible, the F's sprayed saliva. The fall hadn't hurt his mouth any. He winced when Keiko hauled him up by his hands. Storm suppressed a sympathy grimace; Keiko knew exactly how sore his shoulders would be.

"Fuckin-A, ya fuckin' bitches. I'm just helpin' Ken."

Storm realized her mouth was hanging open. It was the guy she'd seen in the dive shop, hanging around with Ken. He'd caught her eye because he'd been shirtless—a bit cocky, she'd thought—and one arm had a colorful tattoo of a bald eagle carrying a round ball with a fuse. He was still shirtless, and the eagle on his deltoid muscle practically flapped its wings with the fellow's aggravation. Those surf trunks looked familiar, too. A wardrobe as extensive as his vocabulary.

"Now you know what we felt like." Stella kicked at the back of his bare heels.

The man gave a little hop and snarled over his shoulder at her. "Ow." He choked back a few indecipherable words.

Stella drew back her sneaker again, threatening. He jerked left to avoid her and bumped into Keiko, who gave him a hard shove, then kept him from falling by hauling back on his arms again.

The women were indignant and showed it.

"You know this guy?" Storm asked them.

"His name's Billy," Keiko said. "He's a friend of Ken's."

Billy glowered at Storm. "Looka that. The fuckin' lawyer."

All three women ignored him.

"We found Damon," Stella said. "He's unconscious and tied up."

Storm pointed toward the inert leg. "Is that Damon?"

"Fuckin' traitor," Billy muttered.

"Traitor?" Storm asked. "Why?"

Billy looked at the blade Stella was holding. "Cuz he gave that to you."

"How do you know I didn't have it in my bra?" Stella asked.

"You could hide a whole tool chest in there, couldn't you?" Billy snickered, which elicited a shoulder-wrenching pull from Keiko.

"You're in no position to be rude."

He grunted out a few more obscenities, then leaned toward Stella. "But you didn't have it in there, did you? We checked."

Stella's smile turned to an expression of disgust and her hand flew to her chest. Billy sneered. "Damon slipped it under the door."

"Why'd he do that?" Keiko asked.

"Wimpy fucker felt guilty."

"Why'd you kidnap us?" Storm asked.

"Orders. We were gonna let you go. No big deal."

Storm doubted every word that came out of the man's mouth. No big deal? She felt like spitting at him, but it wouldn't help. Plus, she'd probably miss and hit one of the women.

"Why did you want us on this boat?" Stella asked.

"Get you out of the way for a while. For your own good."

"Oh sure." Keiko tugged his arms. Tendons bulged all the way from his shoulders up his neck. It looked as if he tried not to cry out.

"Did you break into my hotel room?" Storm asked.

"Your hotel room? Hell, no." He seemed to think for a minute. "The local syndicate might have, though."

"Working with them doesn't bother you?"

Billy looked at her and tried to shrug, but Keiko gave the rope another wrap around her fist, and he flinched reflexively.

"Where's Lara?" Stella asked.

"She's around," Billy said. He acted like she was getting her nails done.

"Where?"

"I don't know. Whaddya think, I'm her babysi—"

"Jesus!" Storm shouted. A silhouette had passed under the boat, visible for a split second in her peripheral vision. She swerved away from it at the same time a swell rolled under the boat. At least she thought it was a swell.

The shadow glided by again, close to the boat's hull. Huge, half the length of the *Quest*. Dark, with a blunt head and a tapering tail. It was a brief glimpse, but every atavistic gene in her subconscious knew that shape.

Chapter Forty-two

The *Quest* took the swell abeam. An awkward and potentially dangerous maneuver, which made Lara wonder what Ken was doing, but she'd had her own trials over the last half hour or so. She sat with her back against the rise of the cabin, out of the view of anyone aft. Not even Ken could see her here, which was nice and private. She needed to think.

About an hour ago, after they were well out to sea, she'd heard a pounding sound and asked Ken, who was at the helm, what was going on. He acted like he hadn't heard her question, but that dildo friend of his started to laugh. Ken shot him a look, and Billy shut up. She liked that about Ken, his sense of leadership. She wished Ryan was more of a leader instead of the pushover he was around his father.

Wait, that wasn't entirely fair. Ryan's friends had a lot of respect for him. He was smart *and* kind. Her problem was his dad, who was an associate of the man who'd ruined her family.

She didn't know whom to trust anymore. Ken and Billy were up to something, and it wasn't good. Billy didn't have enough brain cells to generate a spark, let alone an original idea. Still, Ken brought him into the shop to help out. Ken said Billy had standuplitude. Billy had been in Desert Storm with Ken, and would do what Ken asked him. Ken had brains and some money; Billy had brawn, balls, and he was new in town. Easier for him to get around unnoticed.

Now she just didn't know. Storm, Stella, and Keiko were unwilling passengers on the *Quest*. Ken might be intelligent, but he'd teamed up with Billy, who was neither smart nor kind.

A confused groan escaped her, and Lara looked around, startled by her own anguished noise. Relax, no one could hear her; the drone of the engines and slapping of the sea against the *Quest's* hull would drown out all but the sharpest noises. Was she being betrayed again? By Ken, to whom she'd revealed confidences and allowed into her business?

She did not have good luck with men. Ken, another handsome bad boy, was a shameless flirt who made certain parts of her body feel all loose and liquid. He'd planted the seed of discontent when he asked her why she was marrying the guy who owned the real estate instead of getting it in her own name.

Lara's heart contracted. When Stella introduced her to Ryan, she thought her dreams had come true. In the early days, Ken's suggestions and innuendos bounced off her like rice on a drum.

It had been a black day when she discovered Paradise Consortium, on whose board Obake sat, was a partner with the Tagama's real estate company. They had part ownership in a handful of South Coast properties, among them the shopping center where her dive shop was located.

No wonder Ryan had been flustered when she'd suggested his dad give the land to them for a wedding present. Ryan knew Obake was in on it, despite her family history. The information had practically gutted her.

Stella was clueless, especially when it came to men. Always had been, always would be. Stella adored Ryan. So did Barb, for that matter. In her lucid moments, which were less and less frequent, Barb flirted as if she were the fiancée. Stella had been friends with the elder Tagama for years. Another Obake-corrupted relationship.

Lara's eyes swept the coastline. The *Quest* was miles from Kihei, and approaching the appointment she'd made. Her stomach clenched with nerves. They were about a half mile off shore, in deep water, and out of cell phone range, just as she and Ken had planned.

Three men were on the beach, small in the distance, but Lara could pick out Obake; he was the one in swim trunks and no shirt. He strutted back and forth as if stalking the *Quest*, his blocky, muscled torso the color of oiled teak. He knew she was watching, and he enjoyed the attention.

He'd contacted her, and told her she was lucky that he'd give her a minute or two, the respect due a business associate. She didn't buy that for a nanosecond. He didn't consider women business associates, especially if they were Farrell women. She was the only one who wasn't his whore. Or maybe she was, and she just didn't know it yet.

He told her he'd altered the sales contract that Mary Robbins had with her when her car went over the bridge. He was now the new owner of Michael Farrell's pretty little house on the private beach. Even if someone was suspicious about Mary's death, no one would dare confront him.

But there was something he wanted or needed, because he'd initiated the meet. The ball was still in her court.

Lara's eyes narrowed with hate. His fat feet tainted the sand. He contaminated the whole area: her family land, her nest egg, her place of special memories. The sight made her seethe; it sent her to pick through jagged rubble of her childhood. Memories with teeth.

When had it all fallen apart? Long before Angela started using cocaine and crystal meth. Before Angela decided, like their mother, that success was measured in the men she attracted and the trinkets they offered. Before she dropped out of school. But it wasn't Angela's fault. Barb had the illness, too. Like a nest of termites that ate from the inside until the structure collapsed, Obake had planted the rot.

She thought she'd escaped the shadow that hung over the Farrells. She'd had a chance to throw off the curse. But she'd made choices without knowing where they would lead, and some of them had come back to bite her.

Had she placed her trust in the wrong person again? Ken and Billy had kidnapped three women who were Lara's friends and colleagues. Billy was in Obake's pay, but Ken? She'd believed in Ken.

They'd either shamed or threatened Damon into going along with the kidnapping, but Damon had freaked when he overheard Billy tell Ken they were far enough out to sea to throw the women over. That's when he'd come to her and suggested sliding the blade to the box cutter under the door. Like Damon, she'd been stunned at the plan, and gone along with the idea to help the women.

She hadn't been there when Billy caught Damon at the door to the cabin. Though Damon had been successful at getting the blade to the women, he was now trussed up like a luau pig, ready for the oven. Lara wasn't sure where Storm was, but Stella and Keiko had escaped.

The women were not part of her plan to meet Obake. They weren't to be put in harm's way. No way.

Lara dragged her eyes back to her adversary, who pointed to his watch and shouted something at his two bodyguards. One shrugged, an I-don't-know gesture. Obake yelled something else, and the other guy pulled out a cell phone.

Obake loosened his shoulders by flexing and rolling them, then splashed into the water. He was actually going to swim to the boat. He'd boasted that he would, but she'd argued with Ken about this. When she told Obake she'd be arriving via boat, she was sure he'd have his henchmen find a bigger, faster yacht to intimidate her.

But Ken was adamant that Obake wouldn't pass up the chance to show off his strength, half-nude body, and athletic prowess in front of a female audience. Ken had been right about that part.

Ken, who had loaned her money for a share in the shop. He'd helped her buy all the scuba gear and organized the dive tours. The shark encounter was his idea, and it was a winner. Ken liked excitement, even in the tongue-in-cheek guise of BRA, the Beach

Rescue Alliance. Unlike Ryan, who hid Paradise Consortium's involvement from her, and backed away from arguments. Even when she made him sleep on the sofa.

Ken's ties to Billy were strong. The men had a past, a situation from their service in the Middle East. Lara had overheard Billy allude to a village, which he called by a name she couldn't remember, but she wouldn't forget the insinuation in his voice. Ken had become very quiet.

Lara took a deep breath, and another. She had to keep thinking and stay on top of this. Some of her choices had led down unexpected paths and onto new decisions, then other problems cropped up. It was hard to remember everything. The people involved were pushing her scheme according to their own different agendum, in ways she couldn't have anticipated.

Lara squinted at the water. Obake was doing the crawl, breathing with each stroke. One arm flashed in the sun, then the other, and his legs churned behind him. Not a pretty stroke, too much splash. Lara knew this because of Angela, who was a beautiful swimmer, if only she'd stayed with it.

Look at that. Obake made pretty good time, despite his method. Lara looked at the deep blue and watched for shadows. The sharks should be coming any minute now. Her *'aumakua*.

Chapter Forty-three

"What's wrong?" asked Stella. Three faces, even the belligerent Billy's, stared up at Storm. Anxiety tightened the skin around their lips and eyes.

"I saw something." But it had disappeared, and the boat approached another turning point. She turned the wheel in a gentle sweep this time, unlike the erratic wrench she'd given it when she saw the shark's silhouette.

What else would look like that? Storm looked around. Though they were fairly close to land to see a creature as large as—well, what she thought she'd seen. Fifteen, twenty feet? More than half the length of the boat, but maybe the water magnified it. Lara's *'aumakua*.

"Something in the water?" asked Keiko.

Billy smirked. "Probably a big bad turtle."

Keiko gave him stink-eye and pulled on his ties like he was an unpredictable pit bull.

A thumping distracted all of them. Ken was still in the same position, and appeared to be unconscious. He'd have a hard time moving around with that awful fracture even if he did wake up.

"I don't see Damon," Storm said. The prone form on the port deck was no longer visible. "You sure he was tied up?"

"Yes," Stella said, "but I'll go check." She held the knife blade as if she wouldn't hesitate to use it.

Keiko watched her with an anxious expression, then allowed a movement in the water to catch her eye. "Hey, someone's swimming toward us."

"You're right." Storm stood up. "He looked right at us."

"Yeah, look at that." Billy's voice was amused. "And I have a hunch he'll help some of us out."

"We've got to warn that guy." Storm began to turn the boat toward him. "I think I saw a shark."

"He'll be fine," said Billy. "He doesn't want a boatload of fuckin' women driving up to him."

Storm ignored him.

"Okay, do it. You'll see," Billy said.

Keiko gave him a yank that made him grunt.

"You guys are fucked," he sneered.

Keiko jerked on him again, a surprising burst of strength that made the cords in his neck stand out like cables. He went to his knees, "Fuhhhh—," and onto his face.

Half a second later, Storm's, Keiko's, and Billy's attention was diverted by the sight of Damon edging along the narrow deck between the ocean and the side of the cabin. His eyes, dark with terror, flitted back and forth from the water to Storm's face. Stella held onto his tied hands, but he was unable to hold on to the stanchions that allowed Stella to walk the gunwale with security.

He glanced again at the ocean; at one point, he teetered, and she steadied him. "MMMM. MMMM." He tried to communicate through a gag of duct tape.

"You think he wants to talk to us?" Stella helped him make the big step down to the cabin, where he sat on the gunwale and leaned against a stanchion. She sat next to him. His face was so pale and sweaty he looked like he was made of plastic.

"Where's Lara?" Stella ripped the duct tape from his face.

Storm blinked. He wouldn't have to shave for a month.

The tape's sting had drawn tears. "I tried—"

"I've had enough of this." Stella grabbed his arm and yanked him to his feet. He teetered on the seat cushion just as Billy drew the crew's attention by making a high, nervous sound that hinted at hysteria. His eyes bulged at a sight abaft.

Storm's first thought was that he was taunting Damon, and she gave him a disgusted and fleeting glance. Her eyes went back to the swimmer she'd seen. Where was that guy? Closer than she thought—he was within twenty yards, splashing toward the boat and looking up from time to time through his swim goggles.

She looked down at the throttle and carefully pushed it toward neutral. The last thing she wanted to do was run over him.

"Hey, there are a bunch of people on the beach—" Stella said, but a high-pitched screech from the water interrupted her.

At the same time, a dorsal fin sliced the sea's ripples into a smooth V-shaped stream, then disappeared into the cerulean depths. From her high position on the bridge, Storm watched the huge, dark shape circling the swimmer from below.

The man might not have been able to see it twenty feet below his scissoring feet, but he could certainly feel the vortex of its passing—just as if someone had pulled the plug on a drain.

His head pivoted from side to side. The racing goggles he wore magnified his terrified gaze to a pop-eyed caricature. Billy emitted a series of terrified squeaks. Everyone else gaped, struck dumb by the apparition that glided beneath the swimmer.

The sleek, muscular body flashed to the surface of the water without even a splash. Effortless in its liquid element. Huge. Grinning needles, flat black stones for eyes. Impassive, testing, taking stock. Barely a ripple in its wake.

Though Storm pushed the throttle into gear, twenty yards was too far. The shark moved like a torpedo. The man shrieked again, a guttural and blood-freezing sound. Vertical in the water, he levitated to his waist, while his arms reached for the impassive skies.

Storm opened her mouth to scream, but no sound emerged. It was like a nightmare where she couldn't run, couldn't scream, and was paralyzed by terror. From her elevation, she was the first person to see the enormous creature rise to meet the swimmer.

The man shot into the air. A sheet of white water shielded the collision, though Storm reflected later that perhaps her brain simply blocked a horror she couldn't face. The last image she remembered was the swimmer as he windmilled his arms and flopped over. Then he disappeared.

The shark flashed back and forth, alternating gray and belly-white, a missile of death. The water roiled with activity, and it took the spectators a long moment to comprehend that the attacker wasn't alone. More sharks than anyone wanted to acknowledge thrashed through the pinkish foam.

Riveted by disbelief at what they'd witnessed in the water, no one in the cabin noticed Lara, who crept along the same narrow gunwale where Stella and Damon walked only a few minutes before. A faint smile played across her face.

Nor did any one see Ken make his move. On one leg, he struck like a cobra and shoved Storm from the helm.

Storm flew off the seat at the first blow. Though she landed hard enough to have the wind knocked out of her for the second time that day, she did not have her feet hooked under the footrest.

The *Quest* pitched violently to one side as Ken seized the wheel. He got her steadied just in time to grasp the result of his attack. When the *Quest* veered, Lara, Damon, and Stella, all in precarious positions and stunned by the scene they'd witnessed, were tossed overboard.

Ken shot away from the helm and half-scaled, half-slid down the ladder. The fracture was already bad; impact with the deck shoved the jagged bones through the tender and purple skin above one ankle.

He dashed, bleeding, across the deck. "Lara," he screamed, and dived in.

Chapter Forty-four

Storm stumbled back to the helm. She was hyperventilating with terror, and her hands shook so badly they slid from the round black ball on the throttle. After two tries, she got the engines into neutral so the *Quest* didn't sail away from those overboard. Only ten yards from the stern, the gentle turquoise water had been transformed into a pinkish pool, through which dorsal fins still slashed like butcher knives.

Billy moved fast. He leaped to his feet and climbed, Keiko-style, through his tethered hands. Using the rope that Storm had used to bind Ken, he tied a large loop and lobbed the line into the water.

The sharks hadn't yet responded to the new people in the water; blood and other material in the pink pool still distracted them.

Storm slid down the ladder face out, her feet not even touching the steps. Her eyes were on an implement that she hadn't seen until that very moment. A long aluminum rod with a hooked loop was tucked under the gunwale along the starboard bench. Yasuko's message: *Help Stella and Damon.*

Storm tugged the pole free of its brackets. Billy pulled the taut rope over the gunwale and backed slowly, grunting with effort. A hand, streaming with seawater, clutched the gunwale. Lara slid onto the deck.

Storm thrust the looped aluminum tool toward Stella, who was holding Damon afloat.

"Stella, grab the hook," Storm shouted. "I'll help him next."

Adrenaline surged through both her and Stella, because Stella pulled hand over hand and flopped onto the banquette. Keiko stepped in to wrap her in a dry towel and safety.

Storm returned to Damon, whose hands were still tied behind his body. She hooked the rod into the bonds. "Keep your elbows straight as you can," she shouted, and hauled him up by his straining arms. Keiko got her hand under an armpit. The combination of his hanging weight and hurried tugging dislocated a shoulder, and Damon howled in torment, but the women kept pulling.

She and Keiko heaved him onto the deck with a burst of strength that bent the pole and knocked the two of them onto their rear ends. The three of them lurched against the exhausted Stella, who threw her towel over Damon.

Billy still leaned far over the gunwale. "Ken!" He threw his line into the water.

Ken's face was waxen, glowing like a dying blossom that had fallen into the sapphire depths. He flailed at the moving line, but missed. Billy drew it back and threw it again.

Storm rose to thrust the bent aluminum rod toward Ken's flopping arms, and he managed to wind his fingers through the hooked loop. His injured foot flopped, limp as a dead fish, and a renewed bloom of red curled around his leg. His eyes, blank with helpless terror, rolled between her and Billy.

Storm and Billy saw the huge shadow at the same time. It looped around from under the *Quest* and darkened the water under Ken as surely as a thundercloud overhead.

Billy's voice broke and shrilled. "Don't let go. Hold on, stay there. Don't let go."

Ken's legs thrashed. The pole buckled. Billy gasped, and leaned out to Ken with both arms extended.

Then Ken jerked below the surface like the plastic float on a fishing line. His eyes looked up at Storm and Billy, wide and white as china teacups.

Storm and Billy shouted together. "No!"

Storm yanked the pole, which broke; the lower half fell in the water. But Billy clutched at the sleeve of Ken's shirt, then got a grip on one of his hands. Together, Storm and Billy lifted. Storm dreaded what she might see, a vision that would stay with her forever.

Odd that seeing one leg missing was a relief. The shark made another gliding pass at the blood that ran like an open tap from the truncated thigh, and then dived from sight.

The grinding crunch of the *Quest*'s contact with submerged boulders tilted the boat in the rescuers' favor for once, and Ken slithered over the gunwale onto the deck.

Storm got quivering legs beneath her and staggered to the helm.

Chapter Forty-five

If the seas had been heavy, the *Quest* wouldn't have lasted five minutes. Even so, the boat landed hard. Stella fell, and Storm would have if she hadn't had a tight hold on the ladder.

The boat came to rest at a tilt, its hull shrieking with agony. Its engines were still in neutral, but Storm could hear an uneven thrum that wasn't there before. The diesels caught and sputtered, as if water was leaking into the engine compartment.

She knew nothing about mechanics, but she knew the ocean. They had very little time before a big wave came and lifted the boat. Then the *Quest* would either go out to sea or it would collide with the razor-sharp lava, where it would smash into shards of fiberglass and engine parts.

"Stella, is there a bilge pump?" she called out.

"Yeah," came a muffled reply. "I'm looking for the switch."

Stella was successful; Storm heard the bilge go on. With luck, it would flush enough water out of the hull to lighten the boat. Then Storm would gun the engines and hope for a wave big enough to raise the hull, but not smash them against the rocks. And hope the engines worked. And hope she judged the ocean right. And—

"Stella, is there a radio?"

Stella was out of the cabin, holding tightly to the base of the ladder. "I tried it, but the light doesn't go on."

With that statement, the bilge pump stopped. The electrical system had shorted out.

"Shit," Storm said. Stella echoed her, then hustled back to the cabin to jiggle wires, look for leaks, or just say prayers.

Storm squinted into the black vastness of the ocean and hoped she and Stella would get the engine started before it was too late. In the waning light, it was becoming more difficult to anticipate incoming surf.

What she saw instead was a spectacle that gave hope wings. The bright lights of a good-sized vessel advanced, still far enough away to be visible over the spiky promontory of the bay. Against the indigo sky, the long, sleek vessel looked like a race horse approaching the gate.

"Hey!" Keiko's voice called from below and aft. "Someone's coming."

Storm turned around to confirm, and saw a different sight. Keiko couldn't yet see the seaward craft; her attention was directed toward a small boat that bounded over the waves from shore. The tiny running lights of a dory flickered like uncertain fireflies and its engine shrilled like a cornered hornet. The two men driving the little vessel had the motor maxed.

More lights appeared overhead, accompanied by the boisterous whopping of helicopter rotors. Someone on shore had noticed their struggle and had called for help.

The Coast Guard excels at sea rescues. The helicopter lowered a trained crewman and a stretcher onto the deck of the *Quest*, and the crewman—who turned out to be a woman—strapped Ken in and got him carefully hoisted into the belly of the craft. Billy wanted to go with him, but the rescuer nixed the request. She took Damon, whose shoulder was painful and swollen, instead.

"Anyone else unable to use their arms or legs?"

The answer was an uneasy negative.

"The cutter will evacuate the rest of you."

The crewwoman then gave the group a casual salute and a signal to her colleagues, who pulled her up to the helicopter.

By this time, the Coast Guard cutter had launched a Zodiac, and its skipper pulled to the *Quest*'s port side.

"How many people on this boat?" he asked.

"Seven." Storm counted heads. Damon and Ken had left in the helicopter, and Stella and Billy were stepping in the Zodiac. "Where's Lara?"

Keiko whipped around and without a word, darted back into the dark cabin. A moment later, she re-emerged with Lara, who was still wrapped in a towel. Waiflike, her dark eyes peered out at the group and came to rest on the Coast Guard officer.

"Dad?" she said in the voice of a ten-year-old. "Did we get him?"

Chapter Forty-six

Storm chose to ride with Hamlin and Terry Wu in the dory. The engine's buzz prohibited conversation, and Storm leaned against Hamlin's solid warmth, glad that Terry was piloting. Bouncing along in the indigo twilight, she thought about Lara. And sharks.

Storm had been raised to understand the ocean. Shark attacks on humans, though widely publicized, were rare. When Damon had been forced to creep along the narrow gunwale, he'd been terrified to the point of paralysis. Lara, in contrast, had been rapt.

A chill passed through Storm, and her fingers sought the emerald-eyed pig at her neck. Lara was convinced that her 'aumakua had come to her aid. Her ancestral deity had redeemed itself.

Another insight came to Storm as the dory bobbed across the darkening bay. Lara's superstitious devotion told another story, and it was the tale of a frightened, lonely little girl. A much more solitary woman than Storm had ever been.

Whereas Storm had Aunt Maile and Uncle Keone, who had begun taking care of her when she was young, Lara's family had unraveled. And though people had been there for her, she'd missed their loving intent. As her godmother, Stella was devoted and true. Her father had guaranteed that she was financially secure.

Lara, however, had been handed insults and failure instead of successes and friendships. She taunted Obake, her tormenter, and held friends who could keep her on at even keel at arm's length. Stella and Keiko were her closest allies, and she treated them like the roles she'd given them—employees.

Where was Ryan? Had she betrayed him to be with Ken?

Meanwhile, Lara talked to ghosts. The answer to her question was yes, Obake was scattered to the oceans. But Lara spoke to the people who couldn't care any more, and discarded the ones who could.

◇◇◇

On land, Terry Wu piled Storm and Hamlin into his car. The others were on their way to the police station in Wailuku, where members of several law enforcement agencies anticipated their statements. He did, however, stop at a Bad Ass Coffee shop on the way, where the three of them got hot drinks.

"We've had Akira Kudo, whom you knew as Obake, under observation for a long time, but we sure didn't see the case ending like this," Wu said.

"You were watching him for the prostitution ring?" Storm asked.

"And other things."

"Extortion?" Storm asked.

"I can't talk about it. Even though he's dead, the investigation isn't closed."

"When the shark attacked, I didn't know who the swimmer was."

"Lara did," Wu said. "So did her friends, Ken and Billy."

"How do you know?"

"Phone records and an informant. Billy was a demolitions expert in Desert Shield."

"The bomb last week?"

"We think so."

"Did Ken assist him?"

"Ken and Billy were in the same squad in Saudi Arabia."

"*Auwē.*" Storm slumped against the seat back. "Do you think Lara was involved in the bombing?

Wu hunched his shoulders. "I can't talk about it."

"Is that why the Joint Terrorism Task Force is here?" Hamlin asked.

"Federal agencies are going to scrutinize anything that looks like domestic terrorism. A restaurant blew up and a local politician was killed."

"You knew that Obake's son worked with him, right?" Storm asked. "I saw them coming out of The Red Light together."

"Steven Kudo. He's dead, too."

"He is? When did that happen?"

"A couple hours before the shark attack."

"Did Obake know?"

"Doesn't look like it. The two guys who were on the beach with him are in custody. They're pretty shaken up, and they're talking."

"Did Steven drive a black Range Rover?"

"That was one of his cars." Wu sighed. "This will all hit the papers tomorrow. Another prominent citizen died, too. You'll hear about it."

"I think the son and another guy broke into my hotel room. They stole my laptop and handbag."

"We'll look for them," Wu said. "We've got the car and a warrant to enter his local residence."

"Do you know if Obake or his son threatened Lara?" Storm asked.

"We're looking into that," Wu said.

"You can't say she got a shark to assassinate him. He swam to the boat voluntarily."

"What if you bait the water?" Wu asked. "That's illegal."

"In state waters, but not outside the jurisdictional limit. I didn't see anyone drop bait into the water, and I saw the first shark arrive."

Storm knew the *Quest* was closer to shore than the three nautical mile limit. Though she didn't want to conceal a crime, she also didn't want be lured into incriminating her client. The shark encounter was a public activity, and even if Lara and Ken were baiting the water, it depended where they were when they did it.

Though she, too, had wondered about the variety of sharks gathering around the *Quest*. She'd seen at least four different species, and a Great White sighting, let alone an attack, was extremely rare.

"We'll salvage the boat and search it," Wu said. "Might clear up some questions."

At the police station, Storm was questioned in a room with five officials. Four of them introduced themselves as Joint Terrorist Task Force agents. Carl Moana was the fifth. Moana brought her a cup of coffee and one of the FBI agents, who identified herself as Head of Squad, gestured to a chair that faced a one-way mirror.

"Thank you for speaking to us," she said. It was the woman from the car rental office.

Not that I have a choice, she thought. But she knew what it was like to gather evidence and information.

The law enforcement officials asked about the nature of her business with Lara Farrell, Lara's employees, and the events of the last four days.

"I'm setting up Lara's Limited Liability Company and her bylaws. That's public information," Storm said, "but I'm not free to discuss specifics."

"Look, we understand your reluctance to get involved," another FBI agent said, "but this is a homicide investigation."

"Multiple homicides," said another agent, who took off a jacket that had Bomb Squad in block letters across the back. "This is way bigger than your client confidentiality."

"Where did she get the money to buy her dive boats? How about the expensive diving equipment and inventory? Do you know the nature of her relationship with Ken McClure?" asked the Head of Squad, who leaned across the table.

"She's an experienced small business owner, and I don't know the details of her financing. All I know about Ken McClure is that he worked in the dive shop."

Stella and Keiko would be in similar rooms, and Storm knew the agents would pump them for information about other employees, plus they'd be asking questions about Lara's personal life.

"Do you know Billy Coswell?" an agent asked.

"I met him on the boat today, and I only know him as Billy."

"How did Lara pay you?"

"She sent me a retainer by check when I agreed to help her set up the shop. I haven't billed her for the remainder."

"Did you see Lara with Billy Coswell?"

"No, I got the impression he was Ken's friend."

"Do you think she had knowledge of your kidnapping? If so, do you want to bring charges?"

"No, I represent her and I'm not comfortable with the idea of testifying against her. I can't discuss her involvement until I speak to her. Speaking of, when can I?"

"She's been taken to the hospital," someone said.

After more than an hour of questions that covered topics ranging from Lara's business to the burglary of her hotel room, conversations she'd had with Damon, Ken, and Lara, and the circumstances of her kidnapping, the inquiries began to slow. Storm felt like she'd not only been on a sinking ship, but she'd been put through a wash and rinse cycle, too. She contemplated asking her own questions, but knew she'd have much better luck getting the lowdown if she waited to speak to either Wu or Moana in private.

When the agents collected her contact information and gave her permission to leave, Moana accompanied her out of the room.

"Where are the Tagamas?" she asked when they reached the lobby. She'd tried to keep track of the Feds' questions and the type of information they needed from her. Why hadn't she been asked about Ryan or his father? "I need to talk to them."

Moana's eyes flitted around the room. "Where will you be staying?"

Hamlin set down a five-month-old issue of *Newsweek* and approached. "I made reservations at a Wailea hotel. Use my mobile phone until we find hers."

"I'll get right on that," Moana said. "I think I know where it is."

"Great," Hamlin said.

Wu walked down the hallway toward them, and Storm suspected he'd been behind a one-way window in one of the interrogation rooms. She and Hamlin flagged him down.

"Could you get us a ride back to my car?" Hamlin asked.

"I can't leave now, but I'll find someone," Wu said, and disappeared for a few minutes. When he came back, he had a rookie officer in tow.

Forty-five minutes later, Storm left her clothes in a crumpled heap on the plush carpet of a hotel room and made a beeline for the shower. She made the water as hot as she could stand it and tried out all the settings on the fancy shower nozzle. A half-hour later, she sighed and wrapped one thick towel around her body, another around her dripping hair, and one over her shoulders. When she emerged from the sauna she'd created, Hamlin was tapping at the door to her room.

"Sergeant Moana dropped off your phone and your rental car. We both thought you'd like your suitcase." He handed the bag to her.

"Where was my phone?"

"On the floor of Damon's living room." Hamlin took in her towel attire and gave her a sly grin. "You look more comfortable."

"I am." She smiled up at him and adjusted her towel turban, which was starting to slide. She could tell by the heat that a blush was spreading across her chest and face. "Come in. I'll throw on some dry clothes."

He kissed the tip of her nose as he passed, and headed for the mini-bar. "I'm going to splurge. It's been a hard day."

"You flew from California today. You must be beat."

"At least I didn't get kidnapped. Are you holding up?"

"It's going to hit me, but right now I want answers. Was Lara involved in the decision to kidnap us? Until I saw her on deck, I thought Obake was behind it."

"I think he was. Wu asked me about Billy Coswell. I think Coswell may have done some work for him. It sounds like Coswell threatened McClure and got him to help with the kidnappings."

"Was Obake swimming out to take over the boat?"

"I don't know yet. Did you recognize him as the swimmer?"

"Heavens, no. All I wanted to do was get to him before the shark did." Her voice trembled. "And I didn't make it."

"No one could have, Storm." Hamlin put down the scotch he'd poured and folded his arms around her.

"The only other time I'd seen Obake was when he and his son came out of The Red Light. They had on business suits." One of Storm's towels slid and she grabbed at it.

"People look different without their clothes on," Hamlin said.

Storm's face flamed again, but he'd made her laugh. "That's true." She dug an outfit out of her suitcase. "Give me five minutes," she said, and went into the bathroom to change.

A few minutes later, Hamlin knocked on the door. "Your cell is ringing."

Storm was dressed, but her hair was still wet. She opened the door and took the phone. Stella sounded tired.

"Can we come see you? We need to talk."

"Uh, we were going—"

Hamlin's drink stopped halfway to his lips. "It's okay. We'll get some of your answers," he whispered.

"Sure, Stella. We'll meet you in a half hour. The hotel has a nice pool-side bar."

"We'll be there," she said.

When she hung up the phone, Hamlin gave her a kiss. "Afterward, we'll have a romantic dinner, okay?"

"Thank you," she said, and kissed him. It lasted longer than she'd expected.

"I love your hair like this." He ran his fingers through the wet waves.

"We're never going to make it to the bar."

"Sure we will. We have a half hour."

◇◇◇

Storm introduced Hamlin to Stella and Keiko, and Stella gave him a big hug. "We've heard great things about you."

They had? Oh yeah, she'd told Lara about Hamlin. Lara and Stella probably talked.

Right after they ordered a round of drinks, Storm asked, "Why were we kidnapped? Did Lara know about it?"

"That's what I wanted to talk to you about." Stella's face was lined with worry. "Did the police ask you to file charges against her for kidnapping?"

"I declined," Storm said.

Stella sat back with a sigh. Relief lightened the creases around her mouth. "Thank you. She wouldn't have done it."

"Then who did?"

"Obake," Keiko said. "He was mad that you rescued Carmen and me."

"That's not enough," Storm said.

"He threatened Lara," said Stella. "I heard her talking to Ken this morning. She told him that the flowers in Yasuko's hair were the ones she'd taken to her mother." Stella twisted her hands together. "I was there when she pinned those flowers in Barb's hair."

"You think Obake threatened Lara with Barb's welfare?"

"Yes, I'm sure of it."

"Did you tell the FBI people about this?" Storm asked.

"Yes." Stella nodded. "Was that okay?"

"You need to tell them everything you know. They'll find out anyway, because they're going to grill everyone connected to this event."

"I'm worried that Obake's threat makes it look like Lara made him swim to the *Quest*." Stella chewed a hangnail.

"No one was holding a gun to his head. We saw him leave the beach," Storm said. "And he swims every day."

Stella's shoulders sagged. "I guess."

Storm remembered that Lara had two boats. "Why the *Quest*?"

"That was the boat she used for the shark encounter."

"So she did bait the water."

Stella nodded. "Not all the time, but sharks recognize the sound of the engines and come around. Tourists love it. It's become her most popular excursion."

"Have you ever seen sharks try to bite someone?"

"Never. The divers are in a cage," Stella said. "They don't bite the cage, let alone a person. I don't know why the shark attacked Obake."

"It's her *'aumakua*," said Keiko in a very soft voice, and the words gave Storm chicken skin.

No one said anything for a long moment. Storm broke the silence. "Who physically put us on the boat?"

"Billy and Ken," Keiko said.

"What about Damon? He helped, didn't he?"

"Damon didn't know about the kidnapping until it happened. When he overheard Billy telling Ken it was time to toss us overboard, miles off shore with our hands tied, he put his own safety at risk."

"He was free up until then," Storm pointed out. "And didn't he set me up?"

"I don't think so. He mentioned to Ken and Billy you needed to trade cars, but he didn't know they were going to knock you out," Stella said.

Storm nodded slowly. She remembered the sound of a protest and a scuffle right before the sting of the drug they'd given her.

"How is Lara?" Storm asked. "Can she be questioned?"

"I called the hospital about an hour ago and talked to an orderly I know. He couldn't say much, but he told me sometimes she makes sense, sometimes not so much." Stella hesitated. "And she's a suspect in the restaurant bombing, among other things."

She leaned toward Storm. "Do you handle criminal work?"

"If you're talking about Lara, I'd rather refer the case to an attorney who specializes in criminal law," Storm said. "I can be co-counsel."

"How about Billy and Ken?"

"They need to hire their own counsel."

Storm took a thoughtful sip of wine and glanced at Hamlin. She could tell he, too, was sorting through the available information. There were gaping holes in their knowledge. She needed to ask Lara a laundry list of questions, but she was at the end of a long line of interrogators. And for her client's sake, she needed to restrain her curiosity and find a criminal attorney.

"You're sure it was Obake's men who took you to Pauline's?" Storm asked Keiko.

"Yes, and I signed a complaint against her," Keiko said.

"I can see why he'd abduct you and Carmen, but why Stella and me?" She looked around the table. Keiko and Stella appeared to be waiting for her to answer the question. Hamlin recognized it as rhetorical and raised one eyebrow.

"We don't have all the pieces yet," he said.

Storm slowly set down her glass down. "And why didn't Lara ask for help? From me or from law enforcement?"

"As if you've never tried to handle problems alone?" Hamlin's tone was gentle.

Storm lowered her eyes. "Well, sometimes."

"Obake had friends in local government," Stella said. "He'd already taken Keiko and Carmen to show they belonged to him. He'd threatened you, her lawyer. Lara was frantic, and she trusted very few people."

"Where are the Tagamas?" Storm asked. "I need to talk to them about Paradise Consortium's role."

Sadness lined Stella's face again. "That's the other reason I wanted to talk to you."

Chapter Forty-seven

"Tagama was going to give Lara the land as a wedding present."

"He could do this?" Storm wondered if he had enough control over Paradise Consortium.

"But Ryan didn't tell Lara?" Hamlin asked.

"No, it was a gift. Tagama was going to wrap up the papers and take her and Ryan to dinner." Stella took a drink.

"When did you hear about this?" Storm asked.

"I called Ryan this afternoon to tell him about Obake and Lara."

"What did he say?"

"Not much, he's too upset," Stella said. "Steven Kudo killed his father."

Storm swallowed. "That's who Wu meant? The prominent businessman."

"Tagama left a letter for Ryan."

"Did he tell you what it said?"

"No, he didn't want to talk about it."

Sadness covered the four of them like a damp mist.

"Poor Lara," said Stella.

"Poor Ryan," said Storm.

"Lara made some bad decisions," said Keiko.

Keiko had just voiced Storm's thoughts. She looked at the young woman. Storm had thought no one would rise above the mess Obake had created with his cruel manipulations, but she might be wrong.

Keiko, for the first time in Storm's experience, had on a short sleeved shirt. Her scars showed clearly, but she didn't try to hide them. She didn't twist her arms, though she gave a little shiver and slipped them into the sleeves of a sweater that had been draped over her shoulders. Storm was going to do the same.

"She did make some poor choices, but she was bullied. We're going to get her a good lawyer," Hamlin said.

"We'll take care of her." Storm put her hand on Stella's. "And I'll find out what role the Tagamas played in this."

"I can't believe Ryan would allow anyone to hurt Lara." Stella's eyes pleaded with Storm.

"I doubt it, too. And I'll let you know." Storm paused. "Do you think Ryan blames Lara for his father's death?"

"I didn't ask. He didn't have much to say when I told him she was in the hospital."

"He has a lot to process."

Stella nodded, and changed the subject. "How long are you going to stay?" she asked Hamlin.

His eyes slid to Storm's. "I'll be discussing that with Storm."

A mischievous gleam replaced a bit of the distress in Stella's eyes. He paid the bill, and the four got up to leave. "Any recommendations for a nice dinner place?" he asked Stella.

"The Gaslight. About a quarter mile from here, right on the water. Pricey, but worth it."

"Excellent."

And it was. And so was the walk along the beach to get there, though Storm's mobile phone rang about half way. It was Carl Moana.

"You get your phone and suitcase?"

"Yes, thanks. The car, too."

"This is going to hit the papers tomorrow, so I thought I'd let you know. Ichiru Tagama was working with us." He paused, and Storm could hear the crackling of his car radio. "I mean, local law enforcement agencies."

"What about Paradise Consortium?"

"You knew about that?"

"Sure, it had partial ownership in the shopping center where Lara has her dive shop."

"Yeah," Moana said. "Uh, that part isn't going to be in the news."

"We need to tell Lara about Tagama's role. I have a feeling she thought he was an associate of Obake's." Storm stopped walking. "What did Tagama do?"

"It was an arrangement. Obake kept Tagama on the board of Paradise Consortium so he could keep an eye him. It kept Tagama abreast of the local syndicate's activities. The Feds asked Tagama to encourage Obake to buy into the shopping center under Lara's shop so they had a shared interest."

"Who owned the majority of the shopping center?" Storm asked.

"Mālua LLC owned ninety percent."

"So Tagama could buy out Paradise and do what he wanted with the lease?"

"He bought them out two days ago."

"Is that why Steven Kudo killed him?"

"No." Moana sighed. "Tagama knew they'd killed Yasuko. He knew the police didn't have enough physical evidence to prove it, and he went after it."

"How'd Kudo die?"

"Kudo and his side-kick were both killed with throwing knives. Tagama was good." Moana sounded impressed.

"How did Tagama die?"

"Kudo shot him." A few blats of the radio sounded in the background. "Tagama had a friend in the police, and he called him before he went to meet the two thugs. Tagama knew he wasn't coming back."

"How's Ryan taking it?"

"Pretty rough," Moana said. "His dad left him the whole business, though. He'll pull himself back together. He has to."

"Hey, Moana," Storm said. "Thanks for telling me."

"You're welcome. I didn't want you uncovering any more stones." There was a smile in his voice. "One other thing, but this is my own news. I'm in line for a promotion."

"Congratulations, Moana. You deserve it." Storm thought for a moment. "Do something for me?"

"Yeah, if I can."

"Tell Lara all this as soon as you can, okay?"

◇◇◇

The wine was perfect. So were their dinners and the walk back under the stars. So was the hotel room, the big bed, and the soft breeze that fluttered the gauzy drapes.

Chapter Forty-eight

Monday morning, Grace phoned at nine-thirty to tell Storm that Mark Suzuki called. He wanted to know how she was. The ringing phone woke up Storm and Hamlin, and Grace didn't bother to hide the smile in her voice. Storm and Hamlin recuperated for one more day (and night), then responded to the tug of obligations in Honolulu.

Wednesday morning, Storm sat at her desk and returned his call.

"You owe me a lobster dinner," Mark said.

"You're right, I do. You free tonight?"

Though Storm and Hamlin were on time, Mark was already at the table. He wore an enormous red bib with an advertisement for Marcie's Maine Delicacies printed in big white letters across the front. Since they were at Ruths Chris Steakhouse in Waikiki, Storm figured he'd brought his own supplies. From what she could tell, he had on a clean shirt and tie, but his eyeglasses were, as usual, smudged and slightly crooked on his round face.

The staff seemed to be in on Suzuki's joke. The sommelier wore a big grin the entire time he talked to Hamlin about wine. This wasn't Suzuki's first visit, apparently.

As soon as Hamlin ordered a bottle, Mark leaned in. "So what happened? Don't tell me any of the stuff in the papers. I want the inside scoops."

"When we left, Lara was released from the hospital to Stella's custody," Storm said. "Ryan went to see her this morning."

"And?" Suzuki asked.

"The wedding has been postponed. They're reevaluating the relationship."

"No kidding." Suzuki looked thoughtful. "It was nice of him to go see her."

"Yeah, especially after her involvement with that Ken character," Hamlin said.

"You're jumping to conclusions." Storm frowned at him. "Ryan could have told her earlier about Paradise Consortium's ownership."

"No way," said Suzuki.

"What makes you say that?" Storm asked.

"He couldn't. He had to keep it under wraps."

She eyed Suzuki. "How do you know?"

Suzuki shrugged and drank some wine.

Storm softened. "At least he's giving Lara a chance. Stella told me he brought her flowers."

"Stella's a romantic."

"And what's wrong with that?"

Hamlin broke up the sparring. "In his letter to Ryan, Tagama reassured him that he had faith in the afterlife. He knew his negative karma would keep him from Nirvana this go-round, and hoped his son found comfort in Tagama's belief that he would join Yasuko and begin his atonement for past mistakes. He also mentioned that Obake had an iron-clad alibi for Yasuko's death, and the police didn't have enough to prove Steven Kuko did it."

"Tagama also told Ryan that Obake had found out he was working with the Feds," Storm added. "Tagama was worried about Ryan's and Lara's welfare if he didn't act to end things."

Suzuki shook his head from side to side. "Noble, but tough."

"Ryan is probably the most innocent of the bunch," Hamlin said.

"Wait," Storm said. "Stella and Keiko had nothing to do with Lara's plan."

"That's true. But they knew Obake and what he could do. They knew at least two women who'd died in his operation."

"Stella helped Keiko escape. Both of them have struggled to rebuild their lives," Storm said. "Which reminds me, they've hired an attorney and applied for custody of Carmen."

"Five people died, right?" Mark asked. "Obake, Yasuko, Steve Kudo, the other Yakuza guy, and Tagama."

"Six. The guy who died in the bombing," Hamlin said.

"That's right, Tom Peters, the liquor commissioner," Storm said.

"Have you heard anything about him?" Suzuki asked with a sly smile.

Storm and Hamlin stared at him, and he continued after a weighted pause. "Peters had heard rumors about certain Lahaina bars, and he knew someone on his staff was overlooking gross legal abuses."

Storm narrowed her eyes. "How do you know this?"

Suzuki ignored her question. "On Monday, Peters announced to Wayne Harding that he'd be attending the meeting in Harding's place," Suzuki said. "Big mistake."

Storm sat back with amazement. "Harding warned Obake."

Hamlin spoke up. "Peters was the target? How did they convince him to stick around for the bomb to blow up?"

"Harding was supposed to bring him some tapes. Peters followed the rest of the people to the parking lot, and waited there. Harding, naturally, was late and the bomb went off. It was planted in the shrubbery in front of Peters' car."

"How'd they know he'd park in the right place?"

"Obake and his men made sure it was the closest free space, right next to the entrance."

"I saw the result of the blast," Storm said. "The whole side of the restaurant was gone."

"Billy Coswell set the bomb?" Hamlin asked.

"Looks like it," Suzuki said.

"And he was hired to kidnap us?" Storm asked.

"Obake thought you might have a copy of the sales contract for Lara's Makena place. The contract with the rightful owner, that is."

"Was Ken in on the kidnapping? And how about Lara?"

"Lara didn't know that you three were on the *Quest* until she heard pounding on the cabin door," Suzuki said. "From what we can tell, Ken was pressured into helping Billy, and he bought into the story that you were being held for your own safety and would be released as soon as Lara signed the falsified contract."

"Hold it," Storm said. "Who's *we*? Who are you working with, Mark?"

"Me? I have a consulting firm." Mark lifted his glass for a delicate sip. "Nice wine, Hamlin. Is this the '02 or the '03 Pinot Grigio?"

"Yeah, yeah. Advanced Medical Systems. Come on, Suzuki."

The wait staff arrived with their orders. Storm couldn't believe it; Suzuki must have control over waiter intervention, too. She watched him inhale the aroma from an enormous red lobster on the platter before him. The monster hung off both sides. A cute waitress brought a pot of melted butter and set it next to him. His wide face looked beatific in the candlelight.

She decided to relent for a while and enjoy her *onaga*. Hamlin looked delighted with his filet. They ate and avoided the Maui topic by telling amusing work stories and poking fun at government incompetents. An endless supply of those, they all agreed.

Storm put down her fork for a rest. "Okay, you're not going to reveal your contacts. Or colleagues," she added with a raised eyebrow, and watched Suzuki for a reaction. He attacked a giant claw with a nutcracker.

"Just tell me this," she pleaded. "Remember when I called you from the restaurant?"

"Yeah, I couldn't believe it!" He looked to Hamlin for corroboration. "She calls me from a bar. Here we are, extra careful that Obake can't track our calls—and there she is, outside the restrooms where these guys are trying to pick her up."

"Please. They were blind drunk. And ugly. Did I mention they were ugly?"

"I should try that sometime," Suzuki said. "Hanging around the women's room, I mean," he added quickly.

"They didn't have any luck."

"True," Suzuki conceded.

"So what did you tell that sleaze ball?" Storm demanded. "You know, to get rid of him."

Suzuki extracted a plug of white flesh from the claw and lowered it into the butter. Three times. He raised the dripping morsel to his open mouth.

"Suzuki?"

"I told him you were a secret agent with a license to kill."

Hamlin made a honking noise and raised his napkin to cover a huge grin. Storm glared at him. He was bright red.

Mark's mouth twitched. "Come on, I missed out on all the fun."

"Fun?" She squinted at him.

"Not fun?" he asked, suddenly serious. For a very large man in a big red bib and crooked spectacles, he could have a lot of dignity. It showed up more times than others, and was in full force at that moment.

"No, not fun," she said. "Those were dangerous men, and I was scared witless. There were also innocent people in trouble."

Mark's black eyes appraised her, while Hamlin's had a new glow.

Suzuki raised his wine glass. "My dear friend, you have grown into an amazing woman."

"Suzuki, you're not playing fair."

"I can't. And you don't want me to." Despite the grease on his chin, Suzuki's face took on a solemn sincerity. "Please, Storm. This is an outstanding dinner. It's a pleasure to spend the evening with you both."

When the waiter brought the check, he took it straight to Suzuki.

Storm reached out. "Mark, this is my treat. I promised. I'd be in the trunk of one of Obake's cars if it weren't for you and Hamlin."

"I doubt it." Suzuki looked pleased with himself. "It's my gift to the two of you." He winked. "Teamwork rules."

The waiter appeared and whisked away the leather envelope with the check and Suzuki's credit card.

It was time to be gracious. "Thank you, Mark."

"You're welcome," he said, and sighed with contentment. "I have an ulterior motive."

"Oh, no." Storm groaned.

"Will you call me again for help? Life would be dull without you."

Storm sputtered on her wine. "Suzuki, you're a nut case."

"Could be, but I'm a useful one."

"I'll call you," Storm said.

"I will, too," Hamlin said. "It was an illuminating evening, Mark. Thank you."

On the way to the parking lot, Storm and Hamlin walked hand in hand. Their heels tapped the pavement together, the only sound in the dark street. She broke their comfortable silence. "Hamlin, did I ever tell you about this land my dad left me?" she asked.

"No, show it to me?"

"Yes, I'd like to."

Glossary of Hawaiian words

A bit of history: Until the arrival of the missionaries around 1820, the Hawaiian language was completely oral. The Christian visitors began to record the language and teach the Hawaiian natives to read and write.

There are 12 Roman letters in the Hawaiian alphabet, plus two diacritical marks, the kahakō, which is a line over a vowel, and the ʻokina, which looks like a backwards apostrophe and signals a glottal stop. Because a word with an ʻokina can have an entirely different meaning than the same spelling without it, the ʻokina is considered a letter.

If you spend some time in the islands, you'll quickly pick up these terms. I've tried to use them so you can deduce the meaning from the context, but if you have any doubts or want further explanation, here are translations of commonly used words. Pidgin isn't Hawaiian; it's a combination of languages. When you're *pau*, you'll be ready for your next visit to the islands. *A hui hou aku*!

A hui hou aku—goodbye, or until we meet again

ʻaumakua—a family totem, deified ancestors who assume the shape of plants or animals and helped the living

Auwē—Expression of alarm. Alas, a wail to bemoan something.

hala—the Pandanus tree, whose leaves are woven into mats, satchels, hats, and other useful items

kahuna lā'au lapa'au—experts who heal with medicines made from native plants

kekeface—local pidgin slang for someone with bad acne, literally zit face

kukae—pidgin for excrement, or shit

kolohe—mischievous, naughty, full of fun

manō—general term for a shark

manō hae—fierce shark or fighter

mauka—toward the mountains

omiyage—traditionally Japanese souvenirs, but now used to mean gifts that people take when they're visiting friends or business colleagues

onaga—ruby or red snapper, a delicious fish, also *ula'ula*

opihi—limpet, a shellfish that clings to surf-tossed rocks. Also known as death-fish, because many lives have been lost in harvesting it

pau—finished, over, done with

pua'a—pig

puka—hole, opening, door

tita—local term for a tough woman

wahine—a woman, also wife

wiliwili—a Hawaiian leguminous tree, with short thick trunk, found on dry plains and lava flows

To receive a free catalog of Poisoned Pen Press titles, please contact us in one of the following ways:

Phone: 1-800-421-3976
Facsimile: 1-480-949-1707
Email: info@poisonedpenpress.com
Website: www.poisonedpenpress.com

Poisoned Pen Press
6962 E. First Ave. Ste. 103
Scottsdale, AZ 85251